One Day At A Time

Ian Yates

OTHER BOOKS BY IAN YATES

DCI Carter Novels
One Piece At A Time

OTHER WORKS
Woolwich Shines
The Fighters

Copyright © 2014   Ian Yates
All rights reserved.
ISBN - 10: 1500130052
ISBN-13: 978-1500130053

For my parents.

ONE DAY AT A TIME

CONTENTS

Contents

ACKNOWLEDGMENTS 9

CHAPTER 1 11

CHAPTER 2 15

CHAPTER 3 21

CHAPTER 4 27

CHAPTER 5 34

CHAPTER 6 42

CHAPTER 7 47

CHAPTER 8 52

CHAPTER 9 57

CHAPTER 10 60

CHAPTER 11 63

CHAPTER 12 68

CHAPTER 13 77

CHAPTER 14 80

CHAPTER 15 84

CHAPTER 16 87

CHAPTER 17 90

CHAPTER 18 93

CHAPTER 19 97

CHAPTER 20 102

CHAPTER 21 106

CHAPTER 22 110

CHAPTER 23 115

CHAPTER 24 119

CHAPTER 25 123

CHAPTER 26 127

CHAPTER 27 130

CHAPTER 28 137

CHAPTER 29 142

CHAPTER 30 148

CHAPTER 31 154

CHAPTER 32 162

CHAPTER 33 166

CHAPTER 34 170

CHAPTER 35 175

CHAPTER 36 179

CHAPTER 37 184

CHAPTER 38 188

CHAPTER 39 192

CHAPTER 40 199

CHAPTER 41 202

CHAPTER 42 205

CHAPTER 43 209

CHAPTER 44 215

CHAPTER 45 220

CHAPTER 46 224

CHAPTER 47 228

CHAPTER 48	232
CHAPTER 49	239
CHAPTER 50	246
CHAPTER 51	251
CHAPTER 52	257
CHAPTER 53	263
CHAPTER 54	271
CHAPTER 55	275
CHAPTER 56	283
CHAPTER 57	287
CHAPTER 58	290
CHAPTER 59	293
CHAPTER 60	296
CHAPTER 61	302

ACKNOWLEDGMENTS

As always a huge thank you to Alison, my wonderful wife, for her patience and love as I shut myself away and hammer at a keyboard at all hours of the day and night. You truly are my rock.

Thanks to Ann Carter and Jim Emerson for being the sounding boards for the early chapters of the book. Your positive remarks helped me to continue when I struggled to write. Hope the leg gets better soon Jim. A big shout out to everyone whose name I have used as a character. Whilst the names may reflect what is on your birth certificate, the characters I create around them certainly do not, but you are all great sports for allowing me to do so.

Stuart and Angie, you two are **truly** inspirational. Angie recently fought and survived breast cancer and now goes around giving talks on cancer awareness and how to help prevent it. Stuart has written a book of her struggles through the diagnosis, treatment and recovery. It will make you smile, cry and laugh out loud. It's called *'The Cancer Poems'* by Stuart Wilson.

It is available from Amazon and all profits are going to Cancer charities, please check it out.

I cannot go without thanking everyone who bought a copy of 'One Piece At A Time'. This is for you.

The best thing about the future is that it comes one day at a time.
Abraham Lincoln

'And when I'm finished, bring the yellow tape
To tape off the scene of the slaughter'
Fuck Tha Police - NWA

CHAPTER 1

Mike Mason stirs the simmering pot with a wooden spoon in one hand, while reaching over and grabbing his wine glass with the other. Taking a sip from the glass he relishes the heavy taste of the Merlot across his tongue, and licks his lips in anticipation. Anticipation of the meal he will be serving with it and anticipation of the night to come. He checks the clock on the kitchen wall and sees he still has a half hour before his guest arrives. Just enough time to finish the glass of wine and set the table. He smiles as he thinks of his guest. They only met last week at a lovely little bistro with a well known respect for client's privacy. It was a blind date, set up by mutual friends, but they both overcame their initial embarrassment and hit it off straight away. He takes another sip from the glass and realises he is as nervous as a teenager on a first date. It has been a long time since he has let anyone into his life. He recalls the ugly scenes at the end of his last relationship and shudders involuntarily. He does not want to go through that again. He was in pieces for weeks.

The doorbell breaks his thoughts and he looks back up to the clock with a chill running down his spine. 'Twenty-five minutes early,' he thinks to himself, 'I haven't set the table yet…shit.'

Placing the wine glass on the heavy wooden table in the center of the kitchen, he pulls on the edges of his shirt at his waist to stretch it across his chest, and walks out into the long tiled hallway. His shoes clatter across the small mosaic tiles as he makes his way to the front door. He can see the silhouette of somebody framed in the patterned glass from the street light outside. He checks his hair in the hallway mirror quickly, takes a deep breath, puts a smile on his face, and opens the front door.

'Hi. You're early…' his voice tapers off as he sees a person he was not expecting standing on his doorstep.

'Michael Mason?' an enquiry.

'Yes, umm, can I help you?' he asks confused.

'Michael Mason of Typhoon Scientific Industries?'

'Yes, but do you mind…'

The question is cut off as a gloved hand appears as if out of nowhere and propels him backwards. It sends Michael sprawling onto the tiled hallway floor. He looks up, more in astonishment than in fear as the stranger steps into his house and closes the door behind them.

'I'll take that bottle of Chateauneuf de Pape, the 2006, please.'

Andrew Chinery hands over a fifty pound note to the wine merchant, 'Keep the change.'

He waits whilst the bottle is wrapped in thin, plain, white paper and then passed over the counter to him.

'Thank you, sir. Have a good evening.'

Andrew smiles at the older man in front of him, 'I intend to, thank you.'

He walks out of the small shop and strides over to the waiting black cab. As he gets into the rear of the car, he speaks to the driver,

'Thank you for that. Now, on to our destination please.'

He sits back and enjoys the next ten minutes in silence, looking forward to spending a night out with some good company.

He barely notices when they pull in to an affluent street and stop outside a marvellous Victorian townhouse.

'Here we are, sir.'

The voice of the taxi driver breaks his chain of thought.

'Oh, wow, here already,' he says in surprise.

Andrew digs into his jacket pocket and pulls out his wallet. Glancing at the meter he fishes out another fifty pound note and hands it through the gap in the dividing screen.

'Keep the change,' he says for the second time that evening.

'Thank you sir… thank you very much,' the cab driver replies with a huge grin, 'have a merry Christmas.'

'You too,' Andrew says with a smile, and exits the cab.

His breath is white smoke in the chill of the evening as he surveys the house in front of him. He checks his watch and mutters under his breath, 'Here I come, ready or not.'

He pushes open the small, wrought iron gate and walks up the terracotta tiled path that bisects a compact, but immaculately kept front garden. He is about to push the doorbell, when he sees the door is ajar.

'Expecting me, obviously,' he thinks aloud, and pushes it fully open, calling out as he does so, 'Hello, Michael…it's me, Andrew. Something smells good, I hope you haven't…'

As he steps inside the hallway his foot slips in a wet patch on the floor and he struggles to remain upright, only managing to do so by grabbing the doorframe with his free hand. It is then he notices the bloody bundle on the floor in front of him.

The bottle of wine slips from his grasp and shatters on the tiles, mixing it's dark, red contents with the darker fluid already pooling on the floor from the body in front of him. Andrew's hand flies to his mouth to try and stop the gorge from rising. He turns away from the terrible sight in front of him and fumbles for his mobile phone stabbing in 999 quickly. The call is answered quickly.

'Police, I need help. Something terrible has happened. I think there's been a murder…'

CHAPTER 2

London in December is spectacular. One of my joys since a child has been walking the streets, taking in the sights of the shops and their Christmas trimmings and lights. I am standing with Julia, my fiancée, on this cold December evening, on Brompton Road in Knightsbridge, and staring at the brightly lit façade of Harrods opposite. The lovely old building is festooned with lights, giving off a soft orange glow that bathes us in its ambience, even from across the street. Julia squeezes my hand and looks up at me,
'Shall we go in Peter? We can do the touristy thing and buy a carrier bag. I know mama would like that. She has a collection of the damn things already. She likes to use them when she shops at Asda, she thinks it make her look more affluent.'
Julia chuckles softly and I join in with her laughter before asking,
'How about we get a mug for your father? He can sit in the restaurant with his Greek coffee in it and your mother can unpack her shopping next to him. Make them look like Harrods regulars, eh?'
Julia's smile is brighter than the lights of Harrods and the whole of London combined as she pulls me across the road, dodging the slow moving traffic, and into the most famous department store in the world.
'Julia,' I say, 'go on up to the home-ware department, I just have to make a quick phone call to the office. I won't be long.'

I give her a quick peck on the cheek as I pull out my mobile phone. As a Detective Chief Inspector in the Metropolitan Police Forces Homicide and Serious Crime Unit, I have to keep in regular contact with my office, and it is lucky for me that Julia understands that.

'OK babe. See you in a minute.' And she is off in a whirl of Dolce & Gabbana, Velvet Desert perfume. I love that fragrance on her skin, which is why I bought her a bottle for her birthday.

I watch as she disappears in the throng of Christmas shoppers and slip the phone back in my pocket. I move off in a different direction, ensuring she cannot see me.

'That one please, may I see it?'

The woman behind the small counter looks me up and down before nodding. I don't notice any other movement or signal from her, but I suddenly find a large man in a discreet security guards uniform standing near me. I look at him and smile, 'Afternoon,' I say with a nod.

He just stands there impassively. Watching, but not looking as only a good security guard can do.

'This is a lovely piece, I am sure your...' she pauses to let me finish her sentence.

'Fiancée,' I confirm.

She smiles, 'I am sure your fiancée would love it. The emerald is set in gold and inspired by a bud in blossom. It is understated yet elegant, and the extremely intricate workings of the diamonds in the 18 karat gold are magnificent. The artist is a delightful chap called Theo Fennel, one of the finest workers of jewellery in the world.'

Her description of the necklace I now hold before me doesn't sway my decision. All I can see in my mind is that drop of colour against Julia's neck and I know I must have it.

'I'll take it; it is truly a beautiful piece of jewellery.'

The sales woman smile grows broader, 'We also have a set of ear-rings in the same design,' she brings out another small display case, upon which lie a set of matching ear-rings that catch the light and glisten softly, 'they compliment the necklace perfectly, don't you think?'

I see the price tag and try not to grimace, but she is right, together the jewellery will look stunning on Julia. I can imagine her wearing the pieces on our wedding day and how it will look against her olive skin.

'OK,' I say, knowing when I am beaten, 'it will have to be MasterCard.'

'No problem, sir. I will just have them gift wrapped for you whilst your payment goes through.'

She punches a string of numbers into a small hand held terminal. I cannot help but realise that it is a few numbers more than I wanted to see before I came in, and then she hands the wireless terminal over to me. With a small sigh I input my security PIN number and hand it back to her. An assistant has quickly and expertly covered the two boxes in expensive looking, sparkling paper and popped them in a discreet green bag. Handing my card back with the receipt, the sales woman smiles sweetly, and produces another gleaming piece of jewellery,

'Perhaps you would also be interested in a bracelet?'

I smile as I put away my card.

'Maybe next year, thank you.'

The small bag fits nicely into the inside pocket of

my jacket and I rush off to find Julia, leaving the smiling woman behind me.

I find her looking at a vast array of mugs in all manner of shapes and colours. She is holding a Union Flag covered cup with the Harrods logo emblazoned across it in her hand, and is slowly turning it around as she inspects it. She see's me coming and smiles broadly,
'What do you think of this one? Is it my dad?'
I think of Nektarios, Julia's father and cast an appraising eye across the selection. I pick up a simple coloured travel mug, in black with gold writing.
'This might be easier for him to hold and I think the colours are more his style,' I say.
Julia's smile slips slightly as she considers the practicality of my statement. Nine months ago, her father was beaten and left for dead in a vicious attack. He lost three fingers off his left hand in the assault, amongst more severe injuries, and he is only now managing to move around without assistance. The attack was a result of a long ago feud between Nektarios and an old friend of his, brought about by their love of the same woman. Julia's mother.
'Yes, that would be more suitable for him.'
She blinks back a tear and I put an arm around her and hold her close.
'Let's get him this mug and put it in a carrier bag for your mum. Two birds with one stone then, yeah?'
She nods and places the ceramic mug back on the shelf in front of her. Pulling herself away from me slightly, she prods me in the side, exactly where the jewellery boxes are hidden beneath my jacket.

'What have you got there, Peter?'
Luckily the ringing of my phone stops any explanation I have to give. I smile apologetically, pull the phone from my pocket, and answer it.
'DCI Carter.'
Julia watches my brow furrow at the words I am hearing.
'OK. I will be there as soon as I can...yes ma'am...I will notify Dr Young and his forensics team.'
The phone call terminates and Julia can see by the look on my face that our day trip has come to an end.
'Work?' she enquires, knowing full well what that means for some unfortunate soul.
I nod,
'Come on, let's pay for this and then I will get you a taxi. Please give your parents my love but I think I am going to be late for our dinner this evening.'
She grabs my hand to give it a reassuring squeeze, 'No problem Peter. We all know what you do can't always be done in normal hours.' She looks me in the eyes, 'Stay safe though yeah. Always stay safe.'

After hailing a cab to take Julia back to her parent's restaurant, I call Graham Young, the forensic department chief, and my good friend. I start walking as I talk on the phone. 'Graham, hi, it's Peter. Sorry to disturb your Saturday afternoon but...'
'Peter, no problem. I'm on my way. JD just called and gave me the details. You know, he really is on the ball. Maybe he's after your job?'
I smile at the thought of my partner JD, Detective Inspector Johnathon Dawkins, doing anything to try and usurp me. We have been through a lot of things together and I class him as one of my best

friends. What am I saying? Hell, he is my best friend.

'He can have it Graham. Listen, I am only around the corner from the scene, so I will be there in about ten minutes. I'll meet you there and I presume JD is already on-scene?'

'He said he was on his way when he rang. So much for Saturdays off, eh?'

'That's why we get paid the mega-bucks Graham.'

'Hmm, not sure about that. Maybe I can swing some overtime for this one?' he says half-jokingly.

Shaking my head, even though he cannot see it, 'Not with my budget Graham, but I'll buy you lunch tomorrow.'

'Deal. See you soon to confirm the details.'

I hang up and continue on my way through the expensive streets of Knightsbridge on my way to a grisly rendezvous.

CHAPTER 3

Angela Wilson is watching the commotion across the street from a house almost identical to the one she is standing in. This area of London is not renowned for the flurry of police activity that is currently taking place, and she watches intently as more uniformed and plain clothed officers arrive. She observes that to have money in this neighbourhood means that more police arrive on scene than she is used to in her area of the capitol. Looking behind her, to the man stretched out on the bed, she shakes her head slowly before turning back to the unfolding drama on the street. It is much more fun to watch this than have to return to the almost silent form on the large, double bed behind her.
'What the hell is going on over there?' she questions under her breath.
Not caring as to what her client may think she lights up a cigarette and stares out of the window with curiosity. Taking a deep pull on the filter she realises a problem she may face.
'Shit,' she says out loud, 'coppers all over the place and I am meant to get back before eleven.'
Without turning around she speaks towards the window, but her words are directed to the figure on the bed.
'This is going to cost you mister…and that's even before you get what I came here for. If I don't leave before ten-thirty then it's another grand. No excuses, just payment without any hassles.'

She takes another deep drag on the cigarette and watches with a bored look as the tip glows red. She moves away from the window and takes a few steps towards the bed. The man looks up with a frightened look on his fat, sweaty face. The gag stops the scream from exiting the room as the tip of the cigarette is placed against his inner thigh.
'You won't have a problem with the overtime, will you, love?' Angela asks.
The shudder of pleasure and the rapid shake of the head from her client tell her all she needs to know.
'Good boy…that's all I need to know.'
She moves away from the bed and towards the small bag she brought with her. Pulling out a few objects from within its confines, she looks shyly over her shoulder, 'Now how about we have some fun?'

As I make my way down the street, I look up to the houses around me. This is definitely what they would call 'Millionaires Row', without any shred of sarcasm in the words. My eyes linger on a first floor window opposite as I see a tall, blonde haired woman staring out, watching the goings on of the Metropolitan Police in the house opposite hers. She is only there a moment before disappearing from view. I understand then, that in this area of London we will get no witnesses or any viable sightings of whomever may have perpetrated the crime. Indeed, it was just pure luck on my part, to actually see someone at a window.
Every other house has the blinds or curtains firmly closed against the night. Shutting out the outside world in case it disturbs their viewing of 'Strictly' or some other celebrity rubbish.

I grab the shoulder of the nearest uniformed constable whilst flashing my ID with my spare hand.

'Constable, has anyone canvassed the local area for information yet?'

He looks at my identification and straightens immediately.

'Sir…no sir. We are awaiting instructions from the HSCU…umm..I mean, we are awaiting your instructions, sir.'

'OK. Calm down son. Where is the SOCO?'

The SOCO, or Scene of Crime Officer, is the person in charge until a ranking officer of the HSCU, the Homicide and Serious Crimes Unit, arrives to relieve him or her. The constable points to a squat looking figure talking to a group of people dressed in white paper overalls. I smile as I recognise JD.

'Thanks son. Keep up the good work,' I say as I walk over to my partner.

By some sixth sense, JD turns before I reach him.

'What took you so long?' he says grim faced but with a glint in his eye, 'I've been here twenty minutes already.'

I clasp him on the shoulder, feeling the muscles beneath his bulky jacket react in the way that a piece of granite would…that is, with no reaction at all.

'What have we got here, JD?' I enquire.

'Single homicide. No witnesses, and I have to warn you, it's a bit messy.'

'Aren't they all?' I say.

He shrugs his impressive shoulders, 'Suppose so Peter, but this is a bit more than our average homicide.'

My mind flips back to our last case, a serial killer of women that almost took the life of my sister, and I stay quiet.

'The victim is a Mr Michael Mason of Typhoon Scientific Industries…'

'Shit,' I say, 'he was only on the news last night talking about their merger with…'

'DCI Carter.'

The acting Commissioner's voice breaks into my conversation with JD.

'Yes ma'am,' I say turning towards Superintendent Patricia Wilks, now acting Commissioner of the Metropolitan Police Force since the unfortunate death of Commissioner Derek Temple nine months ago. A full time successor was still to be appointed, but due to recent changes within the forces structure and the subsequent power base given to the Mayoral office, not one of the logical successors was willing to take the plunge and assume the role.

It was seen as too much of a career suicide with very little control over how the force should be run in its daily workings. The new Commissioner would take all the criticism for operations that went awry, while the Mayor's office would take all the credit for solving crimes that 'looked good' for the papers. In my eyes, Patricia Wilks was managing to keep her head above the parapets and keep the force functioning with the very strict rules in place. Her predecessor, with his fast and loose workings, had forced these rules to be put in place by the politicians who had no idea of what it took to be a police officer on the streets of the England's largest city. The problem with staying above the parapet is that it keeps your head in view and it becomes an easy target for cheap shots and cynical criticism.

'Peter,' she says, 'what is the situation here? I've heard it is Mason of TSI. Is that correct?'

'Ma'am, I arrived on scene just a few minutes before you. JD was just briefing me on the situation.'

She turns to JD with a brief smile and a nod of her head, 'Carry on detective, sorry to intrude.'

He nods his own squat head slightly in her direction and continues his conversation with me, 'He was found by his dinner guest of the evening,' a pause as he checks his notebook, 'Mr Andrew Chinery. He says they only met last week through mutual friends and this was to be their first real meeting. The story checks out. I have already spoken on the telephone to the woman who set them up, she was very helpful.'

'OK,' I say, 'what happened? How was he killed?'

JD looks at me like a petulant teenager.

'Without a full forensics yet, it's unsure. Jesus Peter, it's not even been an hour yet.'

'What's your best assumption?' I ask.

The smile returns, slightly,

'Single stab wound to the chest, with a direct, cataclysmic severing of the aorta. Mason bled out in seconds. Even with a paramedic on the scene at the time of injury it would have been impossible to have saved him.'

'Blind luck or purposeful intent?' Wilks asks JD.

'Again, ma'am, without forensics to determine the weapon used and angle of entry, it's too soon to say.'

She turns to me,

'I want a full report on my desk first thing in the morning. Get Graham on this as a priority and I want his report next to yours, first thing.

I know it's Saturday evening and I know we all had plans…forget them. I want answers on this and I want them yesterday. There will be questions asked at the highest level over Mason's murder and I want to be able to have some answers when I am asked on Monday morning.'

She pulls me to one side,

'Peter, this man was a personal friend to many people way above my pay grade, and that includes the PM. I want this case to be prioritised above anything else you may have going in the pipeline. I don't care what you may think,' she says this before I even have a chance to raise an eyebrow in a question, 'this is yours and JD's priority now. Do you understand?'

I can only nod my head. Anything else is not an option at this moment in time. She turns away and leaves as silently as she appeared. She does not even acknowledge Dr Graham Young as he makes his way to the scene, even though he says her name and holds out his hand. He is left, standing there, looking rather foolish as he holds his hand outstretched to thin air. He turns and looks at me, grins and says,

'Guess she's not worried about being on my Christmas card list.'

CHAPTER 4

'I still can't believe we are going through with this.' Zoe Walker is staring out at the TV studio in front of her, but her words are directed to the woman standing next to her.
'Don't worry Zoe, we've been through this with Dr Macauley. She says it will be good for our healing process to get it out in the open, and tell our side of the story.'
Helen Carter looks over at her close friend.
'We'll be fine,' a briefest of pauses, 'you'll be fine. Trust me.'
As they look out onto the studio floor, the assistant waiting with them says quietly,
'One minute ladies. Get ready.'
Zoe turns to face Helen and they hug.
'OK ladies, you're up. Walk out nice and bright…big smiles…you both look great. Three…two…one…and out you go.'

'Ladies and gentlemen, I would like to introduce to you two very amazing, brave and extremely lucky young ladies. You may know them as the 'Ripper Two', but I would like you to say hello to Helen Carter and Zoe Walker. The two surviving victims of the vicious London Ripper attacks from earlier this year.'
The applause is deafening as Helen and Zoe make their way out of the shadows and onto the brightly lit studio floor. The studio audience get to their feet as Helen smiles and waves gently to them.

Zoe keeps her head down and grasps Helen's hand as they move to their allocated places on the sofa. Some of the audience, mostly made up of women, weep openly, and the director is quick to pan the cameras over these more emotional members of the public. Nothing boosts ratings more than tears, sex or blood, she thinks, and this interview should have them all.

'Helen, Zoe, welcome to 'The Breaking Day'. We are honoured to have you here with us to exclusively tell your story.'

The host, a Scottish, middle aged woman, noted for her sensitivity with real-life stories, gestures to them both with a sweep of her hand and the audience refreshes their cheering, raising the volume even higher.

'For those of you, if there are any of you that is, that are unfamiliar with story, and for the rest of us to refresh in our minds those awful weeks of early Spring, here is a short video to remind us all.'

The lights dim slightly as on the screen behind the three women, and on the monitors placed around the studio, a pre-recorded video is played.

The host leans over to Helen, the closest to her, and whispers,

'Sorry I didn't have a chance to meet you both earlier. I am so pleased to see you here and I hope you have been looked after by my crew. We'll just wait for the video to end and then I will ask a few questions. No pressure, just some background from you both and what led up to the kidnappings. You just say what you want, don't feel you have to do anything you don't want to,' she smiles warmly at both of them and pats Helens hand as Zoe leans forward to listen, 'neither one of you has to worry about anything.

We are not live on air, just live for the studio audience. No pressure at all…if you want a time out at any point, we stop recording and wait for you. This evening is all about you and we have all the time in the world'

Behind the women the screen is displaying a montage of the other Ripper victims with their names displayed beneath the images. The final photo is of a heavy-set, bearded man. The caption reads, 'The London Ripper – James Barnwell'.

Zoe turns away as an involuntary shudder runs through her body. The director has one of the cameras on her in a flash to record her reactions and she is the only one in the whole studio and recording gallery to display a smile.

'This is going to be a good one' she states out loud, to no one in particular, but to the gallery in general, 'hold on to your hats ladies and gents and prepare for a rollercoaster ride.'

The coppery, metallic tang in the air is instantly recognisable. Even if you have experienced it only once, you will know the cause of the cloying smell. Unfortunately I have experienced the cause far too many times in my life. In the hallway it is almost overpowering. It doesn't help that mixed in with the scent of blood is the smell of urine and faeces, caused when the victim loosed his bowels at the time of death.

It does not seem to affect Dr Graham Young, the chief of the Metropolitan's forensic department. He is knelt down next to the body in a set of paper coveralls and carefully avoiding the fragments of broken glass from a wine bottle. He is carrying out a brief check on body core temperature and ensuring the victim has no other obvious injuries.

'What do you think Doc?' I ask him.
He doesn't turn around when he answers.
'I would estimate death was sometime in the last two hours. It would have been fairly quick. The blood pooling around the victim is only a small amount of that which would have been caused by the damage to the heart. The rest has pooled in the pericardial sac and chest cavity. It looks as if the stab wound caused a traumatic rupture to the thoracic aorta; he would have stood very little chance of survival even with the best medical care on hand. I don't believe there would have been a way to prevent immediate exsanguination,' he sees the look on my face and sighs, but with a small smile, as if explaining to a child,
'I thought you would know this by now, Peter. Exsanguination…the fatal loss of blood.'
'I don't do medical jargon, Doc. That's your job. What about the precision of the cut? Is that a factor in this? In your opinion, would someone have to know exactly where to stab the victim to get that level of damage?'
Graham now turns to face me.
'Well, I really need to perform an autopsy for that degree of accuracy, Peter. You know as well as I do that any fool that has a connection with the internet can find all the information required with a thirty second trawl through Google and Wikipedia, probably with photos and a horrific video on YouTube.'
JD appears from a door up ahead,
'All other rooms check out Peter. No signs of forced entry at the back door or through any downstairs windows, so it does look like our victim opened the front door to his killer.

The back door is unlocked though and forensics are checking it for prints along with the rest of the house, but at the moment everything looks clean.'
I look down at Graham as he turns back to the body,
'You know Wilks wants this to be our priority don't you Graham? How soon can you perform the autopsy?'
'Tomorrow morning at the earliest. We have a long night ahead of us trying to collect any evidence here.'
As he says this the flash of a camera startles me slightly as the front door is opened. The constable standing in the doorway gets the full glare of my anger as I see reporters standing outside, jostling for position. Another flash as a camera goes off again.
'Shut that fucking door,' I growl at the young man, 'and get rid of those reporters from outside.'
Shutting the door quickly, the constable stops at the threshold.
'Sir, we have been told to re-open the street. Complaints have been made directly to the mayor's office and Commissioner Wilks has ordered that only this house be declared off-limits and a crime scene. She said to let you know.'
I close my eyes and bow my head. I hate the politics that come with the job.
'Right, OK…' I say, 'extend the cordon from the front of the house out to the pavement…no wait, out to the parking area outside of this house and one either side. I'd hate to piss off the whole street just because there has been a murder on a Saturday night.'
The constable opens the door and scurries for cover outside, away from my anger.

'At least he had presence of mind not to step into the crime scene.' Graham helpfully states.
'Fucking marvellous, just marvellous,' I say exasperated as I think of the media scrum that will be developing outside.
Michael Mason is a well known figure to the public due to his recent appearances on TV and his comments in the papers, with his views on drone use, which his company, Typhoon Scientific Industries, or TSI, designs. He has also been of high news value after news emerged of a merger between TSI and a UK owned defence contractor. The drones his company makes have been used throughout the Middle East to supply information back to military headquarters, and more recently to perform precision strikes against high value, terrorist targets. Unfortunately some of these strikes have killed innocent civilians. Just last week a wedding party in Pakistan was hit by missiles fired from one of TSI's drones, causing widespread condemnation around the world.
I remember how Mason appeared on BBC News outside his offices. He was there to announce the breakthrough in his company's fuel cell design. One of their unmanned aircraft had stayed aloft for over 130 hours, beating the previous record by almost 50 hours. Instead he was made to express his regret at the tragedy, but would not apologise for creating the drones that fired the weapons. I couldn't blame the guy. Here he was being pressured to take the blame for deaths in a country the other side of the world so that a journalist could get a sound bite, when, as he rightly said,
'If a bus crashes and people die, do you blame the bus manufacturer? No, I don't think so.

Our products at TSI are used to create a safer world. They are used by governments around the globe to maintain clear and precise combat awareness. Our products save lives by providing a real-time surveillance picture, coupled with a dynamic threat assessment and first strike capability. Without us and our systems, our troops, our soldiers, would need to be on the ground in hostile territory, facing danger at every corner…not knowing what lies ahead. We provide them with the best defence they can be given…distance from the enemy while still watching his every move.'
The questioning from the journalist was entirely predictable,
'But your products kill innocent people…your systems are responsible for killing an estimated 1000 civilians since they were started to be used in a strike role. It has been suggested by the Pakistan government and even Amnesty International that you should stand trial for war crimes because of your involvement in these deaths. How does that, as you put it, 'save lives'? How does the killing of women and children, over 200 children we are reliably informed, amount to anything more than government subsidised genocide?'
The microphone was pushed back into Mason's face as he looked impassively off camera at the excitable, female journalist,
'Don't be ridiculous,' he says, terminating the interview and then he walked back into the building behind him as the camera followed.
I sigh and hope that Wilks will be dealing with the media on this one. It is far beyond my pay scale to have to field questions about the man hated by half the world who now lies dead on the floor in front of me.

CHAPTER 5

The studio audience are completely silent as they listen to Helen and Zoe describe their ordeal at the hands of the New Ripper, aka, James Barnwell. Apart from soft prompting by the host the only sounds emanate from one or other of the two surviving victims.

'You say you were there when some of the other girls were brought in, Helen. How is it that you survived when others did not?'

Helen looks down at her hands clasped tightly in her lap.

'I fought all the time. I fought to stay alive. I fought to keep from being beaten…mentally I mean. I told myself that no matter what was done to me, how much pain and torture I was put through…I would survive.' She looks to Zoe who is watching her intently with tears glistening in her eyes, 'I wanted to live. I think at some point, the others gave up and that was when he…' she chokes back a sob, 'that is when he would come in to the room and take them away.'

After a moments pause, as the audience watches tears streaming down the faces of the three women in front of them, the host, with mascara running, turns to face her audience.

'Ladies and gentlemen, we will take a short break here to let these remarkable women gather themselves,' she lets out a small sob and a smile, 'and I need to gather myself too. I am sure you all understand this is a harrowing tale that we cannot rush. But please, show your appreciation to these two wonderful ladies…

…these two fighters who battled against the odds, and we will be back in a few moments.'

The applause roars through the small studio as the audience rises to their feet as one to show their respect.

Helen grabs Zoe's hand this time, as they are led off the stage by an assistant, backstage to a small, comfortably furnished room. Two soft sofas sit opposite each other with a small table sat between them. A bottle of vodka stands in a metal bucket filled with ice, on the table, and Zoe heads straight for it. Unscrewing the cap she turns to Helen, 'You want one?'

'No thanks,' Helen says with a shake of her head, 'I don't want to lose control out there.' She moves towards Zoe and places a hand on her shoulder, 'Are you sure you want to do that just yet? We still have the rest of the interview to go.'

Zoe slowly places the bottle back in the ice bucket, screwing the lid back on as she does so.

'It's just so hard to go through it all again… I see…I see his face in front of me and I …I…'

Helen pulls her close, 'Shhh, it's alright. You're doing really good. Just a few more minutes and we can go OK? I'll do the talking if you want, no-one will mind. This will be good for us, you know that right?'

Helen brushes a lock of hair from Zoe's forehead and they look in each others eyes with a common bond of horror between them.

Zoe leans in closer and they kiss, briefly, tentatively. Helen's breathing speeds up as she kisses her friend back, and pulls Zoe's body closer to her. The door to the small room opens quickly and they break apart, looking at the host who has just entered.

'I'm sorry to interrupt…ummm…is everything OK in here for you?' She is clearly embarrassed at disturbing a private moment, but she walks confidently into the room, hiding her feelings behind her years of media professionalism.

'I thought, when we go back out there, we could discuss your time together in the warehouse. Your first feelings, what was said, how you reacted to each other. Do you think that would be suitable? Again no pressure, but people want to know you. They empathise with you and want to feel what you felt. Helen…Zoe…any problems with that?'

Still in each others arms in a now seemingly sisterly embrace, Zoe shakes her head and Helens says, 'That will be fine.' There is a brief pause as they all look at each other before Zoe speaks,

'Thank you for being so understanding. It is very helpful to us both.'

It is said with a small smile and the words mean more than just how the questions have been asked in the studio.

'No problem at all. I can't imagine what you've been through.'

The host walks over to them both and gives them both a hug, 'Five minutes and then we go back out. I'll give you some peace.'

With that she turns and walks away, leaving Helen and Zoe to stand there, holding on to each other as the door closes.

'Just a few more minutes, a few more questions, then we get out of here and get home. Sounds good?' Helen is peering into Zoe's eyes as she frames the question. She receives a small nod in response as they hug again.

It always amazes me that in a city of over 8 million people, hardly anyone sees anything when a murder takes place. I have been told it is human instinct to ignore violent confrontations, mostly through fear of injury and harm to self, but people just switch off. Maybe it is a big city thing? I ask myself. I recall an incident in New York that we were made aware of not so long ago, where a homeless man was caught on camera, defending a woman who was being attacked on the street. Surveillance cameras clearly show the man being beaten by the woman's assailants, while New Yorkers walk calmly by, as it all takes place. The woman was screaming loudly for help and no other person stopped or even made a phone call to the police. Is this the sort of society we now live in? I shake my head as I wonder, and bring my attention back to the constable giving me his report.

'No sounds or commotion heard by the immediate neighbours and no suspicious people or vehicles were reported as being seen.'

'What about the woman across the road?' I ask, thinking of the face I saw at the window. I watch as he flicks through his notebook.

'No woman there, sir. Just a man named as a Stuart Masterson, who was leaving to start work. We let him go as he said he saw nothing.'

I frown and turn to Graham,

'I'll see you tomorrow Doc. Your office 9am, I'll bring the coffee,' I shout out to JD who has stepped into the living room off the hall, 'JD, I'm going across the street, there's something not quite right here.'

I hear a muffled response but cannot make out the words.

'Come on constable; take me through the details of Mr Masterson.'

We push our way through the waiting media with the constable giving me the description of this Masterson figure. Flashbulbs are striking their brief glare into my eyes causing me to raise an arm to stop the rapid flashing from blinding me. A voice rings out that I recognise and wish I could ignore, 'Peter…Detective Carter…any chance of a few words about the terrible events of tonight.'
Her hand on my arm slows me down and I turn to see Ann Clarke staring intently at me. Her small digital recorder is raised towards my face,
'Or perhaps you would prefer to talk somewhere in private?'
Her smile is disarming but I know what this woman can do. I reach up and hold her hand, hitting the off button off the small device within it with my index finger.
'This has to stop Ann,' I say quietly, 'enough is enough. You know I am getting married and I'm sorry if I hurt you, but what we have been doing has to stop.'
She brings her other hand up and clasps my hand within her two. She depresses the record button deftly, and pulls our joined hands, slowly, closer to her mouth.
'Why is that, Peter? Afraid that your beloved Julia will find out you've been fucking me behind her back? I won't tell…not unless I have to.'
The words are said quietly, but I know each one will have been picked up by the sensitive recording instrument she holds. I pull my hand away and glare threateningly at her. My problem is that she is like a drug to me, my addiction.

'Your apartment in one hour,' I say, 'we have to sort this out.' and I turn away from her.

'Already looking forward to it, Peter.' She calls out behind me.

The police constable is waiting for me at the gate to the house where I saw the woman looking out earlier. He chooses either to ignore the look of anger across my face, or simply mistakes it for determination to find a killer.

'Who owns this place?' I ask him.

'Umm...' he checks his notebook.

'Get on the blower,' I say with a sigh, 'and find out if it belongs to Masterson or if it is rented to him.'

I leave him at the pavement as I walk through the gate and towards the painted, black, gloss door. I hammer on it three times and press the small, brass door bell button. I hear the chimes resound from inside as I curse myself for getting into such a mess with Ann 'fucking' Clarke.

I let my mind drift as I wait either for the door to open, or for the constable to bring me information. Ann and I used to be lovers before I met Julia. We both thought it would lead to something more permanent, but her job as a reporter and mine as a detective were just not compatible.

I got fed up of being endlessly pumped for information and the last straw was when I found Ann going through my desk, looking for information on a case I was working on at the time. It didn't end well, there were tears on both sides, which I don't mind admitting. We would occasionally meet up, I think the term nowadays is 'friends with benefits', except we weren't exactly friends.

Then I met Julia and managed to break away completely, at least that is, until the kidnapping of my sister Helen, nine months ago.

I was at a low point, Julia was wrapped up in her father's condition, and Ann was there to pick up the pieces. I didn't mean to cheat on Julia, it just happened and has been happening on a regular basis ever since. I hate myself for it, but seem powerless to stop it. Tonight might have changed that, I think. Ann has never stooped to blackmail like she tried just now and I think she must see an end in sight even if I can't. She is getting desperate. The door in front of me opens to break my chain of thought.

'Yes. What do you want?'

'Mr Masterson?' I ask, looking up at the face that is recognisable but I can't put a name to. His greying hair has been coloured to try and hide his true age, but you can't camouflage the wrinkles around the folds of skin in the neck. Not without surgery at least.

'Of course bloody not, who the hell are you?'

I dig my warrant card out and hold it up for him to see.

'DCI Carter, Homicide and Serious Crimes Unit, Met Police. May I have a word, sir…' I look behind me pointedly at the mob of journalists across the street, 'in private would probably be a good idea.'

The constable is about to enter the gate when I wave for him to stop.

'No need for the info son, I know the answer already.'

I turn back to the man I now recognise,

'Now, sir, shall we talk in private or would you like your constituents to see you talking to a police officer on your doorstep?'

The Member of Parliament in charge of Foreign Affairs pulls the door wider and beckons me in with his hand,
'Please, do come in detective…?'
He leaves the question hanging.
'Carter,' I say, 'Detective Chief Inspector Carter.'

CHAPTER 6

'Mason's dead!'

John Miller looks up from his computer screen at the words spoken by his colleague. There are only two of them working this late on a Saturday night at the engineering headquarters of TSI, based on the outskirts of Norwich.

'What? Say that again.' he says, looking across at her.

'There...look, it's on Sky News.' she says, pointing at one of the many monitors that dominate the far wall of the room.

Peering over the rows of computer screens and telemetry equipment, John sees a reporter standing on a London street talking silently to the camera. A ticker report scrolls across the bottom of the screen and gives the information that they cannot hear from the reporter,

'...ael Mason of TSI industries found dead at his London home...BREAKING NEWS...Michael Mason of TSI industries found dead at his London home...BREAKING...'

John is shocked, 'Turn the volume up and get it on the main screen. Let's see what the hell is going on.'

The remote is picked up and a button stabbed repeatedly to raise the volume which quickly permeates around the room from the discreet surround sound system. Another button press and the black and white thermal image pictures on the main screen are replaced by the lone figure of the female reporter.

'…say there were no signs of robbery readily apparent. A police spokesperson has confirmed that Michael Mason of Typhoon Scientific Industries was found dead at the scene but would not comment on the cause of death. Acting Commissioner Patricia Wilks was at the scene earlier and this is what she had to say,'

The picture cuts to Wilks, surrounded by journalists and microphones, flashbulbs popping rapidly as she addresses the crowd,

'We can confirm that Mr Mason has been found dead in his London residence. We cannot and will not speculate on the cause of death at this time. The Metropolitan Police medical and forensics team are on site and we hope to establish a framework of events leading up to Mr Mason's death as soon as is possible…'

'Is foul play suspected, commissioner?' a voice rings out.

'At this time I will only say that until we determine the exact cause of death, we cannot rule that out.'

This statement brings a flurry of questions from all corners that it is difficult to understand any one of them being thrown at her. The picture cuts back to the reporter,

'With a comment like that from the chief of the Metropolitan Police we can only assume that Michael Mason's death was not from natural causes.'

A brief pause as she looks down at a piece of paper in her hand. She clearly has been told to pad out this 'Breaking News' story to keep viewers hooked.

'Umm…as you know Michael Mason is head of Typhoon Scientific Industries. It is a company heavily involved in the manufacture of drones, or UAV's.

A UAV is an unmanned aerial vehicle, and TSI have been supplying their technology to military forces in action around the world and have recently been caught up in disputes about their controversial use. His company was due to unveil a new drone this week that has been quoted as, 'changing the face of surveillance as we know it'. They are also on the verge of a merger with Centurion Defence, a UK based contractor of military equipments. This merger is said to be worth billions of pounds to the company…'

The ringing of the telephone breaks in to the report on screen and the stunned silence of the two people watching it in the room. John slowly picks up the receiver and puts it to his ear. He says nothing for a moment as he listens intently to the person on the other end. Still silent, he places the receiver back in its cradle.

'He's coming in,' he says whilst still staring at the screen, 'He wants to ensure that the demonstration is still ready to go ahead on Monday and Mason's death is not going to stop it. He even said it would raise more publicity for the MASTER prototype,' MASTER is the abbreviation for the Military Aviation Surveillance and Targeting Energy Regenerator remotely piloted aircraft that TSI and Mason created. He turns from the screen to his colleague with a look of disgust on his face, 'the bastard even sounded happy about that last bit.'

'How long will it be until he arrives?' she asks, shaking her head.

'He's driving down from Cambridge now, so he should be here in about an hour, an hour and a half maybe.'

They both look up at the clock with a nervous anticipation of the arrival of their new CEO of TSI.

Sitting in the back of his chauffeur driven Lexus GS 450 h Premier, Jim Emerson is in the process of placing his Blackberry mobile phone back into his jacket pocket, when it starts to vibrate in his hand. Looking down at the caller ID he thinks about ignoring the call from the number he does not recognise, then shrugs his shoulders in an off-hand way and hits the green answer button.

'Emerson, who is this?'

The voice on his phone is well spoken and speaks quickly as if afraid of being cut off,

'Mr Emerson, this is Trudy Cowan of Sky News. Would you care to talk about the death of your colleague, Michael Mason, and tell us your thoughts about the situation? This is not live, but we would like a quote from your company at this terrible time for you all.'

Emerson cannot contain a grin as he thinks of the media circus that is bound to follow the evening's tragic events.

'Obviously it is a terrible personal tragedy Trudy, but it is also a national tragedy as Michael was a visionary and an outstanding engineer. His death could have far reaching consequences for our nation's quest for renewable energy sources, but we at Typhoon Scientific Industries will go ahead with our demonstration of his latest designs this week in honour of his memory. Michael was a very good friend, and as head of TSI, he was also a good boss. His leadership example and the manner in which he conducted himself will live on in the ethics of our company. Our thoughts are with his brother, Jordan, his only remaining family, at this time, and we offer any assistance we can to him.

We also offer our assistance to the Metropolitan Police in finding out what happened on this dreadful night.'

'Mr Emerson, will you be taking control of the company as you are assistant CEO at TSI?'

Emerson looks out of the car's window at the soft English countryside drifting by,

'For the immediate future I will attempt to step in to the sizeable void left by Michael's untimely death, but it will be up to the board to decide on a worthy successor in the long term.'

He did not need to say that he had each and every board member in his pocket. It was a foregone conclusion who would be the new CEO of the company, and with the merger taking place his remuneration package had just doubled with the death of his friend.

'I'm afraid I cannot say any more at this time Trudy. Please, let me contact you directly in the morning when I shall have a statement prepared and will speak to you exclusively. As you are well aware, this is a tough time for everyone who knew Michael, and I ask for a few hours of privacy while we come to terms with tonight's events.'

He can almost hear the eagerness in her voice for the exclusive interview,

'Certainly, Mr Emerson. Please, use this number at any time of the day or night when you are ready to talk. My apologies for your loss and please know that we will deal with your colleague's death sympathetically. Thank you for taking the time to talk to me and I look forward to hearing from you tomorrow.'

Emerson does not even bother to reply as he hits the 'End Call' button.

CHAPTER 7

JD hears Peter saying he is going across the road to '…something not quite right,' and calls back, 'OK, Peter. I'll be across soon,' and turns his attention back to the man who is sitting, in shock, at the large dining table. It acts as a separation between the kitchen and living area in the open plan, ground floor level of the old building. The aroma of the unfinished cooking is still in the air and it makes JD's belly rumble embarrassingly. The man, Andrew Chinery, is staring into the depths of a polystyrene cup of tea as if it holds all the answers to the world's mysteries.
'Mr Chinery… Andrew. Is there anything more you can tell us about the events of this evening? Did you pass someone on the street? Was there any noise in the house when you opened the door?' The woman asking the questions, JD notes, is the new psychologist drafted in just last month to the unit. It's the first time he has seen her in action and, quite frankly, he is not impressed. Why spend all that time getting your doctorate only to end up asking questions that any copper worth his salt would have asked anyway, he thinks to himself. As far as he is concerned they are a complete waste of money and a drain on the already stretched resources of the Met. He is just about to interrupt her banal line of questioning when the man starts to speak.
Chinery looks up, 'I've already gone over this. I saw no one when I arrived, the taxi dropped me off outside the gate and I came straight in because the door was open.

I didn't hear anyone or anything because as soon as I stepped through the door I was a little preoccupied with seeing…him…Michael…on the floor.'

'OK Andrew,' she says softly, 'what about any smells? Can you remember a smell of aftershave, perfume, anything like that, or something else maybe, something out of the ordinary?'

He starts to shake his head then stops suddenly and stares straight ahead,

'Almonds,' he says, 'there was a strong smell of almonds that I thought was something Michael was cooking, but that is not here now.'

JD takes a deep sniff and gets the smell of a rich tomato and basil sauce with something meaty in the background.

'That's good Andrew, very good. What happened immediately after that?' she probes again, gently.

He looks a little embarrassed,

'I turned away and threw up by the doorway. I never thought I would be affected by seeing a person like that, but my head was spinning and I couldn't help myself.'

The psychologist looks alarmed,

'And how do you feel now Andrew? Still dizzy, any other symptoms?'

Andrew looks confused at the question,

'Symptoms? Well I have a cracking headache and I feel a bit weak…is that from shock?'

She reaches out and places a hand on his,

'It probably is, Andrew. I'll just go and get a paramedic to check you over. You will be all right here OK.'

She stands up and motions with a flick of her head for JD to follow her.

In the hallway, with her back turned to Graham's administrations over the body of Mason, she moves her attention to JD.
'Cyanide poisoning. He shows all the symptoms of cyanide poisoning. An almond scent, dizziness, nausea and weakness are all early signs of exposure. I also took a quick check of his pulse just then, it's racing. Get him medical attention straight away and try not to alarm him. I'll talk to the forensics team.'
Without even waiting for a reply from JD, she turns on her heels and strides down the hallway.
'Cyanide poisoning?' JD thinks to himself, 'maybe she's not so bad after all.' He says as he pulls out his radio and calls for medical aid and an ambulance for Andrew Chinery.

'Dr Young? Sorry to bother you, Kate Jeffery,' she stands a few feet away from the kneeling forensic scientist as she talks to him.
Graham looks up from his position next to Mason's body.
'I know you're busy Dr Young, but I think we may have complications in the case here. The witness I have just been speaking to is showing signs of cyanide exposure. I am presuming it was delivered as an airborne agent or in a sprayed liquid form due to the immediate effect and the rapid dispersal before we arrived. I think you should take precautions in dealing with the victim's body.'
Graham turns back to Mason's body and checks around the mouth and nose for any signs. Without looking up, he says,

'No crystals evident here, if what you say is found to be true I would say a gas, probably Hydrogen Cyanide or Cyanogen Chloride was used. What symptoms is your witness showing…oh,' he turns back to face Kate, 'pleased to meet you.'
She smiles pleasantly, 'Likewise Dr.'
'Call me Graham.'
Another smile, broader this time as she looks down at the forensic scientist,
'OK, Graham. Ummm…oh yes, he remembers a smell of almonds before being nauseous and dizzy and he now has a headache and a racing pulse. DI Dawkins is getting him medical attention now, I suspect they will start with oxygen therapy followed by either sodium nitrite or amyl nitrate. Are you feeling any ill effects?'
Graham shakes his head, 'None. It certainly sounds as if you are right to be cautious,' he pauses and turns back to the body, 'one second.'
He leans over and places his face next to Mason's mouth, pushes down on the victim's chest, and takes a deep breath through his nose.
'Dr!' gasps Kate, 'what…'
Graham shakes his head, as if to clear it,
'A faint smell of bitter almonds, a little dizzy, not nauseous…' he pushes himself up to try and stand and stumbles slightly. Kate has to rush forward and support him by gently grabbing him by the arm and helping him stand. Graham nods his thanks as she pushes her head forward to check his facial reaction. Their heads meet with a slight bump and they both pull back with a smile.
'I think you are right to be cautious,' says Graham, 'this opens up a new can of worms for the investigation, doesn't it?'

He finds himself warming to this woman in front of him, maybe the dizziness is not just about the slight traces of cyanide he has just inhaled. The strength and touch of her hands upon his arm causes him to feel reckless.
'Do you fancy a coffee when we finish here?' he asks her.
He watches as a blush rises from her neck and spreads across her cheeks. He breathes a sigh of relief as her smile grows larger.
'I would like that. That would be great…now how about we get you some oxygen to flush out any traces of the gas…that was crazy you know that, right?'
Graham nods again and smiles,
'Quickest way to find out without waiting for test results though.'

CHAPTER 8

I follow the Member of Parliament through the hallway and into a very tasteful, and expensively furnished, sitting room. It is all antique furniture and old style décor. There is a pair of ancient looking Chesterfield sofas that are deep, chestnut brown leather that I don't think are copies. They are placed at right angles to each other with an elaborately carved coffee table between them. An elegant leather faced wing back chair completes the seating area and I wonder at the price tag that the taxpayer has forked out for these extravagant items. Out of place is a huge Sony TV that dominates one wall, currently showing the Sky News coverage of the street outside. Thankfully the volume is muted. He sees me looking at it.

'65 inches of the latest 4K ultra HD TV. I know the chairman of Sony UK and he let me have one before it hits the streets. Unbelievable picture isn't it?'

I ignore his question and look out of the large bay window that shows the same scene as on the television, but from a different angle.

'Luckily I can also use it for conference calls so it was a write off on the expenses,' he continues, motioning to the discreet camera that blends in to the top of the huge screen, 'to be available to the PM at a moments notice has its perks. It's a shame he sometimes has to see me in my pyjamas though,' he lets out a small laugh, 'not a pretty sight I can assure you.'

'Who is the woman and where is she?' I ask.

'What woman? What are you talking about?' He

responds indignantly, 'I am here alone this week as my wife is off doing some charity work…I can't remember which one it is this month as she changes them so damn often.'

I turn to face him and keep my features impassive. I have no wish to show my contempt for this man.

'When I arrived on the scene earlier, I noticed a blonde haired woman looking out from a first floor window. That window was in this building. Now I will ask you again…who is the woman and where is she? I will need to ask her a few questions.'

He stops talking and just looks at me. His face hardens as he thinks quickly through his options. All I can hear is the ticking of a clock as we stand there facing each other. As every good copper knows, sometimes saying nothing can be the best way to get someone to talk. The seconds stretch out and it seems the ticking of the clock gets louder until it is booming in my ears.

'I saw someone waiting at the door, it opened and they went inside. Nothing else.'

The feminine voice breaks the silence and we both turn rapidly towards the source. The woman I saw at the window now stands in the doorway to the sitting room. She is younger than I first thought, early to mid twenties and is stunningly beautiful She is wearing a plain black, sleeveless dress that hugs her body so finely, it may as well have been painted on. In the millisecond of seeing her in the doorway I already notice I can see no discernable underwear lines to disfigure the material. I clear my throat to hide my stunned admiration. She is obviously used to men having this reaction as she smiles slightly, revealing just a seductive amount of perfect, white teeth.

'Uhhm, why don't we all take a seat and I can ask you both some questions.'

I fumble in my jacket pocket for my notebook, feeling like a schoolboy caught with a dirty magazine in the toilets. It gives me enough of a distraction for me to gather my thoughts and tell myself to stop acting like a day one recruit.

She walks into the room carrying a small black holdall with her coat draped over the top of it. She places these items down carefully next to the leather armchair and eases her body down into the seat. I am reminded of a panther I once saw on a wildlife programme. That too was a perfectly choreographed animal with a slow moving, deliberate motion. Then, without warning, it burst into a ferocious, deadly beast with teeth and claws ripping its unwary victim apart.

I must be careful with this one I think.

'OK. Lets start with your name please.'

'Wilson, Angela Wilson.' She crosses her legs and it is all I can do to focus on my notebook.

'And what line of work are you in Miss Wilson?'

'I am an entertainer.'

I look up, startled, and she laughs a small, pretty laugh that sounds like glass breaking on velvet.

'I entertain people that need a break from the monotony of their own, sometimes sad, life.' She glances knowingly across to the minister who is turning a high blood pressure red. 'I provide a service,' she says turning back to me.

'Are you admitting you are a prostitute Miss Wilson?' I ask, putting my pen down against my notebook.

'Detective?'

I nod.

'Detective, I am not a prostitute. A prostitute sells

her body for money. I provide a service that does not involve intercourse. I am a registered business and I pay my taxes. Everything I do is legal and above board and most of all, discreet. I would ask that you would honour my client's discretion also. We are not here to talk about me are we?'

The minister gives her a brief nod as if to give his approval to her statement.

'Is this going to take long?' she asks, 'only I have another…umm…appointment at eleven and I would hate to miss it. It's my uncle's birthday party you see.'

'Uncle?' I query, only to receive a smile and a nod.

'Yes, I have a large family, but he's my favourite.'

Again a smile that makes blood surge through my body. I check my watch thinking of my own appointment with Ann in an hour, 'I don't see why you can't make your appointment in time if I get the answers I want here.'

I address the both of them,

'Who is Stuart Masterson and why was he at your house earlier this evening?'

They turn to each other and I see straight away this is a dead end line of questioning.

'I don't know any Masterson. You say he was in my house? What the…'

I stop the MP before he can build up a head of steam.

'A constable was carrying out door to door enquiries when he saw a man calling himself Stuart Masterson leave your house. It is possible he is linked with our enquiries across the road.' I deliberately look at Miss Wilson, 'If you have any information about this man I need to know it.'

She looks straight at me and shakes her head, her smile disappears slowly.

'He is a white male, approximately thirty to forty years old, dark hair, thin build and around six feet tall. It is a little vague, but does that description ring any bells to either of you?'

Again I am concentrating my attention on the woman to see any reaction from her. Her brow furrows slightly as she processes the information, she reminds me of a young Meg Ryan as she does this.

'That could be any one of a million people in London Detective. I am afraid I cannot be of any more help with that.'

I pick my pen up again,

'Before you watched me walking down the street earlier, did you observe anything…anyone else in the street? No matter how ordinary it may have looked, it might help us catch a killer.'

She bows her head and looks down into her lap before turning to the minister,

'Gerald, would you mind giving us some privacy. Maybe make a quick cuppa, yeah?'

The large man looks at me and I nod my approval.

'Not for me thanks, I will come and get you in the kitchen in a few moments.'

As he walks out of the room I cannot tear my eyes away from the woman in front of me and wonder what she is about to reveal.

CHAPTER 9

'We have a problem.'

Stuart Masterson is talking quietly into his mobile phone as he walks along the dark 4th floor of the multi-storey car park. Stopping at a black Mercedes Benz ML-350 he listens to the clipped English accent coming from the earpiece.

'You know I don't like problems. Is it something that you can handle or do we need to arrange damage control?'

He presses a button on his key fob and the Mercedes indicators flash twice. Pausing with one hand on the door handle he thinks before responding,

'I think we need to get damage control on this. I never got to Mason in time. Someone beat us to it and now I think the police will be looking for me. Our friend Carter was there, but he didn't recognise me.'

'Well at least some good has come from the surgery we gave you.' A sigh breathes into Masterson's ear, 'Get back to the office, I need a full de-brief into what happened and I want to know who got to Mason before us. Did you see him at all?'

'Sir, it was a woman. She was quick, efficient and it was all over by the time I got the front door. I had to rush away as a civilian arrived. I don't know what happened to the woman. She was inside the building when I left and Mason was dead on the floor.'

He opens the door and eases himself into the driver's seat.

'Masterson?'

'Yes sir.'

'Do you think they have the information we were after?'

Staring out across the sparkling London skyline he hesitates before saying the words he knows his boss does not want to hear,

'I am certain of it sir.'

Masterson swears he can almost hear the expletive cross the rooftops in front of him without needing the telephone. Placing his car keys back into his pocket he presses the 'GO' button next to the steering wheel and feels imperceptibly the 3 litre diesel engine purr into life.

'We need to get that information. Did you recognise the female?'

'No. I only saw the back of her head before she pushed her way inside the door.'

The heater is pushing warm air into the cabin now and replacing the chilly December air. Masterson affords himself the luxury of raising the temperature on the climate control a few degrees as he waits for a response.

It is a few seconds in coming, a reflection on the seriousness of the situation.

'Debrief at the firm. Come straight to the basement. I want all the details and I will also want to know from our friends at the Met what they have on this matter. I'll deal with them, you work out what went wrong and I will want to know why you missed your mark on this op. Are we clear?'

The warmth in the vehicle does not affect the chill that seeps into Masterson's bones at these words,

'Perfectly clear sir. I'm on my way in.'

The phone goes dead in his hands and he just sits there for a second contemplating his future. He throws it onto the seat next to him and reaches inside his jacket to pull out a plastic folder containing a few sheets of paper and most important of all, a USB flash drive, the contents of which could be used to secure his future or destroy it. He reverses out of his parking space and decides he has to make a quick stop before making the rendezvous with his boss.

CHAPTER 10

The trip back from the television studio is completed in an exhausted silence. Sitting in the back of the taxi cab hired and paid for by the studio, the two women hold each others hand and watch the bright Christmas lights of London slide by in the darkness of the late December evening. Zoe opens her mouth to say something but notices Helen's drooping eyelids and thinks better of it. As they pull up outside Helen's apartment Zoe has to gently shake her awake.
'We're here babe. Let's get inside, open a bottle of wine and try and relax. Although you look like that should not be too much of a problem.'
Helen smiles sleepily,
'Sounds great. We'll send Ewelina out for a Chinese as well. I can't be bothered trying to cook anything now. I can't believe how much today has taken out of me.'
Ewelina, Helen's flatmate in the rented apartment, had been a great help to them both after their ordeal and even though the place was a bit small for three people to live in full time, they wouldn't think of asking her to leave.
Zoe reaches into her purse and gives the driver a five pound note as a tip,
'Thank you,' she says before exiting the vehicle and walking with Helen to the red brick building. As they reach the front door Ewelina opens it unexpectedly.
'Hey guys, I didn't expect you back so early,' Ewelina says holding the door open for them. She is dressed up and obviously ready for a night out.

'Anyone we know?' Helen asks whilst hugging her. 'Just a guy I got chatting to on the tube this afternoon. Nice man from Brighton looking for someone to show him the sights.' Ewelina smiles, 'Maybe he will take me away from all this and you can have your apartment to yourselves.'

Helen laughs lightly, 'And when that happens he has to pass my approval test,' she counts off on her fingers, 'One; is he rich, two; is he handsome, three; does he treat you right and four, if he passes questions one to three, is he married and if not why not?'

All three women burst out laughing.

Ewelina hugs them both again, 'Don't wait up, I may be late back.'

Helen and Zoe both turn serious and Helen grabs her by the shoulders, 'Just be careful OK. If anything feels strange, anything at all, call us and call my brother. Peter will be able to help. You have his number, yes?'

Ewelina pulls out her phone and presses a few buttons before holding up the screen for Helen to see.

'Speed Dial 1 – Peter Carter Police' is on the screen. 'Just like you said Helen, and anyway, I am always careful.'

With a wave of her hand Ewelina walks away with two pairs of eyes watching her back.

Zoe places her arm around Helen, 'Why don't you get inside and open that bottle of wine we talked about, I'll nip round to Mama Lan's and get us that takeaway.'

Helen is still looking in the direction Ewelina left. 'Yeah,' she turns and smiles at Zoe, 'yeah. That would be good. I'll have the..'

'I know,' Zoe says with a grin, 'Beef and spring onion dumplings and the fried vegetable balls. You are so predictable.'

'Ha, and you with your veggie mushroom rubbish and seaweed salad is the height of impulsiveness.'

Zoe pokes her tongue out playfully and laughs for a moment. She pauses as she is about to say something, mouth slightly open.

'What is it Zoe?' Helen asks, 'Did I say something wrong?'

'No I…I just wanted to say…' Zoe looks up to the sky before grabbing Helen's hands and staring her straight in the eyes, 'I love you Helen.' It is said breathlessly, desperately.

'Oh Zoe, I…'

'You don't have to say it back, not yet. I just wanted you to know how I feel. I wanted you to know…I love you.'

The second time it is said it spills much easier from her lips. She pulls Helen forward in an embrace, they hug and kiss lightly before Zoe pulls away. Helen moves slowly into the building without saying a word while Zoe walks off in the same direction as their flatmate only moments earlier, hoping she has not just made a huge mistake with her words.

CHAPTER 11

'I caught a glimpse of a man going in to the house across the street that matches the description you gave. I recognise him as I have done some work for him in the past.'
I stay silent, waiting for her to continue. She looks out of the window,
'He is a man that you do not want to mess with. In my line of work you get a feel for the men you entertain,' she turns back to me, 'you for instance, you're a curious type. I see no wedding ring on your finger but I sense a certain hesitation in you when you look at me, so I would guess in a steady relationship. Most probably engaged?' It comes out as a half question, half statement.
I smile and nod but say nothing.
'Detective, you have to understand my occupation is of a unique type,' she sighs and looks down at her slender fingers as she slowly rubs one hand across the palm of the other, 'I hurt people and they pay me for it. The clients I have enjoy a certain amount of pain, they get gratification from being dominated by a person like me. I have no qualms about that, each to their own, and the pay is very good. When I was employed by the man I saw today it was,' she raise her head, 'it was different. He paid me to abuse and degrade people he was with.'
'Do you have a name? An address where you would meet? Please, we have to stop this guy before he kills again.'
There is a pause as she chews on the inside of her lip in thought.

'I used to meet him at the Albert Embankment. 85 Albert Embankment.'
She waits to see my reaction.
'Vauxhall Cross?' I ask with a grimace on my face.
'Exactly Detective.'
'Shit.' Is all I can say.
85 Albert Embankment is home to the SIS, or Secret Intelligence Service, also known as MI6. I have had recent contact with some of their operatives and it did not have the outcome I would have expected.
'Can you tell me about the people he had you, shall we say, entertain?'
'Officially, all I can tell you is that I was asked to meet clients at the building and they were all of Middle Eastern descent. Having a woman degrade them was something against their manhood apparently. They made me sign a form to stop me from saying anything else about what went on. I am sorry, so very truly sorry.'
'Who was the contact at MI6?'
I watch as she shakes her head,
'I don't know if I can say. The form was clear about what would happen if I said too much.'
I reach over and grab her hands in mine,
'Angela, this is a separate case entirely. I do not have to divulge how we got his name or where you know him from. This man has probably killed tonight. We have to know who he is in order for us to stop him doing it again. It doesn't matter if he is the Pope, I have to find this guy.'
'Can you protect me?' she asks with a whisper.
Still holding her hands in mine I nod,
'I will protect you. Nothing will happen to you, I promise. We just need this guy's name.'

Quietly,

'OK, OK. He used to call me at my office and specifically ask only for me. His name is Stephens, Neal Stephens.'

I sit back in the chair with a bump, my head reeling. Stephens is the person from MI6 I had dealings with in my sisters case.

'He has changed slightly somehow but I don't think I could mistake him no matter what. His cheekbones are a little fuller and his nose has been altered, but it was definitely him.'

'Plastic surgery?' I question out loud as I think back to our last meeting. Stephens and his boss had pulled the rug out from under our case. They had forced us to shut down our enquiries when we found out the truth behind a string of murders whilst feeding us enough evidence to give closure to the investigation.

'Probably, yeah…that would seem likely,' Angela answers my outspoken thoughts.

What worries me now is the knowledge that Stephens thinks nothing of killing if it keeps with the plans of his superiors.

'Say nothing of this to anyone, Angela. I will keep your name out of this for the moment. I'll put you down as an anonymous source to protect you, but I will need a contact number and address in case I need to speak to you again.'

I look at my watch,

'I will need to see you again. I have some pictures of Stephens that I would like you to look at to confirm his identity but I won't ask you to come to the Yard. I will bring them to you. Is that OK with you?'

She nods as she fumbles in her purse for something,

'Whatever you think best Detective. Here is my card. The land-line is the office and the mobile is my personal number. If you can't contact me straight away, leave a message on the mobile and I will get back to you,' she stands up and smooths her dress down to get rid of any wrinkles, 'may I go now?'

I stand up and reach out my hand to shake hers, 'Certainly. Thank you for your co-operation and your time.'

She holds my hand for a second or two longer than is polite before releasing me and walking to the door.

'Oh wait a second,' I fumble in my jacket pocket and produce a crumpled business card, 'if you need to contact me, this is my office phone and my personal mobile.'

Taking it delicately from me she places it deftly into her bag,

'Thank you Detective,' she says and turns away to bump into her client who is standing in the doorway holding a teapot and some cups on a tray, 'Tea?' he asks.

Angela smiles and reaches up to his cheek with her hand,

'Maybe next time.'

She reaches the front door and opens it just as JD is poised to knock.

'Oh, sorry Ma'am,' he says, 'I am looking for DCI Carter. Is he inside?'

'He certainly is,' she replies as she squeezes past JD's considerable bulk and walks away from the building.

JD cannot help but watch as she glides away, 'Jesus,' he breathes out before heading inside and exclaiming loudly, 'Peter, we have issues here.'

The call from JD catches both me and the Member of Parliament off guard.

'Sorry sir, I have to go. If you remember anything at all about tonight's events please contact my department and I will come right over,' I lean closer towards him, 'I will be discreet with the information I have gathered here today, sir, but I would suggest you need to start acting with a certain decorum and discretion yourself.'

I head towards the front door and JD as the MP bristles behind me, still holding his silver tray of tea at the ready.

'What have we got JD?'

'A huge can of worms, a crazy pathologist and a sick witness for starters.'

I sigh as I close the door behind us and start walking towards the house opposite,

'Tell me about it.'

CHAPTER 12

The security checkpoint at the TSI facility is as thorough as always. It doesn't matter who you are, from the head of the board to the milk delivery, you will go through the same process. It is a fact that it is harder to get into or out of the complex here in Norfolk than it is to get into any military establishment in the country.

Jim Emerson is ushered respectfully from his car and into the building through a chain link corridor. The slight drizzle forces one of the guards to shadow him with a black umbrella bearing the TSI logo until he reaches the protection and warmth of the search area. The driver of his car follows behind, turning his collar up against the droplets of rain that fall lightly on his head and shoulders. Even if they must be searched the same, some things are different when you help run the company.

Behind them in the bright sodium glare of the floodlights the car is being meticulously examined. A team of two sniffer dogs are being encouraged to seek out anything out of the ordinary. One animal is specifically trained to identify explosive substances, the other is there to hunt down any human stowaways. When the dogs have finished their sweep of the car, three men move in to check the vehicle.

A slim man in black overalls with 'TSI SECURITY' neatly stitched on the left breast gets down on his back and crawls under the car. His head-torch flicks from side to side as he inspects any dark crevice for recording devices or other unexpected add-ons to the vehicle.

The two other men who are both dressed in the same uniforms, work their way through the interior with hand-held x-ray devices before turning their attention to the boot and engine compartment. Ten minutes after the car has arrived it is declared all clear following the rigorous search, and the team leader, who has been watching from inside the building behind a one way blast proof window, steps back and presses a small button to announce the all clear to the other security detail who are with Emerson and the driver.

Emerson is relaxed and composed. He is sitting in a soft leather chair and sipping an espresso from a small, clear glass coffee cup. The body scan showed nothing out of the ordinary as he walked through. His company mobile phone has a chip inserted to allow it through the machine. The driver is not so fortunate to have such a device. His cell phone has caused the machine to warble a soft warning to the security staff without causing alarm to the person inside the body scan equipment.

'Sir? What do you want us do?'

The question comes from a stocky, crew cut, middle aged man who materialised next to Emerson as the first alarm sounds emanated throughout the room. He too is dressed in the same black coveralls as the rest of the staff with the exception that on the right breast of his the word 'CHIEF' is emblazoned in gold lettering.

'He knows the score. Teach him a lesson.'

The Chief doesn't move an inch away from his superior but nods almost imperceptibly towards a camera placed high up in the corner of the room. The warbling stops to be replaced by a stringent sounding buzzer and a red strobe light starts to flash lazily.

Inside the scanner the driver looks up startled as he sees the light and sudden realisation dawns on his face. He starts to feel around his body, patting his pockets before alighting on the hard, oblong object in his jacket pocket. As he touches it his head drops and Emerson smiles as he sees the man mouth, 'Damn it,' behind the security glass. The driver slowly brings out his mobile phone and holds it up.

'Into the chute please.' A metallic voice commands through hidden speakers.

Turning in a half circle he places the phone into a drop down box that has appeared to the side. It closes with a snap and the phone disappears from view.

'Now strip and place your clothes in the chute when done.'

Knowing he has no choice the man in the scanner reluctantly complies.

Emerson smiles as he watches.

'Sir, they are ready for you. Would you like to wait for…him?' The chief nods towards the man undressing in front of them.

'I don't think so, Chief. Do a body cavity search and then turf him out. There is no room for any mistakes in my company.'

'Yes sir. I'll call him a taxi.'

'No. It's his mistake. He can find his own way back.'

The Chief knows better than to say anything more. He nods and motions with one hand for the chairman to walk through a set of doors that lead into the facility.
'Oh and Chief...find me a new driver will you. Someone reliable this time.'
'Yes sir. I'll get onto it straightaway.'

The doors lead into another secure area where a guard seated inside a glass walled room checks Emerson's identification against a match on a computer screen. The guard nods towards a small device on the wall and Emerson moves his head forward to line up his left eye for the retina scan. A second later a green light flickers on and a soft clunk is heard.
'OK sir, please come through the barrier.'
Emerson walks into the floor to ceiling metal cage and pushes the bars slightly to rotate the secure revolving metalwork. As he attempts to walks through the bars they jolt to a stop after performing just a quarter turn. He looks impatiently to the guard in his booth, his eyebrows raised in anger.
'Sorry sir, it's been playing up lately,' the guard presses a button to manually release the lock on the mechanism, 'I'll get maintenance on it again.'
As Emerson walks through he shakes his head and mutters,
'You do that son.'
The brightly lit corridor he faces is flanked by offices for the security staff. He walks past these, following the corridor is it makes three 90 degree bends before opening out to a large landing at the stop of a concrete staircase. The cool air form the air conditioning below adds a chill as he walks down the steps and into the heart of TSI.

The bunker is three stories of high tech equipment and enough computing power to blow Microsoft out of the water. The huge facility is a relic from the cold war. At one time it would be manned by hundreds of Royal Air Force personnel as they watched the skies around the UK from deep underground. Secure communications links from the outside world fed in data from long range air defence radars, AWACs aircraft, naval ships and satellite imagery. From here they could direct fighter aircraft to intercept long range bombers from Russia before they got close enough to drop their deadly cargo. The complex was built to withstand anything but a direct hit from a nuclear weapon and it was virtually impregnable to attacks from the outside, be they either physical or electronic.

With air scrubbers, water treatment, electricity generators, workshops, sleeping facilities and even a gym and two restaurant style food halls, it had everything to keep hundreds of people alive in relative comfort if the worst was to happen. Emerson wished he was the one with the foresight to buy the place when it came up for sale, but, as always it was Michael Mason that was the forward thinker of the company. The whole complex including the grounds outside cost less than Mason's townhouse in Knightsbridge to buy.

The company had spent almost the same amount to equip the space with state of the art equipment and it had come close to bankrupting them, but orders started coming through and for the five years after they started work from here their profits had increased each year.

It helped that there were wars being fought on two fronts and their products were in high demand. It was then that Mason decided to expand the company. From small scale projects with high product turnover they expanded into Unmanned Vehicle technology and Mason was especially intrigued by the fuel to flight ratio. He had spent millions on developing more efficient systems and the unveiling of their new unmanned platform would have been his crowning glory, not just for the military, but also for the world as a whole. Emerson shakes his head as he thinks all this, 'How naïve can you get,' he says aloud as he walks through the concrete lined corridors.

To stop any blast waves from explosions on the surface reaching the manned areas, there were many right angled corners with blind corridors branching off to catch the pressure of an explosion. Finally he reaches the huge metal blast doors that mark the entrance to the main complex. A flashing strobe light and a klaxon mark the automatic opening of the heavy, hydraulic doors. Emerson waits as they take the sixty seconds to fully open before striding through. An armed security guard nods as he walks past and continues down to the main control room.

Emerson presses his hand against the scanner outside the door and waits a moment for the system to recognise his prints before the door swings inwards silently.

It is surprising that only a team of two is needed to run the facility during the quiet hours.

'Miller, bring up the stats for the MASTER mother-ship, Susan how are the fuel cells working?' Emerson commands softly as he enters.

John Miller presses a few keys on the back-lit keyboard in front of him and the large screen brings up a wire frame image of an aircraft and a list of numbers next to it. As Emerson reads through the list, Susan Ewan, John's assistant, reads from her own computer screen,
'Fourteen cells have been recovered and replaced in flight. The homing beacon is working well apart from a slight glitch when passing close to the RAF radar site at Trimingham.'
'What sort of glitch?' Emerson asks without taking his eyes from the screen.
'One of the replacement cells became disoriented, possibly by a burst of high power RF. It attempted to lock on to the beam but gave up after…let's see…umm, 3.6 seconds, before resuming its course to the mother-ship. We had it return here immediately to check for damage but none was found.'
'How close was it to the radar?'
'250 metres.'
'Hmmm. See that it doesn't happen again. I want a safe distance set up of 500 metres from any equipment transmitting more than 300 kilowatts.'
He points to the screen,
'Bring up greater detail on the nano-generators I want to know why there was a dip in power two days ago?'
Susan is ready for this question but she did not think Emerson would have picked up on it so quickly,
'We had a power cut in the area on that day. The ambient backscatter was reduced until the power was restored. Not a fault with our equipment, sir.'

Mason's breakthrough in energy harvesting was a device that 'sucked up' radio waves as they travel through the air. These nano-generators could harvest the energy from television, satellite and radio broadcasts as well as the minute signals given off by all electrical items and convert it into useable electrical power. The electro-active polymers used to create the generators were not cheap, but they allowed the aircraft to recharge its batteries continuously. Coupled with the autonomous, replaceable fuel cells meant that in theory, the aircraft would never have to land.

The fuel cells were the selling point. The mother-ship was just a state of the art remotely piloted surveillance vehicle, but the way it was refuelled was where TSI would make its fortune.

Each fuel cell was an autonomous, unmanned aircraft in its own right. Stored within the main ship were thirty fuel cell docking areas. The cells created energy by the conversion of water into hydrogen. A clean, green resource. When close to exhaustion, a fuel cell would send a signal back to base requesting a replacement. One of two things could then happen;

The nearly empty fuel cell could detach itself from the docking bay and return to base directly, or, it could be used as a mini surveillance platform sending information back to its controllers via secure radio link. At any point the fuel cells could also be used to create a small squadron of unmanned aircraft with a limited kill potential. The fuel cells could be directed onto a target and made to explode using their hydrogen tanks as the explosive.

The damage radius would easily take out a car or small truck and more could be directed onto the target very quickly if anyone survived. The MASTER mother-ship could stay on station for two hours even if all fuel cells were used in this way, giving more than enough time for fresh cells to be sent up to replenish it.

'I want a full check of all MASTER systems by 0800 hours and I want to see the full details of the last seven days flight recordings in my office immediately,' Emerson walks back towards the entrance to the control room, 'and call in Ethan. I want to know exactly why we had a glitch with the fuel cell. I'll be in my office.'

The doors open as he approaches and close softly behind him.

'Well that went better than expected,' John says as he starts collating the information for Emerson.

CHAPTER 13

I cannot believe it has taken me forty five minutes to get away from the crime scene involving Mason. As a DCI there is not much I can do apart from watch and ensure the crime scene is not tampered with. I told Ann I would be with her within the hour. I am late by thirty minutes.

I reach her apartment block and press in the four number key code to let myself in. As usual her lift is out of order and I smile slightly as I think of the health benefits the bad maintenance of the elevator will have on my body.

As I climb the stairs I run through my mind the conversation we will be having. I have to break away from her now or she will be forever a part of my life that I do not want. I know the following few minutes are going to be ugly but I have to do it if Julia and I stand any chance of a future together. I steady my nerves as I climb the stairs but I know it will not prepare me for what I have to do when I get to her apartment.

Her front door is ajar. That should have sent my alarm bells ringing straight away.

I push the door open almost carelessly; I have seen enough human destruction tonight without thinking I will see more in the next few minutes. Her body is pushed almost carelessly into the corner of her soft L-shaped sofa. I remember making love to her in that very same position on more than one occasion in the past, but this time her body looks like it has been forced into place.

'Ann!' I shout.

I rush forward and pull her backwards towards me. One hand goes directly to her throat as my head bends down to her soft lips to see if I can feel or hear her breathing. I feel her soft, slow pulse under my fingers as I can sense her uneven breath in my ear. I pull my mobile phone from my jacket pocket and dial 999 as I look around the room for any signs as to what may have occurred over the last few hours.

'999 emergency, how can I help?'

'This is DCI Carter of the Metropolitan Police. I need an ambulance and a crime scene unit at my location, I am an off duty officer requiring immediate assistance with an unresponsive casualty. Do you understand?'

'Sir, please confirm your badge number.'

I repeat my Metropolitan Police badge number and am acknowledged with,

'Right away sir.'

I hang up and again rapidly survey the room for any clues. On the heavy coffee table a set of papers are placed as if she was reading through them. I have to do a double take as I see the documents have the TSI logo emboldened across them and the word MASTER in thick capitals at the top of the page. They are too far away for me to reach without letting go of Ann so I have to peer at them from where I sit. I cannot make out much, but I do see what appear to be plans of a large aircraft with numbers and details in one corner.

'Oh Ann, what happened here?' I ask breathlessly as I hold her in my arms.

I do not hear the paramedics arrive as I hold her in my arms. I barely notice the flash bulbs from the cameras as they capture me holding her in my firm embrace.

Two hours later as I stand outside the Emergency Department of University College Hospital, I think to call Julia.

'Julia, hi babe,' I say with a smile on my face, even though I find it hard to do so.

'Hey Peter,' she says, 'how are things going?'

'Sorry I never made it to the meal this evening. Please give your family my best wishes. I don't think I will be home tonight either. There have been, um, …complications.'

'OK. No problems,' she says sleepily, 'You just make sure you look after yourself OK?'

'Yeah, I'll do that sweetheart, goodnight.' I reply as I end the call.

I place the phone back into my jacket pocket and feel the hard jewellery box from earlier in the evening and it feels like a lifetime ago. My mind is swirling as I look through the large plate glass window towards the woman, my lover, who is lying on the hospital bed with tubes and machines attached to her frail body.

'What the hell is going on here?' I ask myself.

I don't get any answers. I wasn't expecting any.

CHAPTER 14

'Where the hell have you been? You were meant to come here direct from the incident site and report your findings.'
These words are declared with a sense of anger. Stuart Masterson just smiles,
'I created a distraction.'
The man on the other side of the small room explodes in anger,
'A distraction! A fucking distraction! Who authorised you to do such a thing and why should you have to carry out such a, what did you call it...a fucking distraction. Who the hell do you think you are?'
Masterson smiles, thinking back to many such extravagant gestures he has witnessed in the past,
'I am the man that keeps pricks like you out of the public eye and safe from investigations by the powers that be. Without me and my distractions you and your department would be nothing but a speck of shit on a minister's shoe. Do you understand that?' he raises his voice in sarcasm,
'Sir.'
The man the other side of the room adjusts his tie theatrically before placing both hands on the table in front of him,
'Tell me more.'
Still smiling, Masterson takes off his jacket, places it on the back of the chair in front of him and sits down.

'I thought it prudent to follow your instructions and find what information our police friends had on Mason's murder. I overheard a reporter talking to Carter and arranging a meet for later so I followed her to see what I could learn. I was hoping to pump her for information after Carter had left but unfortunately someone had beaten me to it. As I was waiting for him to leave there is suddenly a roar of sirens and the police and an ambulance turn up tearing into the building.'

'What was their meeting about? The reporter and Carter I mean. Did you find out?'

Masterson shakes his head, 'Not sure, there was no way to get a listening device inside at such short notice, but I do have a few photographs from the scene. As luck would have it, the ambulance crew were being shadowed by a cameraman who is doing a piece on the state of the NHS. I flashed him my badge and asked for the camera's memory card. Of course he spouted freedom of press so I had to coerce him slightly.'

The man across the table grimaces slightly,

'What is on the pictures?'

Masterson pulls a USB stick from his pocket,

'I copied them across to this, he still has the originals to use as he sees fit.'

'I thought you said you coerced him?' it is said with a sneer as if he is disgusted with his methods.

'I did, and you now owe me Five Hundred Pounds for the pleasure. It's not all about violence. Now do you want to see the pictures or not?'

He gets a nod of the head towards the flat screen display with a laptop attached,

'Plug it in there.' is the command.

After a few seconds delay as the memory stick is read, a folder opens with hundreds of images within. Masterson works his way backwards from the most recently dated. On screen, Peter Carter is shown standing over the prone figure of a female in the back of an ambulance. Like a slow motion replay in reverse we see how the woman is taken from the ambulance and moved back into the apartment building before being taken off a stretcher and placed in the arms of Carter as he sits in a small living room.

'OK Masterson, what am I looking at here?'
Masterson scrolls a few pictures forward,
'This one I think is one that will interest you.'
The image shows two paramedics checking the body of the woman whilst Carter stands to one side staring down at a coffee table.
'And why is this interesting?'
Masterson taps a few times on the laptop's keyboard and mouse buttons and the image zooms into the corner of the coffee table that Carter appears to be studying.
'Is that…?'
'Yes it is. Those are Mason's documents concerning the MASTER prototype.'
'Where are they now?'
Masterson presses another button and the images flick forward. The picture on screen shows Carter in the background placing a sheaf of documents into a plastic folder, 'CLICK', and the image changes to show how he is seen placing them into his jacket pocket.

'We need to stop publication of those photos, I will sort that out under National Security measures, no editor will dream of publishing them with that order on them, and I need those documents,' he turns to Masterson, 'at any cost.' he repeats for emphasis, 'At ANY cost.'

CHAPTER 15

Helen cannot believe just how tired she still feels as she wakes up to the sound of a kettle boiling from the kitchen. The piercing light coming from the windows makes her look around in confusion as she realises she is asleep on the sofa in the living room. Her eyes settle on the digital clock on the front of the satellite receiver and she watches as the green readout changes from 07:53 to 07:54. She raises her wrist to confirm the time on her own watch and is incredulous to think she has slept through the whole night.
'Hey sleepy head, fancy a coffee?' Ewelina's lilting Polish accent makes Helen turn to her with a smile on her own face. She stifles a yawn and stretches her arms over her head.
'I didn't hear you get back in. How was the date?' Ewelina raises her mouth in a sly grin as she replies, 'I only just got back, why? Did you miss me?'
Helen laughs, 'You dirty little stop-out. No wonder you are up so early, or have you not slept at all.' Ewelina turns her back on Helen and heads back into the kitchen, 'Oh I've been to bed…just never managed to get any sleep.' She says as she disappears from view.
'Coffee, strong, two sugars,' is Helen's command. Again the disembodied voice, 'On it's way babe, shall I make one for Zoe?'
Helen shakes her head, 'I can't believe she left me on the sofa. I'm going to give her such a beating…'

she pauses awkwardly as she thinks of their history together.

'I'll go and get her out of bed. I must have already been asleep when she got back with the Chinese last night. She must have decided not to wake me.'

'You were snoring pretty loudly when I arrived.'

'Fuck off, I don't snore…much. Anyway where's my coffee you whore, and don't forget Zoe likes it milky!'

'Whores get paid. I would gladly do all that again for free.'

Helen snorts laughter as she clambers off the sofa and makes her way to the bedroom where Zoe is sleeping.

'Zoe,' she calls out sweetly as she pushes open the door, 'oh ba-abe, why did you…'

The question trails off as she sees the bed is empty and still made from the day before.

'Zoe?'

She walks back to the kitchen, 'Have you seen Zoe since you got in?'

Ewelina is just stirring the hot drinks with a teaspoon, 'No, isn't she still in bed?' she says without pausing.

'The bed hasn't been slept in. I don't think she came back home last night.'

Helen turns and runs from the kitchen towards the low table where here keys and mobile phone are lying. She grabs the phone and quickly rushes through the menus.

'No calls, no messages. Zoe, where are you?' she cries out.

Ewelina, hearing the anguished tones in the outburst, hurries through to be with her flatmate. She pulls her phone from her purse as approaches and checks for any missed calls or messages too. There are none.

'Try and call her, Helen. See if she is staying…I don't know where, just see if she answers.'

Helen is already nodding as she holds the phone up to her ear to listen to the electronic ringing tones emanating from the handset.

After five rings it is answered,

'Hi, this is Zoe, I am not available at the moment so please leave a message on my voicemail and I will get straight back to you when I have a little more time. Thanks…byeee.' BEEEEEP.

Helen slowly lets the phone drop from her ear as she turns to her friend,

'Something's happened, oh God, I know it, something has happened to Zoe.'

She stabs away at the keypad again. This time the phone is answered on the first ring.

'Peter, it's me. Something's wrong, somebody has taken Zoe.'

I hear the desperation and fear in my sister's voice as I sit in interview room number four at the Met's Headquarters. I look up at JD as he crosses his arms and turns his head to the woman sitting next to him.

'DCI Marie Phillips, internal investigation interview of DCI Peter Carter paused.'

I nod my head in thanks and speak softly into the mouthpiece,

'Run me through it from the beginning Helen. Let's see if we can sort this out.'

CHAPTER 16

Acting Police Commissioner Patricia Wilks is sitting at her desk holding a report in her hands. Her coffee, which she picked up from the canteen on her way in, stands rapidly cooling and untouched on her desk. She is normally in work early to review the night's investigations but this morning is earlier than normal. Her head of Homicide and Serious Crimes Unit has been cautioned and is currently in an interview with the Metropolitan Internal Investigations department.
'Can you be sure he has been giving information to this reporter?' she asks the man who she rushed out of her comfortable bed to meet at her office.
'Ma'am, we have been following DCI Carter closely for the last nine months. We were given information by an outside agency that all was not above board and correct and...'
'What outside agency, John? Where did they get that information and why do you so blithely believe what you are told?'
DCI John Midgely knows he must tread carefully here, 'Ma'am, obviously we check any accusations against any officers on the force. We especially check these allegations when they come from another government department, which in this case is MI6,' he holds his hand up to stop Wilks from speaking, 'I cannot and will not go into any greater detail on this matter. The document you hold there shows a brief history of dates and times of the meetings, in private I must stress, of DCI Carter and Ann Clarke over our surveillance period.'

Wilks places the sheets of paper on to the desk in front of her and folds her hands over the top of them.

'So why are you interviewing him now? What has happened that has made this,' she waves her right hand over the desk, 'to make this seem more than two friends meeting?'

Midgely tilts his head slightly to one side, 'You don't know?' it starts as a question and is repeated as a statement, 'You don't know. Ann Clarke was found beaten and unconscious in her apartment last night. The only person with her was DCI Carter.'

'Circumstantial to say the least and I think...'

Midgely interrupts her, 'She had been reporting from the scene of Mason's murder earlier that evening where Carter was in charge. What got our attention is that he was found with documents that could only have come from Mason's residence and we have proof that he was sharing these with Clarke.'

He pulls out an envelope from within the briefcase next to his chair, 'These pictures were taken by an independent photographer who just happened to be with the ambulance crew that turned up at Clarke's apartment.'

He spreads out a few photos across the desk towards Wilks.

'These pictures clearly show the documents in question on the table and here, here we see DCI Carter picking them up and placing them back in his jacket pocket.'

'How did you get these pictures so quickly?'

Midgely looks slightly embarrassed.

'They were brought to our attention by a request from MI6 to block them for NS reasons.'

Wilks leans forward, 'Why would these by a risk to National Security and why would MI6 be getting involved…again? John, come on. There is something not quite right here. Who at MI6 is your contact? Who is supplying you with this information?'

'Ma'am I can't…'

'Bullshit, John!' Wilks explodes furiously, 'Someone is trying to harm the reputation of one of the best officers on this force and I want to know who. Do you know the history between Carter and MI6? Do you know they stopped an investigation he was working on that involved his sister, again claiming National Security interests? They threatened his career, John. Did your contact tell you that? They are not above the law. Whoever is feeding you false information and sending you on a wild goose chase is not above the law.'

'I will have to discuss this with my superiors. I understand you want answers, but you must realise we are in the middle of an investigation and we must be careful.'

Wilks pushes herself back into her chair, 'Are you suggesting that I am under some form of suspicion too?'

'Ma'am, we are in the middle of an investigation involving one of your officers, we have to be careful that loyalty does not come into question here. I am not saying you are under investigation, but we want no-one to confuse matters or have a biased view while we do our job. I hope you understand.'

Wilks stares at the man before her, 'Oh I understand Detective, I understand perfectly.'

If looks could kill, Midgely thinks, his department would now be investigating his murder.

CHAPTER 17

Compared to the calmness of the previous day, the control room is now a hive of activity. Emerson, standing in the centre of the room, watches as his team of engineers and scientists are scrutinising every facet of the MASTER's readings as they are relayed from the aircraft.
'We have the firing range online at Holbeach, sir,' A voice searches him out in the controlled chaos, 'All targets will be ready for go at eleven-hundred hours as requested.'
He looks down at his watch. Three hours to check the waiting dignitaries through a modified security procedure and show them what MASTER can do.
'Are the NanGens ready for refuelling?' he used the abbreviated, self made word for the Nano Generator fuel cells.
A serious looking, young blonde woman looks up from her panel with the report,
'We have forty-three cells ready for sending to the MASTER, seven undergoing maintenance and just one that is being investigated for it's tracking errors from this week. MASTER is fully loaded with thirty cells, all fully charged. MASTER systems are in power save mode and regenerating power, we are in a positive energy situation with MASTER.'
'Tracking?' he calls out.
'All systems operational. No issues reported with fuel cell or MASTER tracking during docking and re-engagement.'
'Weapons and Counter-Measures.'
'Systems check in progress, one moment…'

Emerson turns towards the location of the voice with a frown threatening danger across his face. Before he can react the voice continues,

'Ninety per cent capability on weapons drop. Three NanGens showing red. Working on it now, sir.'

His frown deepens and he strides over to the group of four people who are all bowed before their computer screens as if in prayer.

'What's the problem?' he asks bending down to join the group in their huddle.

'Telemetry is indicating a hold on these three.' The engineer points to his screen showing a box of thirty squares. Three of them are blinking red whilst all the others are a steady green.

'As you can see they are all in the same quadrant and we are concerned it is a MASTER docking problem.'

Emerson sighs angrily, 'Have you tried re-docking?'

'In power regen mode it's not possible sir.'

Emerson stands up and shouts around the room which turns silent immediately,

'Listen up people. We are hours away from the most important demonstration in this company's history. We need to get it right and we need to start sparking for fucks sake. Get these NanGens redocked NOW. I want 100 per cent serviceability on MASTER or there will be repercussions. Get it done.'

As he marches out of the room, it stays silent for a moment before faces swivel back to their monitors and they continue their work.

'Fucking idiot,' is said softly from one corner, just loud enough for everyone to hear. It raises a few laughs but these soon fade out as everyone again concentrates on their own equipment.

Orders and commands are relayed around the room through microphones and headsets in muffled, soft voices. Electronic commands and corrections are transmitted from consoles to the MASTER aircraft in order to fulfil Emerson's instructions. Some of the assembled engineers may not respect his authority, but they are scared of it. It takes just ten minutes for the three fuel cells to un-dock themselves from the MASTER mothership, perform a quick functional self-test as they fly alongside their much larger companion and then re-engage with it.

'All systems are green,' is the relieved call as the process ends, 'best let the boss know.'

Emerson is standing in his office, adjusting his tie in the mirror when the phone on his desk rings. He smoothes a hand through his hair, takes a moment to admire his reflection, and then he answers the call. Listening to the voice on the other end he nods, 'Good' is his only response as he places the handset back into the cradle.

'Now let's go part some governments with their hard earned cash,' he says to the empty room. 'It's show time.'

CHAPTER 18

After I finish my call from Helen I look back to the woman sitting opposite me.
'Are you charging me with anything?' I ask.
'DCI Carter, you are under investigation for inappropriate behaviour with Miss Ann Clarke, a reporter with 'The Metro' newspaper. This interview is to determine the facts around your relationship with Miss Clark. We want...'
I break in and repeat more firmly, 'Are you charging me with anything, detective?'
The room falls silent and I notice JD is trying not to smile. I shake my head slightly in his direction and he stops himself.
'If you have nothing but the fact I was at Ann's apartment, that I found her injured and called it in, then I am out of here.'
'What about the documents? Mason's documents? What were they doing in the apartment with you both and why were you there in the first place?'
I stand up and ignore her questioning, turning my attention to JD.
'Zoe is missing. She didn't get back to Helen's last night and she is worried. With the shit they have been through I want to make sure she is OK.' I turn back to DCI Phillips, 'I presume I will be suspended while you investigate me?'
Her silence says all I need to know.

'Right, JD, you are on Mason's murder. The documents I found at Ann's house are somehow related to this. Get them back and get the forensics guys on them for any prints,' I stare at the female officer across from me, 'that is if these muppets haven't ruined them already.'

Phillips bristles but says nothing and so I continue, 'Get Luke on the case. I want him to check out if there is anyway he can get into Mason's computer setup and see what contacts have been made recently. I don't understand that stuff but I know he can do wonders with it. I want some answers about why Mason was killed, maybe then we can start looking for a suspect.'

I walk over and bang on the interview room door to be let out,

'I'm off to see Wilks and then I am going to see what's happening with my sister. Interview fucking terminated.'

I don't bother to knock and just forcefully push open the door to her office.

'Do you know I've been suspended…again?' I burst out.

Wilks to her credit does not even flinch as she remains seated at her desk,

'Ah, Peter. Glad you made it. This,' she points behind me to a man I do not recognise, 'this is DCI John Midgely from Internal Investigations. He has just been bringing me up to speed on their work.'

Her face turns into a puzzled mask, 'Suspended? Who said you were suspended?'

I stop, suddenly aware that nothing was said to that effect and I had assumed it would be the case. I turn defensive,

'Well aren't I?' is all I can ask.

Wilks again looks over my shoulder,
'Is he?'
I turn to face the man who appears to hold my career in his hands. He stands up and offers me an outstretched hand. I don't want to take it. Like most police officers we are wary of anything Internal Investigation team are up to, especially when it's concerning yours truly.
'John Midgely,' he says.
I shake his hand, 'Peter Carter, but I guess you already know that.'
He smiles to try and defuse the situation but he might as well strike a match next to a leaking gas bottle. It just makes me want to punch him in the face.
'Why don't we all sit down, Peter. We can finish your interview here with the Commissioner present and clear the whole thing.'
I turn to Wilks who nods her approval from her seat. I pull up a chair and sit between the two.
'Peter,' Midgely announces, 'I am only going to ask you three questions. You answer them and we are done, no suspension, no loss of pay, no recriminations. Are you alright with that?'
I nod warily, the alarm bells in my head are threatening to shatter the windows with their urgent tones.
'Are you in a sexual relationship with Ann Clarke?'
I feel my cheeks start to burn. I nod.
'I need to hear it Peter, are you and Ann Clarke having a sexual relationship?'
'Yes,' I say quietly.
'Have you divulged any sensitive information to Miss Clark during the periods of your time together?'
'What? No of course not. I...'

'Peter...' Wilks warns.

I close my mouth. Midgely smiles.

'What are technical documents from TSI and Michael Mason's safe doing in Clarke's apartment and why did you take them?'

I want to reply that he said only three questions but know it would come across as petulant and childish. Instead I give the only answer I can, 'I don't know,' I say as I look him directly in the eye, 'I don't know is the answer to both questions.' I hope he cannot see the icy grip on my heart that fear has caused.

The reality is that I took them because I could see how bad it would look for me to be meeting a journalist, in her apartment, just hours after a prominent businessman's murder, and have incriminating evidence linking us together from the scene. I was trying to save my career and quite possibly my future relationship with Julia. I could see all of that slipping away from me now and I am scared. More scared than I have ever been in my entire life.

CHAPTER 19

Pulling the bloody organ out of the body in front him, Graham Young places the heart into a shallow metal bowl on his right hand side and looks at the digital readout.
'Heart weight 324 grams.' He says out loud for the recording device.
He removes it from the stainless steel weigh scales, rinses the surface with water to remove the remnants of coagulated blood and places it down on the surgical steel surface in front of him for closer inspection.
'No signs of disease indicators or lesions to pericardial sac or outer walls of organ. It does however show a mottled appearance conducive with trauma as well as an irregular shape, i.e. non conical. Penetrating injury to thoracic aorta with subsequent tears in the circumflex branch of the left coronary artery and the inferior vena cava looks to be caused by some kind of long, thin bladed implement. In my opinion, exsanguination would have occurred within minutes without prompt medical care.'
He peers over and looks inside the body cavity.
'Large amounts of clotted blood in aortic cavity concur with preliminary findings.'
He moves back to the heart and picks up his scalpel,
'Commencing transverse section incisions of the coronary arteries to check for any signs of calcification and tortuosity…'

For the next minute there is just the sound of Graham's breathing within the room.
'Low to mild calcification, no impact on the probability of survival for the victim. I will now commence dissection of the heart, which due to the trauma upon it, will be completed using the roll out method.'

Four and a half hours later with the full forensic autopsy complete, Graham is standing at the sink washing his hands and wondering what is going on with Peter Carter. They have been friends since Peter attended a lecture that Graham was holding, and it was from there that the job offer was made for him to move South, from Leeds to London. He picks up his notes and walks out of the 'Cold Room', as he likes to call it, across the hall and into his rather spacious office. He places the paperwork onto his desk and picks up the phone. After two rings it is answered,
'JD, it's Graham. I have just completed Mason's autopsy and it is as expected with cause of death likely to be traumatic damage to the heart. I am waiting on lab results for evidence of cyanide poisoning from blood and liver samples as well as scrapes made from Mason's mouth and nasal cavity.'
'Thanks Doc,' is JD's response down the phone.
'Any news on Peter?' Graham asks almost timidly.
'He's been to see the Commissioner after his run in with the Internals and I've not seen him since. He's pursuing something to do with his sister, that's all I know. How long until the report is ready for the file?'
'Oh… give me an hour and I'll bring it up.'

'No need for that Doc, I'll send someone down and…'

'JD, I need the exercise. It does me good to get away from this house of the dead. Besides, I am worried about Peter.'

'Me too, Doc. Me too. See you in an hour.'

Graham hangs up on JD and with a sigh powers on his computer to start typing up his findings from the autopsy on Michael Mason.

After sitting in on the interview with Peter earlier, JD has been liaising with the cyber crime unit to see what they can find on Mason's computer equipment. Luke, the Met's own wunderkind with IT, is explaining patiently the process he is working on.

'Gaining access to the operating system is relatively easy. We didn't need to spend too much time on that. As you can see it is the files that are encrypted and that makes it a lot tougher for us. Mason looks to have been using a modified script based UNIX encryption. It has a large SALT value that will take time to break.'

JD breaks in, 'Salt? What's that?'

Luke pauses to compose his answer. He knows how to relay the information in 'techno-speak' but he has to translate into simpler terms.

'SALT is a way to make passwords harder to crack. We used to run what we would call 'dictionary attacks' on passwords. Our software would run a huge database of words against the password until it cracked it. This is because in the good old days passwords were recognisable words so people could remember them. Did you know that for years the most common password in ALL systems was 'Password'?'

JD looks uncomfortable when he hears this.
'Maybe you had better change your password eh, JD?' Luke says with a smile.
'Anyway, what SALT does is insert random data in the password string to protect it, and this means it can take a huge amount of time to crack it depending upon the amount of data included. It looks like Mason was using 24 Bit SALT to encrypt his files so this could take some time. Sorry JD.'
JD places his hand on Luke's shoulder,
'Good things come to those who wait. Is there any information that is useful for us on Mason's machine?'
'He was a very careful man. It appears he only used a works VPN for connection to the net and then only to access files from the TSI servers. What is odd is that he has no internet history, no cookies, no Emails, in fact nothing to say that he used this PC for anything other than work. Even solitaire has never been used. Was there another PC in his house. A laptop, a netbook, maybe even a blackberry?'
JD looks thoughtful, 'Nothing that was brought in. Why?'
'Well if he used this machine to work from home, how did he contact his colleagues at TSI? Where are the Emails, the documents back and forth...'
Luke turns in his chair, 'Flash drive,' he exclaims, 'he used a USB flash drive.'
His chair swivels back to the desk and his hands fly across the keyboard. A new window opens up on the monitor in front of him.
'There,' he points at the screen, 'drivers for a Kingston USB. He must have transferred everything across to that and physically delivered

his work to others or he had a dirty machine to use for that purpose.'

'Why would he do that?'

'I don't know JD. Perhaps he was worried his work was being monitored from the TSI servers. By using another PC connected to the internet he could pass his encrypted files to anyone he wanted without being spied upon from within his own company.'

'How can we prove that?'

'I can check for spyware embedded in his system and see where that leads us. I should be able to find out what was being looked at and where it was being sent. Most companies have this enabled, I mean, we do at the Met.'

He stops what he is doing, his hands poised above the keyboard.

'You never heard that from me, JD.'

'No problem, Luke. The secret's safe with me,' he pauses, 'would Internal Investigations have access to that information?'

Luke nods, 'It was their system in the first place. They use it to trace any spread of sensitive information from within the Met. It is quite damning evidence.'

JD thinks of Peter and the interview earlier. If he thought he was worried before it has suddenly tripled in value.

'Shit. Luke, call me when you have anything, I have to go and make some phone calls. You have my mobile number yeah?'

Luke nods as he once again turns his attention to the keyboard, 'Will do, JD. No problems.'

JD walks away from the young man, thoughts whirling in his head from a hundred different scenarios.

CHAPTER 20

Alex and Jenny are in deep discussion as they take their dog, Max, for a walk in the small park near their home.

'But you're not getting any younger sweetheart,' Jenny says smiling at her husband, her Trinidadian accent brushes across him with its gentle tones.

'I know, I know, but retiring so young…what if we can't manage on the pension, what about the kids, what about…'

Jenny cuts him off mid sentence, 'There is always something we can find to stop us doing what we want to do. Why not look at what we need to make it happen.'

Alex sighs, he knows Jenny is right but to give up work and move to a foreign country in his mid 50's is a big step. They had already bought a small holiday home on the island of Corfu with a view to retiring there. The dream was to take advantage of the milder winters and enjoy living in the sun whilst they could still enjoy it. But then the banking crisis hit, and overnight those dreams turned sour. Investments were lost, their income decreased while their pension age was increased. The value of their house had been slashed by a third in a matter of weeks.

Alex absent-mindedly throws the ball that Max had dropped at his feet and smiles as he watches the dog chase after it excitedly.

'Sometimes I wish I had been born a dog. No cares, no worries, just give me food, love and the occasional run around on some grass and I'm happy.'

That's when the moment of truth, as he called it later, hit him. If he worried about everything then they would never manage to live their dream.
'OK Jenny let's do it. I'll cash in and take the early redundancy offer. It's not what we expected but what the hell. We'll put the house on the market and see what happens there.'
He pulls her into his arms and kisses her passionately on the lips before whispering in her ear,
'But you have to tell my mother!'
They pull away from each other, both laughing.
'Do you mean it, Alex? Do you really mean it?' She asks, her mouth in huge smile revealing her perfect white teeth.
He kisses her again and says, 'Let's do it.'
Even Max seems excited with the joy on his owners faces. He runs back to Alex's feet, his muffled bark grows louder as he drops his toy, ready for it to be thrown again.
Alex bends down and picks it up, slightly light headed with the decision he has made. A new life, a new world for them both. His smile fades as he grasps something that is not Max's tennis ball. He looks down questioningly at the object he holds and lets out a disgusted cry as he recognises a dismembered human hand within his own. He drops it in revulsion and rubs his hand against his trouser leg as if to remove the taint of it. Jenny screams in horror as she too realises what lies before them. As Alex pulls out his mobile phone to call the police all he can hear are the screams of his wife and the excited barking of his dog as it jumps around the gruesome find at his feet.

I have been at Helen's apartment for just five minutes when I get the call. I have not been suspended but I have been momentarily removed from the Mason case pending the results of the inquiry by Internal Investigations. The phone call comes as a relief to me, not because it means more work, but because when I arrived at Helen's, Julia was there comforting her. The look on her face told me she had taken a guess at what had been going on between me and Ann. The nail in the coffin was the paper lying on the table in front of them. Splashed all over the front page was a picture of Ann in her living room with me cradling her in my arms.

I didn't need to read the headline, it was the caption beneath it that grabbed my attention, 'Ann Clarke and her partner DCI Peter Carter at the scene last night.'

Both of the women in front of me had been crying and both shot me venomous looks. Luckily Ewelina rescued me by asking if I wanted a cup of coffee or tea, that paused the accusations for a moment or two and then the phone call came in.

'We have a female body found in Brockwell Park. The SOCO has asked for you specifically.'

'Why me?' I ask.

'It has to do with your sister's case, sir. First indications show it to be a similar MO as that.'

My skin turns cold and I look at Helen with growing dread. Her face drops and turns pale, 'What is it Peter? Oh God...no, please, no.'

I keep looking at her as I say to the despatch controller I will be there as soon as I can. Brockwell Park is not far away from my sister's apartment in Clapham.

'Helen, we don't know anything yet. A body has been found, a female body, and I have been called in to co-ordinate. I promise to let you know anything more as soon as I know myself.'

'Peter,' Julia's voice is soft but it slices through me like a scalpel blade, 'Peter, when you are done with that we need to talk.'

I nod my head. I can't bring myself to say anything more. I watch as she takes her engagement ring off and places it on the table in between us.

'It is up to you if you bring this with you, but at the moment I am not sure I can wear it.'

Silently I reach out and pick up the ring. I know I should be saying something here but my mind is numbed by the fact that we may once again have a serial killer on the loose. What scares me is the fact that he may be tying up the loose ends left from his last spree, one of which is missing and the other sits before me.

I turn away so neither of them will see the tears burning my eyes.

'Your coffee, Peter,' says Ewelina as I brush past her and out to a crime scene that fills my heart with ice. It is now I am beginning to wish I had been suspended.

CHAPTER 21

It is an all too familiar scene as I make my way towards the crime scene at Brockwell Park. I am forcing myself to concentrate only what I am going to find here and not the events of the last twenty-four hours. It is tough to do.

I look up at the sky. It is one of those beautiful December days. Clear blue skies with a sharp chill in the air that makes you catch your breath. The trees hurl their leafless branches to the heavens and pray for life again, and I remember I am here to see another lifeless form. One that has no hope of rejuvenation once the warmth of spring comes back.

I see JD talking with the Scene Of Crime Officer, the SOCO, and a feeling of déjà vu hits me. He catches my eye and finishes his conversation then walks over.

'The Mason case is on minimal hours for now, Peter. Wilks is putting all our manpower on this. It looks bad I have to warn you.'

'Is it…?'

He nods his head, 'It looks like it. The marks on the body seem to bear resemblances…' he trails off and looks at me with compassion, 'she's over here.'

He leads me towards a small clump of bushes at the base of a huge old oak tree.

'She was found a few hours ago by a couple walking their dog. The dog actually brought them part of the victim, a hand.'

I say nothing as we walk past the uniformed policeman standing guard on the perimeter. They deliberately look away as I approach. It seems obvious to me that news of the internal investigation has spread far and wide in the department.

A flag in the ground and a small blue tent stand guard over the discarded body part as an indicator for the forensic team. A larger, white, pop-up tent has been erected near the base of the tree. JD and I are handed a pair of white, paper coveralls and plastic bag booties. These we put on in silence and we make our way forward into the tent.

A forensic photographer is taking photographs and we watch as her assistant holds a steel ruler next to parts of the remains on the ground and the flash explodes in a burst of white light. I want to look away but I can't. The image in front of me will remain burned in my soul for an eternity.

Zoe's body is lying prone on the bare earth. Her clothes have been folded neatly to one side, along with her dismembered limbs. The arms are folded at ninety degrees at the elbow and placed together like a couple of carpenter's set squares. The legs are perpendicular to these and lie straight out. Only one hand lies atop the clothing, next to a dirty looking tennis ball.

'The dog's ball.' JD explains.

The torso shows the scars from Zoe's past abduction and torture. Scars made by my sister as they had to fight to stay alive. Her head rests atop her small breasts, the eyes wide open and staring accusingly at me. *Why didn't you save me?* I can almost hear her saying. Written in blood on her abdomen are two words that send a chill along my spine.

'MISS ME?'

JD is watching my expression as I take in the scene before me. He grabs my arm and leads me out of the zone of death.

'She was killed elsewhere and dumped here. We are not sure what time, but we have a team checking the CCTV footage from last night along her last known route and also the routes into the park. There is no way he could have managed to dump the body here without being caught on camera somewhere.'

'Stephens?' I ask.

JD shrugs his shoulders, 'He was responsible last time and got away with it due to his connections. He's my first suspect I'd like to question. Do you think we could get Wilks to put some pressure on the spooks?'

It's my turn to shrug, 'I'll get on to her straight away. I think I had better do it in person.' I pause and look at my old friend with pain behind my features, 'I have to tell Helen.'

'Peter!' a cry from behind us causes us both to turn in that direction.

Helen is struggling with the two uniforms as she tries to break her way through the blue and white perimeter tape.

'I'll come with you.' JD says.

I nod my thanks. No words are needed with the big man. Still in our paper coveralls we make a long walk to my sister. She sees the look on our faces and starts a low wailing,

'No..oh no, oh no no no no…'

I start to run towards her and grab her in my arms holding her tight.

'I am so sorry, Helen. So, so sorry.'

She pulls away from me and the hatred in her eyes stops me in my tracks.

'You caused this. You!'

She turns and runs back towards her apartment. I go to follow but JD stops me with one of his big hands on my shoulder,

'Give her time, let her process this. I'll send victim support over to be with her and put a uniform with her for protection, just in case.'

I watch as my sister disappears from view and I am wondering if everything in my life is turning to shit. I rip off the paper suit and plastic boots and shove them into the hands of one of the constables, 'I'm off to see Wilks.'

CHAPTER 22

Emerson is in his element. The gathered ministers and military hierarchy from many different countries are his type of people. He knows how these people work, or so he believes. He spends a few seconds with each, handshaking, accepting condolences for Mason's death, before moving on to what he considers the next source of income. All the people in the room are here for one thing, ownership of the MASTER aircraft. Well he has a show for them alright, he thinks, get your chequebooks out and let's start a bidding war. When he finally reaches the platform with it's curtained off area he addresses the crowd.

'Ladies and gentlemen, thank you for your patience with our security measures and may I welcome you cordially to the unveiling of Typhoon Scientific Industries new surveillance and targeting unmanned aircraft.'

He smiles and catches the eyes of certain ministers. His voice turns sombre, 'When I and my good friend, Michael Mason, designed this aircraft we thought we would both be here today to share in it's premiere,' he pauses for dramatic effect and looks off to one side as if to compose himself, 'unfortunately the world is not a safe place. We realised this when we created this company. Today is a day for Michael, and I dedicate the success of this venture to his memory.'

A small patter of applause rises up to him.

'But the world stops for no man and I know he would have wanted this demonstration to continue, so without further waffling from me I present you the TSI Military Aviation, Surveillance and Targeting, Energy Regenerator, or MASTER aircraft for short.'

The curtains behind him open and models of the aircraft come into view for the crowd to see.

'Please take a few minutes to get a close up view of our display. Many of them are interactive and explain the options that are available on MASTER should you wish to have these features.'

As he is speaking a large screen flickers into life showing the MASTER in the air.

'We have ground based cameras tracking the aircraft in flight and we will provide a real time demonstration of it's capabilities in just a few moments. First, take a look around, have a glass of champagne and ask any questions you have to myself or my staff at any point. Thank you.'

He steps down from the platform and picks a champagne flute from one of the waiters, 'To Michael,' he says quietly, but just loud enough to be heard by a majority of the crowd. There is a general murmur of agreement as they each raise their own glass in support.

'Holbeach range online. Rapier battery ready, still awaiting confirmation from REAPER.'

The voice rings out across the control room from a speaker high up in the corner of the room.

'Contact Waddington and get that REAPER confirmation. Without that it is only half a demonstration.' The command comes from John Miller who is in charge of the control room while Emerson does his 'pressing of the flesh' upstairs.

'OK people, go or no go on your systems. Talk me through it.'
'Weapons, go.'
'Counter-measures, go.'
John listens as each of the operators around the room checks off in their pre-defined sequence. The last voice to ring out is,
'Comms, go'
John smiles as a small cheer ripples around the control room,
'Calm down everyone, we have a long way to go yet.'
He picks up the phone in front of him,
'All systems green. We are ready for the go.'
On the other end of the line a technician flicks a switch twice in a pre-arranged signal. Emerson has been waiting for the blinking light.
'Could I have your attention please? The demonstration is about to begin.'
He picks up a small remote control, takes a deep breath as he looks around the room, and begins the most important presentation of his life.
'At TSI we are at the forefront of modern battle field thinking. Fast and accurate target acquisition with a rapid response is the mantra of our armed forces. Dominate the air and you dominate the ground. MASTER gives you the power to do that. Present surveillance systems allow multiple targets, at the most possibly five or six to be assessed consecutively, but this is over a very limited range. MASTER allows over thirty targets to be addressed consecutively and independently targeted by its own on-board weapons systems over the whole battle space and beyond.'

He presses a button on the remote and the large screen shows multiple displays. A few fingers point at the screen as they recognise the residences they were staying at the night before.

'This recording from earlier today shows twenty-five of you making your way here over a *forty mile radius,* proceeding on your way to our location this morning. Each feed is from an autonomous surveillance and weapons platform that is linked to MASTER.'

A worried voice breaks out from the French delegate,

'You say autonomous *weapons* system. What if a malfunction caused it to attack us?'

Emerson addresses the well dressed French woman,

'In the event of any attack the operator has a chance to over-ride the system to prevent the unfortunate mistakes that we have all seen in the past. Only in the face of attack to itself or the MASTER mothership will input from an operator be deemed unnecessary. In this situation it will destroy the aggressor using any weapons at its disposal. This morning all weapons were disabled to enable us to fly in this country and abide by CAA rules. In a moment you will see how we can react in a multiple threat environment on a free fire range with the assistance of the Royal Air Force and the Army.'

He nods his head at the two multi-medalled, uniformed officers at the front of the crowd.

'The demonstration you are about to see is, in essence, a free for all. The army has installed a Rapier surface to air missile system from the Royal Artillery to protect the land based targets such as would be used in a hostile forward operating environment. The RAF, in co-operation with the US Air Force, has gladly sent up a modified REAPER remotely piloted aircraft in an attempt to destroy our own unmanned MASTER. They have both been told to destroy our aircraft with all of their capability. By the way, the modified REAPER has been loaned from the USAF. It is one of their first air to air fighter capable UAVs that will be going into operations in the near future.'

He presses another button and the screen once again shows the MASTER in flight.

'Ground based cameras will be capturing the demonstration. When it is finished we will have time for questions as the MASTER returns from the demonstration area.'

'If it returns,' says a clipped Oxbridge voice from the bespectacled RAF officer. A small titter of laughter politely follows from the assembled group.

'Quite right, Air Vice-Marshall,' Emerson says with a smile. Inwardly he is thinking, let's see who's laughing last you prick. He nods towards the technician who is still on the phone to Mills in the control room.

'We have a go. Repeat, we have a go,' is said into the mouthpiece.

All eyes are transfixed on the screen as green text appears at the bottom of the screen,

'Systems Ready – Automatic acquisition and targeting in place.'

CHAPTER 23

The guard sitting in the small booth next to the blast door checks his watch again.
'Just forty more minutes,' he says to himself and stifles yawn. All of the security personnel hate this area of the complex. Stuck in a glass walled booth, opening and closing the heavy doors is just so monotonous. A buzzer sounds and he looks over to the small monitor on the desk in front of him to see a man and a woman pushing a wheeled trolley down the corridor to his station. He flicks a switch and opens the external communication link.
'Where are your passes?'
The tinny quality of his voice is heard from the small panel set just left of the heavy metal doors. The woman looks around as if wondering where the voice is coming from. The guard smiles slightly as he sees her confusion.
'You need passes to enter this area. Are you lost?' He asks.
The man with her points to the wall panel and the woman comes over. The guard is looking straight down her cleavage from the cameras vantage point and he suddenly thinks this job is not so boring after all.
'Umm, hello, we were told to bring some refreshments down from the meeting room above. Nobody mentioned any passes to us.' She says into the speaker and microphone.
'Well Miss, I'm sorry but I can't let you in without proper authorisation. You will have to go back and get it before you can come through here.'

He watches as her face drops on the camera as she realises her mistake. She turns to the man with her, 'Bob, run back up and let Mr Emerson know we need passes to deliver this to his team.'
Everyone knows Emerson's reputation. The guard knows to cross him or cause him any minor complaint is career suicide. He makes a snap decision,
'Wait. Mr. Emerson sent you down?'
The woman nods outside.
'Stand back and wait for the doors to fully open. I will have to search you before you enter.'
He clicks off the communication and presses a large red button whilst thinking he will enjoy the next few moments of the search. The woman outside is quite stunning, he thinks. He adjusts his belt with pistol holster attached and steps outside his booth to usher them in. He is smiling as the door opens wide enough for him to see the woman standing there. He is still smiling as the 9mm bullet from the silenced Berretta PX4 hits him square in the nose and barrels through to destroy his brain. He collapses in a silent heap, dead before he hits the ground.
The woman presses the transmit button hidden in the pocket of her jacket and says,
'We are in.'

Upstairs in the conference room all eyes are on the screen as they wait for the demonstration to begin. Only the Air-Vice Marshall notices one of the waiters place down the tray of canapés and reach into his jacket. He raises his head inquisitively and his eyes widen in shock as he recognises the outline of a dangerous looking machine pistol drawn from within its confines. He gasps and starts to reach for his mobile phone when a womans voice rings out from next to Emerson.

'Ladies and gentlemen, if I could have your attention please.'

Everyone in the room turns towards the source of the voice to see a tall, olive skinned woman holding a pistol to the head of James Emerson. There is a general burbling as people start shouting out or looking around in frenzy.

'Thank you,' the woman says and smiles to the group. 'If you look around you, you will notice that we have you in a rather, shall we say, compromising position. My people are armed and will use their weapons if they need to. The doors here have been made secure and it is just our luck that anyone attempting to break out, or in, is going to need a small army to get through. Don't you just love the Cold War technology? I want you all to remain calm and perhaps you will walk away from this without anyone getting hurt. If you follow my commands you will all be home to see your families and friends in no time.'

The RAF officer has his hand in his pocket. He feels the smooth screen of his phone and swipes a finger gently across the surface. In the quiet room the soft tones of his mobile coming to life are deafening. He freezes in place as the woman turns her gaze upon him. She nods her head and he feels a strange sensation around his neck. Forgetting his phone he takes his hand out of pocket and brings it up to his throat. There is a whistling sound he can't quite locate the source of and he looks down at his hand which is covered in blood. The army officer takes a step forward to help him.

'Nobody move or you will be next,' the woman commands.

A few people turn away from the figure in front of them as it slowly sinks to its knees, and the blood pumps its way out of the severed throat.

It is only as his vision fades and his breathing becomes ragged does he even realise what has happened to him. In some strange instinctive reaction, he uses his fingers to push his spectacles back up the bridge of his nose, heaves a last breath, and lies still.

The waiter standing next to him is holding the thin bladed knife down by his side as he bends over and fishes in the dead man's pockets. He pulls out the mobile phone and smiles up at the woman.

'Your attention please,' she shouts out to the horrified crowd, 'rule number one…no attempt to communicate. Your phones and radios will not work anyway for we have a multi-frequency signal block in place.

Rule number two…do as I say, when I say it and exactly as I say it. As you have seen, your lives are worthless to us. Now, please would you all sit down. We may be here some time.'

She looks around the room at the confused and mostly terrified people. She points her gun at the French minister who is silently weeping, 'I said, SIT DOWN.' This time her command is followed. She smiles a thin lipped, vicious smile and turns to Emerson.

'Now you and I are going to have a little talk whilst your friends here enjoy the show.'

She marches him away from the front of the group and into a small room to the right of the large screen.

CHAPTER 24

I am furious as I march into the acting Commissioner's office. Luckily this time she is alone.

'We need pressure put on MI6 to release Stephens, or Masterson as he is calling himself now, to us.' I burst out as I enter.

Wilks looks up at me, her face pale as she talks on the phone. She holds up her index finger in the universal gesture of 'wait one second', and her serious look stops me in my tracks.

'Yes Prime Minster, he is with me now.'

My anger vanishes as I hear her words.

'I want a resolution to this too I can assure you Prime Minister…thank you sir…yes sir…goodbye.'

She hangs up and just stares at the phone for a moment before turning her attention back to me.

'Peter, we have a situation. As of immediate effect you are no longer under suspicion of any wrong doing in the Mason case. We have a confession.'

I shake my head as if to clear it,

'What?' I say, 'Who?'

Wilks opens her desk drawer and pulls out a remote, points it at the screen in her office and presses the power button. BBC 24 news blinks into life from the large plasma display. I watch as a balaclava wearing person is gesturing to a man next to her. Another button press and the mute is lifted to reveal a woman's voice.

'We are not affiliated to any terrorist or religious groups. Our aim is to raise awareness of the thousands of murders that are being carried out in our name by this hateful government and its allies.'

I read the ticker going across the bottom of the screen,
...group holding TSI CEO, James Emerson hostage. Claims responsibility for Michael Mason killing...BREAKING NEWS...Unknown terrorist group holding TSI CEO... the message repeats itself. On screen the woman continues as she gestures to the man who I now know is Emerson,
'This man and his company are culpable for these murders in the same way as our governments. They will all be brought to justice for their war crimes.'
She points a pistol at his head,
'We can dispense this justice, along to the dozens of minsters and military generals we have in our custody, or...' she pauses and removes the gun from view, 'we can let you decide to try them in a court of law. We have only two demands to be met to allow these people to live. One, all drones and UAV's to be removed from the borders of Pakistan and Afghanistan, the killing there must stop, and two, a promise that those who perpetuate these war crimes are brought to trial in a neutral country.'
Wilks mutes the volume again as the woman starts to read out a list of government officials names,
'Not surprisingly they want the heads of state from the UK and Israel and the US president amongst many others to stand trial.'
'Do we know who they are?' I ask, all thoughts of Zoe's murder forgotten for the moment.
'That's the worrying part. Nobody has a clue. They have appeared out of nowhere. The NCA, MI5, they had nothing on their radars about this, or at least they are not sharing it with us if they did. The good thing is we know where they are and who they have as hostages.'

I sit down opposite my boss.
'What can I do? What can you tell me?'
She sighs and pulls a notepad full of illegible scribbles towards her.
'They are holed up in an old military bunker that was sold to TSI for its base of operations. They have as hostages, 49 various defence personalities from across the world, including our own defence minister and foreign affairs minister.'
I think back to the interview I had yesterday. I did not particularly like the man, but I have no wish to see him dead.
Wilks continues reading,
'There are also 66 staff and security personnel that work at TSI who we also fear have been taken hostage, and that includes their CEO, James Emerson. Emerson is the man in the video, if you hadn't guessed.'
I look back at the screen which has switched to showing a video of a strange looking aircraft, the caption reads LIVE FEED.
'Turn the volume up ma'am, what's this?'
She hits the remote's buttons again.
'…been informed that the group have also taken control of the fully armed TSI MASTER drone aircraft. Reports are coming through that this will be targeted at what they are saying, are 'legitimate targets' in the capital. TSI industries were scheduled to perform a demonstration of this new unmanned aircraft today and this is the reason so many defence attaches and military personnel are at their location. We have not been told what may be legitimate targets…ahh…wait one second…yes, OK, we are going live to Downing Street where the Prime Minister is about to make a statement.'

The screen goes black for a millisecond before the famous door and railings of Number 10 Downing Street come into view. Instead of the two unarmed policemen who are normally stationed outside the door in their day glow vests, there are two officers from the Specialist Firearms Command, SCO19, dressed head to toe in their black Nomex coveralls and each armed with a 9mm Heckler & Koch MP5 sub-machine gun. They have also a tactical leg holster with a Glock 17 9mm pistol, and these guys must be worried as they are also wearing their PASGT ballistic protection helmets. I am sure that above them, out of view of the cameras, there are more specialist officers with sniper rifles and optical equipment checking for any suspicious activity within the immediate area. We don't yet have anti-missile systems on the roof of Number 10, like the Americans have at the White House, but I have no doubt it will not be that far in the future with the threat we have just been issued. The black gloss door opens and the familiar figure of the Prime Minister steps out and walks sombrely to the lectern at the pavement's edge.

CHAPTER 25

The two Royal Air Force pilots watch on the 42" plasma television in their crew-room as the Prime Minister begins to speak. Squadron Leader Gary Thirlway takes a sip of tea from his insulated mug and winces at the taste.

'Where do they get this crap from?' he says placing the metal mug down on the table next to his battered armchair.

Before his colleague, Flight Lieutenant Paul Ferguson can answer, a strident klaxon and flashing red light interrupts. Their reactions are immediate as the two pilots of the Quick Reaction Alert (South), respond to the alarm. Both jump from their chairs and run for the door, pausing only slightly to grab their helmets from the stowage area next to it. The klaxon has alerted the ground crew and they are already on the way out of the building, beating the pilots to the hardened aircraft shelters, and opening the large steel doors to allow the aircraft a safe exit.

'See you up there.' Gary shouts across to his wingman as they head in different directions to their respective aircraft. He sees a smile cross his friends face,

'Catch me up when you are ready, old man.'

Gary flashes a grin back as he runs on to his own Typhoon Eurofighter jet.

'What's the score, chief?' he asks to the senior technician who is standing next to his aircraft and directing his engineering crew as they prepare it for take off.

'Hi sir, QRA scramble called in for an unidentified target. More information in the air is all I have been told.' He checks his rugged computer tablet, 'Aircraft Yankee Delta fully serviceable, four air to airs on board plus 500 rounds of ammunition available for use.'

Gary starts clambering up the thin metal steps and enters the familiar cockpit of the RAF's most advanced fighter aircraft. The low rumble of the generators is replaced by the high pitch whining of compressors as the two enormous jet engines beneath him pulse into life. He starts running through the modified pre-flight check list as the Senior Aircrfatsman, or SAC, tightens the seat harness around his body. The noise now is so loud that they have to communicate by hand signals. The SAC taps him on the shoulder and shows the three ejector seat pins he has removed from their positions. Gary is now sitting on another set of live rockets that are ready to propel him skywards in the event of an emergency. He gives his own thumbs up and goes back to checking his equipment. Before he clambers down the steps the SAC plugs in the communication cord to Gary's helmet. The chief's voice enters his head from the inbuilt speakers,

'All systems green, weapons hot. Prepare for canopy in three, two, one…'

The siren from the aircraft is heard even over the engines as the canopy closes around Gary. It clicks into place and the pressure inside the cockpit is equalised as the seal is made. The engine sounds fade dramatically with this final operation.

'Sir, have a safe flight. Handing you over to visual control, see you back here in time for tea and medals.'

The chief removes his own long cable from the side of the aircraft and takes a few steps back. He gives the pilot a thumbs up and smiles. Gary gives his own thumbs up and a small salute. The ground crew direct him forward onto the taxiway with their hand movements and Gary is pleased to see he has made it out in front of Paul.

'Old man my arse,' he thinks to himself as moves forward to the runway threshold and waits for ATC to give him the go.

'QRA One, this is Tower. Clear for take off, vertical ascent to 25,000 feet, bearing 137 on completion and await vector from fighter control, over.'

'Tower, QRA One, that's a roger, vertical to 25, bearing 137, check.' Gary replies into his mouthpiece.

His adrenaline is flowing as he pushes forward on the throttle. He holds the brakes until he feels the aircraft vibrating like an angry tiger waiting to pounce. The computer flashes a green GO signal and he releases the hold on the beast he now controls.

Both aircraft force themselves through the damp air as if controlled by the same entity. Gary is pushed back into his seat with the power of his engines. He watches his instruments with intensity, gasping for air as he pushes against the g-forces on his body.

'Rotate' he says simply.

The two aircraft, as one, punch a hole in the sky as they throttle upwards. The roaring engines emit a long yellow and blue jet of heated air and fire behind them as they take off in a vertical dance against gravity.

On the ground, in the off duty quarters for the rest of the RAF stations personnel, people groan as the rumbling of the engines set off car alarms around the site.

CHAPTER 26

Graham Young is looking across to the naked body lying next to him. After the workload of the last two days he had taken a few hours off to relax. Being head of his department did come with some perks such as the ability to take an hour or two off. He made a call for a coffee date and could hardly believe how it ended up like this. He reaches out a hand and traces a finger along the contours of the soft skin from the shoulder blade down to the hip. A sensual shudder passes through the womans form and she murmurs. He thinks it sounds like a cat purring and brings his head forward to kiss the nape of her neck to see if other sounds will emanate from her. He feels himself becoming aroused again. God, this woman is amazing, he thinks.
She turns around, slowly, to face him and he finds his fingers tracing a line down her breasts. He looks into her face at her lazy smile and can't help but smile back,
'Well hello, Dr Young,' she says with a raised eyebrow as feels him pressing against her body, 'I see both of you are awake.'
She reached down and touches him lightly causing him to catch his breath.
He kisses her gently on the lips before pulling his head back,
'Kate, I thought I said to call me Graham.' he says in mock anger.
She grasps him a little tighter in her hand,
'I was speaking to him,' she says and starts laughing.

He moves in to kiss her again when his ringtone starts to go off indicating a message.

'Oh shit,' he mumbles into her flesh as they kiss. He leans back in the bed and reaches over to the nightstand to read the text displayed on the small screen, 'duty calls it seems.'

Another ringtone calls out and Kate reaches for her own phone too. They both have the same text message,

'ALL PERSONNEL TO REPORT FOR DUTY. NO EXCEPTIONS. OPERATION FORTUITOUS IN FORCE.'

'What does this mean?' Kate asks Graham as he is already making his way out of bed and pulling on his clothes.

'It means the shit has really hit the fan, or it means the shit is going to hit it imminently. FORTUITOUS is the sign that an immediate threat is underway. Kate, we have to go in.'

He grabs the TV remote and turns on the small set in the corner of the room.

'If it's bad the news channels should know about it already,' he says as he bends down to pull his socks on. He stops and looks up to the screen as he hears the voice of the Prime Minister.

'…evacuation of all public buildings is a priority. COBRA is in conference to discuss our reaction and tactics against this threat. I urge all Londoners to stay calm, at this time we believe the threat to be targeted at government and authority buildings only. We will not bow down to terrorism and we will never follow any demands made by any terrorist organisation. I remind you all that we have measures in place to keep our city and its inhabitants, safe and out of harms way. There will

be no questions at this time, I am sure you understand that time is of the essence. Thank you.'
He turns and walks back towards the two armed policemen as shouts from the assembled journalists follow his every step.
'I guess that answers any questions we might have about the text then,' Graham says.
Kate starts picking up her clothing as they both wonder what is happening,
'Where the bloody hell are my knickers?' she asks loudly.
They both look at each other and burst out laughing at the same time.

CHAPTER 27

Masterson is fuming with himself. The documents he left with that damn reporter should have been in the public domain by now. Even his beating of the woman had been a way to garner even greater publicity for the blueprints. He knew that no single company, or government, should have control of the technology that TSI had produced.
Unfortunately his boss was not of the same mind. Masterson knows that there are other plans for the MASTER aircraft than that even Michael Mason had envisaged.
He twirls the USB memory stick between his fingers and wonders what to do with the information contained within its aluminium body.
'Fuck it,' he spits out and reaches for his phone.
'Hi. I need your help again. Can you come to my apartment and we'll discuss it?' he listens to the response, 'look, I wouldn't be asking if it wasn't important, you know that.'
He lets his eyes drift out of the window where he watches the London Eye drift slowly on its axis, 'See you in an hour.'
He sits there twirling the USB stick whilst his mind does its own insane whirling as he wonders if he is going to go through with his plan.

I am still in Wilks office when my phone rings in my pocket. I pull it out and don't recognise the number on the display. I almost don't bother to answer it, but on a day like today I can't take any chances.

'Carter.' I answer.
'He's contacted me again. He wants me to meet him.'
My confusion is short lived as I suddenly put a face to the voice.
'Angela? What are you talking about?'
'Stephens called me just a moment ago. He says he wants me to go to his apartment for something, something important. What should I do?'
My mind is right back to the scene of Zoe's body earlier this morning. I want Stephens or Masterson or whatever he is calling himself,
'One moment, Angela.' I cover the mouthpiece with my hand, 'Ma'am, is there anything I can do with what's going on or do I concentrate on the case in hand?'
She has been busily sending messages out from her computer and she waves me away,
'Carry on with the Mason investigation. We can't do much about this mess at the moment until we have more information. I guess MI5 and the anti-terror squad will be taking the lead on this.'
She stops typing and looks over her monitor at me, 'I want you on Mason's murder, not your sister's partner. Are we clear?'
I nod, 'Crystal, boss.'
Leaving her office I turn my attention back to Miss Wilson,
'Sorry about that, where and when does he want you to meet him?'
'He wants me to go to his apartment in an hour.'
'Where are you now?'
She gives me her address and I look at my watch,
'I'll be there in fifteen minutes. I'm coming with you. There are a few things I need to discuss with our mutual friend.'

I terminate the conversation and head for my office to pick up my car keys. I cannot believe my luck, Masterson handed to me on a plate and the fact that I can claim a connection to the Mason murder will keep me off the hook with Wilks. I almost smile but the image of Zoe's body again flashes through my mind and my face drops into a determined frown.

JD looks up as I walk in. Seeing my face he sits up straight in his chair,

'Looks serious, what's up Peter?'

I open my desk drawer and pick out my keys,

'I've got a lead on Masterson,' I pause and look at my partner, 'do you fancy paying him a visit with me?'

'Sure, no problem. But who is this Masterson guy?'

I realise that I have not had chance to discuss the details with JD,

'I'll tell you it all in the car.'

We arrive at the address Angela gave me and she is already standing outside, waiting.

'So, Masterson is Stephens and he was at the scene of Mason's murder?'

I nod my head to JD's question.

'And she knows Stephens from her line of work as a…what did you say she called it, an entertainer of men?'

I nod again.

'You think he's involved in Zoe's murder, or at least has some knowledge of it because of his involvement in the Barnwell murders too?'

I nod for the third time.

'So he's now called Masterson, he's had plastic surgery to alter his appearance because Stephens is officially dead, he's implicated in the murder of two people in two days, one the highest profile assassination since I can't remember, the other your sister's girlfriend,' he sees my dark look, 'just saying it as I see it, Peter. And now we are going to his apartment to question him with a person he has used in the past to terrorise Middle Eastern suspects.'

'That's about right,' I mutter angrily. Even as he has been saying it I realise how foolish it all must look.

'OK by me, let's do it,' he says as Angela approaches the car. He reaches into his jacket and pulls out a 9mm automatic pistol.

'Jesus,' I exclaim as he removes the magazine, cocks the weapon to clear it, before firing off the action with a click and replacing the magazine.

'What the hell are you doing with that?'

'Didn't you get the text? We are on OP FORTUITOUS. All fire-arms trained officers are to carry a weapon on duty.' His face looks at me incredulously, 'You were going to see this guy without a weapon?' He lets out a long sigh through clenched teeth, 'You're crazier than I thought.'

Angela taps on the window to hide my embarrassment. As she bends down I catch a glimpse of her cleavage and fell the familiar rush of attraction. JD cannot help but notice too and lets out another sigh of an entirely different nature.

'Dangerous times my friend. These are dangerous times we are living in.'

His words echo in my mind as I open the door and let her into the car in a swirl of perfume and arousing pheromones.

'JD, this is Angela Wilson. She's a witness in the Mason investigation. Miss Wilson, this is Detective

Inspector Dawkins, my partner. He has been brought up to speed on the case.'
JD turns in his seat and holds out his hand for her to shake,
'Call me JD, pleased to meet you.'
Angela smiles, showing a glimpse of her perfect white teeth,
'Pleased to meet you too, JD. I wish it could have been under more favourable circumstances.'
JD turns his considerable frame back to face the front again. He is grinning like a Cheshire cat and his neck has turned a bright shade of red that threatens to rise up to his already pink cheeks.
I just look at him and he shrugs back at me with that insane grin on his ugly mug. In the rear view mirror I catch Angela staring at me with the smile still fixed on her face and I understand the reason for JD's blushing. She truly is a remarkably attractive woman.
I put the car into gear and pull out into the almost deserted streets.
'It looks like most people are taking the PM's advice and staying away from the city today,' I say.
'In my opinion, that means the terrorists have already won. If we can't live our lives without fear, well isn't that their whole plan?'
JD and I both say nothing to her words. We know that you should be fearful every day. It's not just terrorists that kill, maim and put ordinary people in harms way on a daily basis.
We continue on in silence until I pull up at the impressive entrance to the underground car park of Masterson's apartment building.
'You go in first,' I say to Angela, 'you have ten minutes and then we are coming in. Go along with whatever he says, we will be right outside the door.

When you hear us knock three times, that is your cue to step to one side. We will be coming in fast and hard. I will call you one minute before we enter, if he has a weapon tell me that you are sorry but you are busy on Saturday. OK?'
Angela nods her head. I am impressed by how she shows no fear but painfully realise she has probably been in far more troubling situations than this. We all step out of the car and walk towards the building. JD and I follow her in as she waves to the security guard on the front desk,
'Hi, Alan. How are the kids doing?'
'Fine, Angela,' he says smiling back, 'just fine. Paul's just been picked for a trial with London Welsh.' he says with obvious pride.
Angela does not even pause as she walks past him, 'Well if he follows after his father in the muscle department he'll be playing for England in no time.'
The man beams, 'Not a chance, I'm pushing him to play for Wales. I don't care if his mother's English, he's playing for my country.'
Angela lets out a musical laugh,
'That's not fair to the English is it?'
With those words we enter the elevator together.
'So you have been here a few times?' I ask.
'Some of my best clients are here. Alan gets a little kickback now and then to keep him sweet.'
'What about coming in here with two strange men?' JD raises the question before me.
She reaches out and presses the button for the top floor,
'Men, women, sometimes an animal or two. My clients have certain desires that sometimes require more than just little old me.'

Both JD and I stand there speechless as the elevator rises rapidly upward. Angela just smiles demurely in the reflection of the polished metal walls.
'Oh if only *these* walls could talk,' she purrs as she strokes the surface gently and looks up at the camera in the corner, winking at Alan who is no doubt watching from his desk downstairs.

CHAPTER 28

The doors to the control room burst open and John Miller, along with the rest of the TSI technicians and flight control staff, turn towards them.
'Who is in control here?' a womans voice shouts out.
Miller stands up,
'That would be me, what can I do for you?'
The bullet hits him high in the chest knocking him backwards over the console he had been working on. He feels no pain but is unable to move as he struggles to breathe. It feels like he has been pinned beneath a large, heavy yet soft object. He looks down the length of his body and sees a red patch spreading across his chest and soaking into his shirt. His last thoughts before darkness takes over are, *my wife will kill me. This is a new shirt.*
'Is there anyone else who thinks they are in control here?' the woman shouts out again to the stunned room. No one speaks up,
'Good. Everyone move away from your consoles and stand against the side wall. Which of you are the manual flight controllers, the pilots?'
No one moves. She levels her pistol at the nearest person to her, 'Who are the pilots?'
The man holds his hands up and starts to whimper. She watches as a dark stain appears at his crotch. The guns report is lost amongst the screams of the people next to the man whose head now resembles a burst watermelon as he crumples to the floor. She switches her aim to the next person in line who is covered in blood, fragments of bone and brain matter,

'Where are the pilots?'
This time she gets the response she was after.

Emerson looks at his captor with a mixture of disgust and fear as he sits on the floor in front of her.
'What do you hope to gain by this?' he asks.
The look of contempt on her face is apparent,
'It's people like you that have fucked up this planet. You sit here, thousands of miles away from the destruction your machines are causing and count your money with a fat smile on your face. All you see is profit, not the pain, the misery, the children and babies slaughtered in their thousands so you can drive around in your fancy car and not have a care in the world. If only you could pump your millions into doing good for the world instead of destroying lives.'
Emerson sees his chance,
'Don't you understand that is what we are trying to do?'
'Oh shut up. How? By bombing people out of starvation and poverty for oil and gas? When has that ever worked?'
'We don't do that. We are creating new technologies for creating energy without the need for fossil fuels, we…'
'You create mass forms of destruction that keep the people down in foreign countries so governments can destroy any will power of the people to stop their tyrannical forms of land and oil grabbing.'
She takes a deep breath, 'Don't even think about saying you do anything else or I will shoot you here and know.'

She raises the gun to his face and pulls back the hammer with her thumb. Time seems to slow down for Emerson as he watches her finger begin to tighten on the trigger.

He raises his hands to his face as if that could deflect the bullet and closes his eyes.

'Now you know what it is like to stare death in the face. It's not nice is it? Not knowing if this breath is to be your last. That is how millions feel every time they hear one of your killer drones fly overhead. It is constantly looking down the barrel of the gun and wondering if it is your turn.'

Emerson gingerly opens his eyes to see the woman's face inches from his own. He flinches as she spits at him,

'You worthless piece of shit.'

He wipes the spittle from his face with the sleeve of his jacket and turns his face away from hers.

He faces her again as she starts talking once more, 'You know I wanted to kill you first. Mason was the brains behind the whole thing, you I just thought of as the money man. The one who sells death to the highest bidder. It's a shame really because I would have loved to see you bleed out in front of me like him. Did you know it took him a good five minutes to die? I even sprayed cyanide in his face to make his last few breaths as torturous as I could. He lay before me, gasping and choking on his own blood as I laughed. We were persuaded to kill him first, after all, you cut off the brain and the rest of the body dies as well. Even if you live, you will be nothing because you are nothing.'

Emerson cannot help but laugh in a sad manner, 'If only you knew what you have done.'

The kick to his side is painful and he feels a crack as if one, or possibly more, of his ribs snap under the pressure.
'I've had enough of this. Tell me the self destruct codes for the drones in use in Afghanistan and Pakistan.'
Emerson's mind is clouded with pain.
'What are you talking about? There are no self destruct codes.' he says gasping for breath.
'Of course you would say that. We were told you would. I wonder what motivation is required to bring you around to our way of thinking.'
She points to one of the men in the room, 'Bring her in.'
Emerson looks up to see his personal secretary, Claire, dragged in by the hair and dumped on the floor in front of him.
'Take off your clothes,' the woman demands.
Claire looks at him, eyes pleading through her tears. A kick is sent out that connects to her thigh and she screams out in pain.
'Take off your clothes,' is the repeated order.
She starts to unbutton her blouse, tears streaming down her face. Emerson is forced to watch as she strips down to her bra and panties and stands there shivering, not with the cold but in fear.
'All of the clothes.'
Claire shakes her head and gets another kick, this time to the back of her calf. She collapses to the ground clutching the injured limb.
'Mr Emerson,' it is said dripping with sarcasm and contempt, 'take off her underwear for her. It wouldn't be the first time, we know all about the two of you.'

He closes his eyes and sighs sadly. When he opens them again a knife has been placed against Claire's throat as she sits in front of him.

'Take off her underwear. I shall not repeat myself again.'

He slowly reaches out and places his arms around her back to undo the bra strap. As he does so he leans in to her and whispers, 'I'm sorry,' into her ear. Pulling the thin material from her shoulders he lets it fall to the floor.

'Now the panties.'

His eyes lock onto Claire's as he hooks his fingers into the band of the flimsy cotton. He cannot manage to get them away from her body as she is pushed down in the sitting position. She is grabbed roughly by the arms and yanked upright. Wanting to get this over with he pulls them down quickly and looks at his sometime lover standing before him, naked and crying.

The woman walks over to his side,

'What are the codes?'

He shakes his head again, close to tears,

'There are no codes. Our systems do not have a self destruct built in them.'

'Do it.' the woman says.

He is forced to watch as Claire is dragged over to the heavy wooden table and slammed down upon it.

Outside the gathered crowd of hostages can only listen to the inhuman screams pierce the air as they watch the MASTER in flight on the screen in front of them.

CHAPTER 29

The Cambridge offices of TSI are situated on the outskirts of the city on a non-descript industrial estate that is full of new technology start-ups and high end industrial buildings. It is from here where the money is made and the deals are struck. If the bunker in Norfolk is the brains, this is the heart of the company. Pictures of the area are currently being transmitted from the wide angle camera aboard the MASTER and shown on the large screen in the conference hall. The images are also being relayed on to the major news networks and streamed live on the internet.

Back in Norfolk, the small flight room situated in the heart of the bunker is cramped and smelling quite foul. The lifeless bodies of the two pilots lie crumpled in the corner and one of them has soiled himself in death as his bowels relaxed. Their unique keys have been used to allow two of the terrorist attackers access to the flight controls. The timing of the group's assault could not have come at better time as the weapons system are already 'hot'. This may have saved the lives of a few people outside the room, thinks the female who posed as the waitress. She is almost as ruthless as her sister who is upstairs with Emerson. Between the two of them they are a formidable force to be reckoned with and should not be underestimated, as many men, and also women, have found out to their cost.
'Send out two of the nano-generators. Focus the cameras on the back of the buildings. Target the…'

A small red cross appears on the screen where she was pointing. She smiles,
'You know what I want, very good. Send in one, then another 15 seconds after the first. If we don't have the required effects send in one more.'
The multiple screens in the flight room show two separate pictures as two of the fuel cells detach themselves away from the MASTER.
'Let's show them we are serious,' she says to the room.
Outside in the main control room the technicians watch the unfolding events with rising excitement. Even though they may be about to witness an act of random violence, this will be the first real test of their years of dedication to the project and they have been waiting to see it in action for a long time.

Wilks is sitting in a small room deep beneath the heart of London. The COBRA members are all here and she, as acting Commissioner of the Met, has a place at the table. There has been much discussion over the terrorist crisis but it seems that no-one wants to make a decision about hostage rescue just yet.
One of the military figures is on the phone to a colleague from a small base near Hereford. He thanks whoever is on the end of the line and addresses the room.
'Prime Minister, the SAS have two teams on standby for just this type of event. Unfortunately it is viewed as a suicide mission and would also likely end up with all hostages being killed.'
The man at the end of the table rubs his eyes tiredly before speaking,

'I thought our special forces were the best in the world, General. Please tell me why they have said they won't do it.'

'It's not they won't do it, sir. They have taken a look at the plans of the bunker and, well, sir, it was built to withstand an all out nuclear attack. With all of the security measures in place we stand no chance of gaining access unless we can get to someone on the inside. We need an opening that doesn't need a thousand tonnes of TNT to force an entry. If you give the orders, they will do their best and I assure you they are the best at what they do. But this might just be asking too much of them. It's not some embassy in the middle of the city,' the General sees the look from the Prime Minister, 'with all respect, sir.'

'Alright General,' the PM sighs, 'who can tell me what's happening with the drone aircraft, this MASTER, or whatever they have called it.'

The defence minister leans forward,

'QRA jets from a base in Lincolnshire have been scrambled to provide protection for London. Four more aircraft and crew are being prepared to allow for twenty-four hour coverage and defence of the skies above the city. At present, TSI's aircraft appears to be in a holding pattern in the Cambridge area. We are not sure if this is a failsafe or if the terrorists do indeed have control of the aircraft. We have also placed the army on alert and they are deploying anti-aircraft units at key locations around the city. These are last ditch surface to air batteries that will be available for use in the next few hours. It is helpful that the streets are relatively quiet.'

The Prime Minister looks at Wilks,

'Commissioner, what is happening on the streets at the moment.'

She clears her throat and glances only momentarily at the notebook in front of her,

'We have had some disturbances on a few of the normal patches, nothing major. The Muslim community has come out and deplored this action of the taking of hostages and have offered to mediate if it turns out this is a breakaway Islamic group. We are getting reports of peace supporters trying to drum up support for a rally they hope to walk tomorrow, finishing at the Houses of Parliament. We are of course attempting to dissuade this due to the proximity to a political location and the possibility of civilians being in the line of fire if the worst happens.'

The PM scratches his chin, his fingers rasping through the stubble of his five o'clock shadow,

'What do we know about Michael Mason's murder? I am presuming this is connected.'

'Sir, we don't yet know. It appears the fatal stab wound was completed by someone with an intimate knowledge of anatomy and there are indications that a poison, cyanide, was also used in the attack.'

An aide enters the room and whispers in the PM's ear who nods as the information is relayed.

'It appears we have a developing situation,' he says as the aide moves to the side of the room and turns on the large, flat screen attached to the wall.

It bursts into life showing an aerial shot of an industrial complex. The aide begins a running commentary.

'This is the TSI head office in Cambridge. The pictures are being relayed by the MASTER drone itself, through the Norfolk complex and direct to the news feeds who are lapping it up. They have put a five minute delay to the feed in case of deaths on the ground. This was transmitted just under three minutes ago and has not yet been broadcast by the syndicates.'

On screen the picture turns to a soft focus black and white,

'This is now a thermal imaging picture. The military prefer this type of imagery for targeting on the battlefield.'

He points to a dark mass at the rear of the building, 'This is the storage facility for TSI's hydrogen fuel cells. They have a licence to create and store their own fuel for use in the building. They have been supplying energy to the national grid system for the last 14 months.'

A small object appears from the top of the screen and flashes bright white as it hits the storage tank. The thermal flash is a bright white blossom that lasts a few seconds on screen.

'The tank has just been hit with one of MASTER's nano-generator in weapons mode. Luckily the tank is designed to withstand small explosions like these and it appears that just two of its three skins were damaged by this first strike.'

'Thank God for that,' the science advisor whispers.

'I am afraid this is not the only strike, sir.'

The advisor visibly pales, 'You mean there has been…'

'I am afraid so.'

Another rapidly moving object hurtles in to the cooling, light coloured mass at the centre of the screen. The thermal camera is completely blanked out with the resulting explosion and it switches back to raw optical. The scene of devastation on the ground sends groans around the room.

'Unfortunately, the second weapons delivery ruptured the fuel tank itself.'

The camera zooms back from its fairly limited view.

'Our analysts are estimating a blast radius of at least one kilometre and damage out to perhaps four or five.

'Casualties?' the PM asks.

'Within one kilometre, almost total annihilation. Out to two kilometres, 50 -75%. The five kilometre radius shows signs of improvement for the casualty figures, maybe 15%.'

'What about deaths?'

The aide looks distraught,

'Those are the mortality estimations, sir. With the amount of industry and housing in that area, the A14 running through the blast zone,' he pauses, 'we are saying that the number of deaths will be in the thousands, worst case scenario possibly even double figures. You must realise that the center of the city is within four kilometres of the blast.'

The PM slumps back in his chair and looks like he has aged ten years in ten seconds.

'God help us all. Tens of thousands…gone.'

The silence in the room as we watch the destruction on the screen before us speaks volumes for the country's state of mind. Cambridge looks like it has been wiped off the map.

'I want that drone destroyed. Send the aircraft in immediately.'

A phone is picked up and rapid orders are softly spoken. For the first time in over seventy years aircraft are about to go into battle over UK airspace.

CHAPTER 30

JD and I get out of the elevator a floor below Masterson's and tell Angela we will walk up the last flight of stairs to avoid any chance of him seeing us. She stays remarkably calm and once again I am impressed by this strong, attractive woman in front of me. She is the complete opposite of Julia. A wave of regret washes over me as I think of my fiancée, hopefully my fiancée still.
'You know, Peter, I've been thinking about Zoe's murder. Do you really think that this guy is behind it?'
I pause on the stairs,
'I don't know, but he's the only lead we have. What about you.'
He stands on the step beneath me,
'Something's not right with it. I think back to the other murders and there are just too many irregularities. Zoe never went missing; she was killed on the same day. Her clothes were folded next to her body and the main difference is with the hands. It's similar but not the same.'
'You think we have a copy-cat killer?'
'I think it's a possibility we need to explore.'
'OK. Listen, I've not been with it the last few days. So much stuff going on, a lot of it personal. When this finishes I am going to take a few days off, maybe longer. I can't let my personal life affect the job. I'm telling you because I'm putting you up to run the department while I am away.'
'Jesus, Peter, it sounds like you are thinking of quitting.'
He sees the look in my eyes,

'You *are* thinking of leaving, aren't you?'
I turn away and continue back up the stairs.
'I don't know JD. I need to sort my life out, work out just what I want. At the moment the job is dragging me into places I can't control. It forces me to make decisions against my better judgement. It's made me think that life is cheap and…'
He grabs my arm to stop me,
'Peter, if anything I would say it has taught you the opposite. You see death and violence and, yes, it numbs you. But it makes you want to see more of life, makes everything we do more vibrant. That is why we take risks, to prove that we are alive. This thing with Ann, that was a risk. You wanted to prove to yourself you were still alive, still willing to take a gamble. Peter, sometimes a gamble is lost. That is what happened with you. It doesn't mean you have to throw it all away. I know how much Julia means to you. Fight for her, fight for the two of you.'
I sigh but say nothing and head back up the stairs until I reach the door to the top floor of the apartment building. I look through the small glass window and can see Masterson's apartment door. As JD catches me up, without taking my eyes from the door I say,
'Thanks JD. It means a lot.'
'No problem mate. Now, how do you want to play this out? You said fast and hard. Does that mean you want me to go old school on this guy?'
I shake my head.
'Let's see what he has to say. He's involved with the Mason case somehow but I also want to see how he reacts to Zoe's murder. Keep your weapon holstered but available. We both know what he's capable of.'

'Holstered but available. Yeah, right, cheers for the great advice as always,' he says and punches me in the shoulder good naturedly. A good natured punch from JD is about the same as a full swing from a normal sized person and my shoulder slams into the door painfully.

'Ooops,' is all JD can say.

He pulls out his radio and I put my hand over his, 'What are you doing?' I ask.

'Informing control of the situation.'

'Not yet. What if he has a scanner or even a police radio? He is MI6 remember. It's fair to say he could be monitoring us.'

Without warning, Masterson's apartment door opens and he pokes his head out of the gap. He catches me looking directly at him,

'Shit!' I exclaim, but then he does something I was not expecting. Masterson walks over to our position and pulls the door open.

'DCI Carter, DI Dawkins. Good to see you again. Won't you come on in?'

JD and I look at each other, both thinking just how strange this day is becoming and wondering what is going to happen next.

'Please sit down. Coffee, tea, something stronger perhaps?'

Masterson's apartment has a sweeping view of the London skyline. The Thames and especially the London eye dominate the view, dwarfing even Big Ben and the Houses of Parliament beyond. Angela is sitting in a soft arm chair, her smooth, long legs crossed demurely but showing just enough flesh to raise your heart rate.

I attempt to take control of the situation,

'We need to ask you some questions. First do I call you Stephens or Masterson?'

'Neal Stephens is dead Mr Carter, we found, sorry, you found his body a few months back if I recall. My name is Stuart Masterson. I consult with government agencies on many different contracts and subjects but mainly defence orientated. I think that should suffice for the background for now.'

He sits down at a large, modern, glass dining table. 'What do you need from me Chief Inspector?'

I struggle to maintain my composure. Sitting in front of me is a man I have had visions about for the last nine months. Luckily for me, JD pipes in, 'What happened to cause the death of Zoe Walker in such a brutal manner?'

'Zoe Walker? What are you on about?'

JD continues his line of questioning,

'A body was found that has been confirmed to be that of a Miss Zoe Walker, one of your victims…I'm sorry…one of Neal Stephens and Jim Barnwell's victims that escaped being abused and dismembered last year. Come on Neal, oh sorry, I keep forgetting it's Stuart now isn't it,' he says sarcastically. 'You must remember her. She escaped alive with Helen Carter.'

I glance over at JD as he uses my sister's name. I am still to come to terms with the degradation and inhumanity she had to deal with during her ordeal. 'I know who Zoe Walker is detective but I didn't know she had been murdered.'

'What makes you say murdered,' JD looks at me, 'we didn't say murdered.'

Masterson sighs, 'Two detectives from the homicide unit of the Met show up asking about a body. What conclusion would you make from that?'

I step in, 'Mr Masterson, can you tell me your whereabouts for Saturday evening please.'
I feel my anger rise as I see him smile. My whole body screams at me to reach out and smash it off his face with the maximum force I can muster, but instead I grind my teeth to almost their breaking point. The ache in my jaw helps me to focus and it forces me to reduce my violent intentions towards this man in front of me.
'I was watching you enter the reporter's apartment after you had vacated the Mason murder scene.'
I feel a cold chill make its way down my spine.
'You were following me?'
'Quite the opposite it seems. You were on my trail.'
A rumble of thunder rolls through the room as I stare at him. It makes Angela turn to look out of the window and her face wrinkles into a light frown.
'Hmm, strange, not a cloud in the sky.' she mumbles half heartedly before turning her attention back to the room.
'So you admit you were at the scene. What were you doing there and why were you at Ann's apartment later?'
'Why don't you both sit down, this is going to take a while and I am sure you would like to take notes.'
He gestures to the empty chairs at the table where he is seated. As JD and I pull out a chair each, he turns to Angela,
'Be a love and put the kettle on will you. My throat is parched.'
Angela gets up and makes her way to the kitchen.
'She appears to know her way around your place pretty well,' I comment, 'tell me how you know her.'

'We have had business dealings in the past, but I am sure you are well aware of that. Angela is a special character, Chief Inspector, and a person whom I have grown attached to over the years. We had a personal relationship for a while but, ahhh, you know how difficult it can be to hold down a steady relationship and a career at the same time, don't you?'

I feel my phone vibrate against my chest from my jacket pocket, but choose to ignore it. I see JD dig into his inside pocket and pull his own phone out. He reads the message written there and looks up at me. I have never seen him look this way and my first thought is that something has happened to Helen.

'Peter...' he gets up without saying another word and walks towards the television to pick up the remote control. The screen bursts in to life showing the National Geographic channel.

'How do I switch to a news channel?'

'Channel 151,' says Masterson, a look of confusion on his face.

As JD presses the numbers into the remote, the room falls silent as we see the carnage being broadcast in front of us. It is the caption at the bottom of the screen that has caused our shock.

1000s KILLED AND INJURED IN CAMBRIDGE TERROR ATTACK - LIVE

What causes me to turn away is the sound of Masterson's voice.

'Oh shit. I'm too late.'

CHAPTER 31

'Q1 this is Control, Q1 this is Control, over.'
Gary stops looking at the rising column of smoke to the North and thumbs his transmit button.
'Control, Q1. Go ahead, over.'
'Q1 be advised of transmission on tactical two one, uplink of data in progress, HAZARD will be loaded in three, two, one…do you have visual, Q1.'
Gary flips the electronic visor down and his helmet's Hazard Awareness Zone, Augmented Reality Display, HAZARD for short, springs to life. It brings a 3D representation of the battlefield as an overlay to the view he sees from the cockpit with his own two eyes. It gives the pilot a greater advantage in a combat situation by supplying real time data from all battlefield surveillance units in one easy to interpret feed.
'Control, HAZARD is good, switching to tactical two one.'
Reaching out with his left hand he deftly touches the large LCD display in the centre of his console and presses the 'TAC' readout. He waits a millisecond as it turns from red to green and then says out loud, 'Voice on…Freak two one.'
Turning on the voice activated suite of controls in the aircraft he changes his frequency to that of channel 21 in tactical mode. Voice control allows for more rapid response in a combat role. Gary can now change frequencies, deploy counter measures, select weapons systems and fire them without removing his hands from his control stick or throttle.
'Tac two one this is Q1, over.'

'Q1, spoof kilo eight four zero, confirm.'
Gary scrolls through the display and brings up his communications confirmation screen. There is always a threat that the enemy will gain access to the frequencies that are being used by the aircraft. A spoof confirmation reduces the risk to almost nil that false orders will be given. Gary runs through the list to grid kilo and looks down the numbers to find the one starting with 840. He reads out the last three numbers to confirm he is possession of the same grid and confirm his identity then repeats the process in case that one grid has been compromised. Finally satisfied that both stations on the communications network are who they say they are, the transmission proper can begin.
'Q1, wait for message from Papa Mike, over.'
He is taken aback as he answers, 'Roger.'
Papa Mike, PM, the Prime Minister. Things must be more serious than he thought and he brings his head around to look at the rising column of smoke in the distance again wondering if this is connected.

'The country's fate is in your hands,' he instantly recognises the distinctive voice that resounds clearly through his headset, 'a terrorist attack of a nature not seen before has been committed on this country. Your orders are to intercept and destroy the unmanned aircraft that has been hijacked by an outside agency and to do so at any cost. This is not a drill, you will be the first pilots to attack an aircraft in UK airspace since the Battle of Britain and the stakes could not be any higher than they were then. I will hand you over to the chief of staff, good luck gentlemen.'
The transmission goes silent for a second before a new voice comes over the tactical radio,

'Q1 and Q2, your rules of engagement have been changed to reflect the current situation. All weapons are hot. I repeat ALL weapons are hot. You have a free fire order to remove this aircraft from our skies. Collateral damage is not an issue, the MASTER aircraft must be stopped. No confirmation required, systems show green at my location. Happy hunting gents.'

The transmission ends and Gary can't help but exclaim, 'Fucking hell.'

'Roger that Q1, but your microphone is live.'

Gary blushes beneath his helmet but hopes that his little slip up will be understood. It is unprecedented to be given the order to destroy a target with no matter what damage is done to civilians or infrastructure around it.

Information starts to overlay his vision as the fighter controllers and airspace operators feed tactical data directly to him and his aircraft. A flashing red triangle shows their target and a bearing and height is automatically fed into the aircrafts flight computers. All Gary has to do is say, 'Course accept' and then follow instructions that direct him and Paul towards the rogue unmanned aircraft. He says the words and pushes forwards on the throttle to ignite his afterburner and eat up the eighty or so miles to the target.

'Q2 follow my lead, we are going in hard, fast and hot. I want you to keep a watch for threats and friendly's in the area.'

'Q1 roger, one threat, four Charlie Alphas in vicinity.'

Gary checks his own display again and see's the four civil airliners Paul spoke of. With the major London airports as well as Stansted and Luton all within twenty minutes flying time it is a stroke of luck there are not more. Then he realises that NATS, the National Air Traffic Control Service, have probably diverted all other flights away.

It is only a matter of moments before they are in missile firing range. Gary focuses on the red triangle in his vision, 'Identify Zombie One', the letter and number Z1 appear over the triangle. He moves his eyes away from the target and sweeps the horizon. He sees the four yellow circles from the HAZARD showing the civilian flights. In rapid succession he tags them all, 'Identify Alpha one,' he moves his focus to the next, 'Alpha two, Alpha three, Alpha four.'

In a few seconds he has tagged all aircraft in his battle-space to reduce a friendly fire incident.

'Paint Zombie one,'

A low pitched humming sound is heard as one of his air to air missiles starts to actively seek the target. Gary notices the Z1 symbol make a rapid left turn towards the nearest airliner. The airliner must have received instructions from NATS as it makes a slow rolling turn to the left to try and move away from the incoming aircraft but it is too slow. In his display, Gary watches as the two symbols converge until Z1 and C3 are sitting on top of one another.

'Son of a bitch,'

It is an old Cold War era Soviet trick of having a military aircraft come in under the radar by flying underneath and slightly rearwards of a commercial flight. Gary had read about it and seen photos but never expected to witness it being done for real. The humming in his helmet changes pitch as his weapons systems lock on to the much larger target they are presented with. He realises that to fire a missile now would destroy both aircraft. He switches off the targeting system.

'Q1 this is Q2, what are you waiting for?' says Paul's normally easy going voice now sounding slightly anxious.

'I'm not going to be the first pilot to shoot down an airliner with a missile.'

'Our orders state we have a free fire zone, collateral dam…'

'We approach to visual range, switch to guns, come up behind it and destroy the drone with slow, easy bursts. That way there is less chance of killing the 200 plus civilians on that airbus.'

'Roger Q1, you're the boss,'

'Don't forget it Q2, this is my call.'

As they approach the two aircraft in front of them, they reduce speed to match and pull alongside. The MASTER has not moved from it's location less than twenty feet below the aircraft it almost matches in size. Gary switches to the universal emergency frequency and notes the tail number of the airliner.

'Heavy five five one four, this is Royal Air Force Q1 off your port wing. Do you have visual, over'

He watches as a face appears in the cockpit side window and gives a thumbs up.

'Air Force Q1, we see you. Please explain the situation, over.'

The American drawl is calm and confident sounding and Gary feels a sense of hope that this could become a win-win situation.

'Heavy one four, you have a hostile aircraft shadowing you. Do not descend, I repeat do not descend. We are going to remove the threat with controlled bursts, do you understand.'

IN the RAF pilot's peripheral vision he notices the passengers are taking photos from their vantage points at the windows. The flashes of the cameras are a little distracting but he attempts to focus on the cockpit only.
'OK, Air Force Q1, give me a moment to inform my souls on board of the fireworks display and get them strapped in. Good luck.'
He reduces speed and allows the two aircraft to pull ahead slightly,
'Commencing in one minute, Heavy one four.'
He receives two clicks on the microphone in confirmation and understands the pilot is probably already on the tannoy system asking everyone to remain in their seats and fasten their seatbelts.
Gary lines up a few hundred yards behind the MASTER and immediately starts to feel his own aircraft being buffeted by the jet wash and slipstream of the two flying ahead of him. He is so intent on keeping his aircraft flying straight and true that he fails to see a small object detach itself from the MASTER.
'Watch out!' Paul shouts out a warning which causes Gary's head to raise instinctively.
He sees something fly under the nose of his plane and jerks back on the stick in reflex, but it is too late.
The nano-generator flies directly into the right hand side air intake of the fighter's engines and explodes. The small charge rips a hole in the fuselage and sends shards of red hot metal up into the cockpit and through the aircraft. One piece, less than 1cm across, rips a hole in a fuel line. The fuel jets out in a high pressure mist and touches the glowing shrapnel where it explodes into a rapidly

expanding fireball that blows the port wing off the body of the fighter.

Gary valiantly attempts to correct the roll but the aircraft knows it is a fatal catastrophe and does what its computers tell it to do. Gary feels straps tighten across his legs, chest and shoulders to bring his body and limbs into the smallest possible package as an explosive charge blasts out the bullet proof glass above him and rockets fire his ejection seat out of the doomed aircraft.

Gary looks up to see Paul's fighter jet in the wingman position and screams aloud in horror as he realises what is about to happen.

The ejection seat, travelling at over 300mph smashes him into the bottom of the second Eurofighter Typhoon aircraft, destroying its main computer systems and disabling one of the engines immediately. Paul attempts to control his stricken aircraft as it rapidly loses power. He looks up to see the two other craft move away, the civilian aircraft in one direction and the MASTER in another as it makes a turn that points it towards London. Paul keys his microphone to warn of the ongoing situation but doesn't get a chance to say anything. A small, ungainly looking, toy aircraft sized object appears next to his cockpit. He smiles at the appearance and dies instantly as it explodes just inches away from his face.

Wilks watches as the Prime Minister closes his eyes and lets his head drop slightly as the images before them unfold.

'Damn it, he should have used his missiles,' the General shouts out.

The PM slowly shakes his head,

'No…no. He did the right thing,' he raises his head and re-opens his weary looking eyes, 'I hope we can all be as brave when the time comes. What are our next options, people?'

The table and the room stay silent in shock, and in recognition that their options are limited.

CHAPTER 32

Luke is still working doggedly away at the files on Mason's computer. He has had some success and has managed to retrieve a swathe of e-mail addresses and subject headers. They look fairly innocuous to him, but he's not paid to make that kind of decision so, he bundles what he has together in an e-mail and sends it on to JD. He turns to his other PC where he has managed to hack in to the TSI servers at their head office in Cambridge. He finds it strange that such a high tech company like TSI with contacts spread around the defence world has failed to protect itself from a simple backdoor hack. It was found in the IT management software given out by Microsoft called, 'Performance Assurance for Microsoft Servers.'

Basically it has allowed Luke access to an account user name and password through the IT suite that then allows him to run batch scripts, or programs. One of these programs was then used to create an administrator account for Luke and he now has full control of the TSI servers. He flexes his fingers by interlocking both hands together and pushing forward,

'My precious,' he states aloud as he brings his hands down to the backlit keyboard in front of him. 'Let's see what Mason had been doing in the last few weeks.'

He knows that officially he should have sought approval before going in, but he also knows the pressure that Wilks is under and, since she is the one who brought him into the Met's services, he has a soft spot in his heart for her.

He starts running a simple SQL query with Mason as the base component, when the connection is closed unexpectedly. He attempts access repeatedly but each time is rebuffed with phrase, 'network not available.'

He checks other connections to the outside world and pings a server he has running at his home and finds no problems.

'Huh, guess they sorted out their security issues. Oh well, I suppose we will have to do it the old fashioned way.'

He picks up the phone and dials the number for TSI's headquarters. The strident tones of an unobtainable number roar down the phone to him. He hangs up and sits there in concentration,

'Shit, have I just killed their servers.'

He turns back to his console and checks for any sign of damage he may have caused by his illegal intrusions but finds that the only error is the network issue. He sits back and purses his lips together,

'What is going on?'

'Luke, Jesus, Luke. Why are you still in here?' the young woman's voice breaks his confused concentration.

'Hmm, what?'

'Come out and see this. You will not believe what has just happened.'

He slowly eases himself out of his chair and stretches a few times before heading outside of the computer forensics labs. He sees a group of his colleagues and a few men and women in uniform clustered around the television in the small self-serve canteen and crew-room area.
'...fuck did they manage that?'
'...many dead?'
'...sister at University must...'
Snippets of conversation break through to him as walks along the corridor to the irregular gathering. He pushes his way through, following the woman who called him out.
'It's Cambridge, Luke. The business and technology park there. They are saying it was some kind of explosion at TSI's headquarters, hydrogen or something like that caused by a terrorist take-over of their new drone.'
Luke's mouth drops open as he watches the screen as it shows a repeat of the earlier footage. A flash of white light and then the pan back to reveal the devastation in full colour. He turns suddenly and pushes his way frantically through the group and runs back to his console.
Something in one of the e-mails from Mason has created a spark of curiosity in him from the pictures on the television. At least now he knows why he lost access to the servers at TSI.
His fingers fly across the keyboard and he pulls up the list of encrypted e-mails. He quickly scans down them and sees what he is looking for.
'SUBJECT: Actions in event of hostile takeover.'

At first he thought it would be about the company, its shareholders and what to do in the event of a company battle for majority control. Now he thinks it might be far less mundane. He attempts to open the file but the contents are still encrypted, 'Right you bastard, I am going to break you.'
Luke bends over his keyboard and starts attacking the encryption with all of the dark IT skills he has acquired and mastered over his years.

CHAPTER 33

Emerson is staring in disbelief at the broken and bloody body in front of him. In the space of less than an half-an-hour it has been reduced from an attractive woman into a disfigured piece of meat. He turns away and vomits again, this time he only manages a dry heave. The barbarism of the two men whilst the woman questioned him repeatedly about kill codes has left him reeling. It is one thing to see death and destruction on a computer screen from thousands of miles and the violence he has just witnessed in front of him.

'Take him back outside,' the woman says to the two bloodied and gore covered men, 'give him time to think and we'll bring him back in soon.'

Her radio beeps twice and she walks over to pick it up from the chair where she placed whilst the interrogation was taking place.

'Is it done?' she asks.

'You will not believe how successful our little demonstration has been. Can you see the display?' The voice of her sister comes through clearly from the bunker below.

'I will see it in a moment. I'll make the call.'

She pulls out her mobile phone and calls a number from memory. A man's clipped English accent answers almost immediately,

'Hello, who is this?'

'I take it you have seen our display of force?'

'That was not part of the plan. What the fuck do you think you are doing?'

'There has been a change in the plan. I hold the power now, not you.'

'You little bitch. Why the fuck do you think I should even listen to you? Why, I should hang up now and let you rot you...'
'Shush, shush, shush,' she says softly as if talking to a petulant child, 'hang up if you wish but then I walk out of this room and announce to the assembled crowd of dignitaries, that I am holding hostage by the way, that this little incident was sponsored by the British government and the head of MI6.'
She pauses and listens to the quiet line in her ear, 'That's better. It's much nicer when you calm down and stop swearing.'
'What do you want?' he does not yet sound the way she wants him to, which is defeated.
'I will call you back. Don't go anywhere.'
With that she hangs up and walks outside to the large room to see the demonstration her sister was talking about. Her smile as she watches the images on the screen is like that of a child as it enters Santa's grotto for the first time. It is a mixture of awe, joy and pure unadulterated pleasure.
She turns to the crowd of people, looking for one person in particular. She finds him staring defiantly back at her from the edge of the room. Raising her arm she points directly at the older man. He stands up, his face a mask of hatred directed at her. A guard steps forward to beat him back down to the floor,
'Stop! Bring him into the room. I need to talk to him.'
She turns and walks confidently back into the bloodied and stinking office space to wait for the man to be brought to her.

Emerson watches with red-rimmed eyes as his captor and tormentor turns her back to him and walks back into to that terrible room. A hand reaches out and touches his shoulder and a small bottle of water is placed in his hands,
'Thank you,' he croaks, 'thank you.'
'What happened in there? Are you hurt?' a man's voice asks.
Emerson looks towards the source to find an army officer staring at him intently.
'No, not me. They…they killed Claire, my assistant. They want some kind of information they think I have.'
'What information? Did you give it to them?'
'No, no I can't. I don't have it.'
The officer looks around at the guards,
'Listen, as long as we don't do anything stupid they leave us alone. What information are they after? Maybe I can help.'
Emerson takes a sip from the water bottle,
'They want the kill codes of the drones, all the drones.'
'And with these codes they can control how we operate in any theatre. I see why they want them, but why didn't you give them to her? It would have saved that woman's life? Is it to protect our troops?'
Emerson shakes his head and snorts, 'What? No. If I give them out it would ruin the company, ruin me. Everything I have worked for would be worthless. Everything I have done would be for nothing.'

The officer pushes himself away from the dishevelled looking Emerson with disgust clear on his face. He opens his mouth to say something but nothing comes out so complete is his disbelief in the words he just heard.
Emerson just watches the screen in silence as it shows the two fighter jets closing in to the MASTER.
'This should be interesting,' he says, and takes another sip of water.

CHAPTER 34

Helen and Ewelina sit on the couch together, and just like the rest of the world, look on in shock as the terrible events of the day unfurl before them. The TV commentators are already comparing it to 9/11 and there are rumblings that attacks on the Muslim population will increase.

'Why don't they realise that it is the way they are reporting this that makes people hate whole religions instead of just the radicals,' Helen asks the screen as she raise her arm towards another 'expert' on unmanned aircraft that the news channels have dragged out from a shady hole somewhere.

Ewelina places an arm around her shoulders,

'It has always been the same. In Poland we had the Russians come in and tell us what religion was right and wrong. If you disagreed, you went away in the bad days of my parents and grandparents. It will never change.'

Helen tilts her head to one side and rests it on her flatmates comforting arm.

'I have friends in Cambridge, I hate what has been done as much as the rest of the world, but I am asking myself, what brought them to such measures. They don't go out and suddenly decide to do this for no reason. Have we brought this on ourselves do you think?'

Ewelina also brings her head down until it touches her friend's own. They both sit that way and watch the unfolding drama on the television.

'At least Zoe is not around to see this. It would have destroyed what little faith she had left.'

Ewelina gently strokes Helen's face as tears roll softly down her cheeks. It is not long before both are quietly sobbing as they hold each other.
Theirs are just some of the millions of tears that are being wept this day.

Graham drops Kate off at the entrance to her building and drives his car, a vintage Jensen CV8 in sky blue, to the underground car park of his own offices. The 305 bhp Chrysler 361ci V8 engine sounds like a powerful speedboat's outboard motor in the confined space of the garage. Graham cannot help but smile. Pulling into his reserved parking slot, his smile fades as he recalls the task he has set himself for this afternoon, the unwelcome autopsy of Zoe Walker.
Hi sits behind the steering wheel feeling the vibration of the engines heavy notes rock his body as he steels himself for the task ahead. After a few seconds he twists the key to switch off the engine, and with a sigh, extricates himself from the vehicle. Five minutes later he is in his office and starting on his first coffee of the afternoon that is just one of the many that day from his personal Krups coffee machine which sits on the sideboard in his office. He pulls out the case file on Zoe and skims through the pages of what some of the homicide detectives call, the Murder Book. Taking a sip of coffee he closes the buff coloured folder and opens his desk drawer. He pulls out a small, digital, silver voice recorder and a package of unopened AA batteries. He removes the ones in situ from the device and places fresh ones in. The old batteries go in to the desk drawer for later use in remote controls.

There is still plenty of life left in them, unlike the people he works on, but he doesn't want to risk running out of power for the digital recorder halfway through his task. He finishes his coffee and throws the small paper cup into the bin as he walks out of his office and heads towards what he refers to as, 'The Cold Room'.

The autopsy room he enters is one of the largest he has worked in. There are eight dissection tables available for use and a viewing gallery. Today the curtains have been drawn around the windows of the gallery for privacy and there are no other procedures scheduled to take place either.

'Hi, Dr Young,' Chris Harris the APT calls out as he steps through the heavy double doors.

An APT, or Anatomical Pathology Technologist, is there to assist in all aspects of the autopsy. Graham takes a swift look at the examination sheet and sees that Chris has already photographed and weighed the remains of the body within the body bag prior to the external examination.

'You've been busy I see, Chris. How are the exams coming along?'

Chris was in training to make the step across from APT to forensic pathologist, a step that Graham was only too happy to help with.

'Going well Dr Young, just one more year then I'll be after your job.'

Even behind the mask, Graham can see that Chris is smiling.

'With days like today I will even help you fill out the paperwork. I think I am getting too old and too tired to continue.'

Chris puts down the implements he was preparing and places his gloved hands on the side of the steel table in front of him,

'You are one of the most dedicated and professional surgeons I know, Dr Young. If it wasn't for you and your support, I would not be in the position I am in. Your work here gives closure to families who feel they have lost everything. You help to give them hope.'

'Hope?'

'Yes, hope. It is the evidence you find in this room that determines what type of justice is set. Our findings convict criminals who think they have got away, literally, with murder. It is what happens here today that determines that a young woman did not die in vain and...'

Graham holds his hand up, 'This is from the foreword of my book isn't it?' he lets out a small laugh, 'Thanks, Chris.'

'You're welcome, Dr Young. I know this is almost a personal one for you today and if you think I am ready I will gladly complete the autopsy under your guidance.'

'Chris, you are ready, more than ready in fact, but I owe it to this girl, and also to a good friend of mine to give this my utmost attention. The next is yours, I promise you.'

Chris nods sombrely as Graham pulls on a set of surgical gloves and presses the record button of the small silver device in his hand.

'Forensic autopsy, case number 131122452. Caucasian female identified as Zoe Walker. Age, weight, identifying marks, etc recorded as per examination form. Carrying out visual external examination...'

The next four hours pass by in a blur as the two men perform their 'danse macabre' around the brutally dismembered body of the young woman before them, looking for clues and evidence to pinpoint her slaying on someone or something. At the end of it, Graham is exhausted.
'I'll finish up here, Dr Young.'
'Thanks Chris. I'll get this typed up with the findings and get it up to homicide. Chris?'
The young man looks up, 'I meant what I said, the next one is yours with my supervision. You're a ready and capable physician.'
Depositing his gloves, face mask and surgical gown in the hazardous waste bin, Graham leaves the ghoulish sight of a grinning Chris, sewing up the remains on the stainless steel table behind him. He heads back to his office to type up his conclusions.

CHAPTER 35

'What do you mean you're too late?' I ask Masterson as he stares at the screen.

'This,' he points towards the television, 'this is what I have been trying to stop.'

He reaches into his pocket and I see JD put his own hand into the confines of his jacket.

'Easy big man, you don't need that. What is it anyway? Standard issue Sig? You would need to be this close to do any damage.' He looks at me, 'May I?'

I nod my head and he slowly pulls his hand out of his pocket holding a small USB stick.

'You remember my boss?'

I nod again.

'Well the information on here is worth an awful lot of money and lives, and he wants it. Our government wants it, everybody's government wants it.'

'What is it?' I can't help but be drawn in.

'On here are the full schematics of the MASTER aircraft and the dockable fuel cells along with all the software required to keep it in the air. Mason knew he had created a monster and this demonstration today was supposed to show the world the cutting edge energy innovations he had discovered whilst showcasing the potential terrible repercussions of using his technology.'

We all look at the TV. It is JD who voices our thoughts,

'Looks like he got his way.'

'What are you doing with it in your possession?' I ask.

'Mason trusted me for some reason. I had escorted him as part of MI6's overseas security details when he was in Afghanistan working on their last unmanned aircraft. We hit it off, he's a,' he has to pause, 'he was, a really likeable bloke.'

'But what are you doing with it?' I repeat.

'Mason wanted this to go public. It's worth billions but he was willing to give it away. I think all the death and destruction caused by his products finally got to him. Being branded a baby killer and harassed every time you go out can probably do that to a person. Well, he wanted out of the circus especially after the warnings he received.'

My interest is piqued,

'Warnings? Who was warning him? How was he warned? What…'

'Whoa, whoa, whoa. Slow down. He told me he had made it clear to his company that this was the last aircraft he would work on and he wanted most of the technology to be shared to create cleaner and cheaper energy for all. This didn't go down so well with certain members of the board as I am sure you can imagine. Apparently there was a huge argument mostly centred around profit, loss and the survival of the company.'

'And this was when he started receiving his warnings? Did you see any of them?' JD asks.

Masterson shakes his head,

'I was just told of them, although Mason did inform me that it wasn't just his company that had started with the threatening letters. He mentioned he was getting a lot of pressure from oil producing nations and he received personal visits from the US ambassador, which started off friendly enough but soon turned quite nasty, informing him he should not release the information.'

'Why would so many people be interested in an unmanned aircraft?' I ask.
Masterson shakes his head,
'You still don't see the big picture do you? The oil is running out, natural gas is being held at ransom by places like Russia and China, our electricity is getting more and more expensive to produce and green power is beginning to look like an expensive proposition that can't keep up with demand. Mason had created a clean, renewable energy source. And more importantly, it was cheap to manufacture. If you control a multi billion dollar industry, what would your reaction be?'
'So you're saying this is all about money?' I say.
JD turns his head towards me with his words of wisdom,
'Well that has been the root of all evil since time began. How many cases do we get that are all about the money?'
I nod my head,
'Fair point,' I bring my focus back to Masterson, 'Do you have any proof of this?'
'Only what's on this memory stick. Mason wanted it released in case anything happened to him. I was going to get Angela to leak it through the press.'
'Why ask her to do that? Wouldn't that place her in danger?'
He shakes his head,
'She has no involvement with any of this, unlike me. If I were to be found out doing something like this, let's just say I would disappear very quickly. My boss has a far reaching grasp and does not take kindly to what he would see as a personal betrayal.'
I look out of his window at the London skyline and take a deep breath.

'So let me just get this straight,' I say whilst staring out of the window, 'Mason was murdered for the information on that stick, you're saying it could have been the oil companies to protect their interests, the Americans to protect their oil revenue, or even our own government to keep this information secure.' I turn back to face the room and see Masterson nodding. 'Yet you have no proof to confirm any of this and you are not willing to blow the whistle yourself because of the danger you would be in.'
'That pretty much sums it up, yes.'
I lean back in my chair and let out another loud sigh as I weigh up the options,
'What can we do to help?'

CHAPTER 36

'Leave us,' she says sternly.
The two armed men flanking the small man turn and leave. She stares with anger at the man before her until they close the door, then she rushes forward with a grin on her face.
'Did you see? They will surely give us what we want now.'
They hug and kiss.
'Do they suspect?' he asks as he pulls away slightly.
'How could they? They are so in shock and I...'
'I meant your men.'
'Oh. No, they think this is all about stopping the drone attacks.'
'And you are sure of their loyalty? They will do what needs to be done when the time comes?'
'It is beyond reproach,' she smiles thinly, 'would you like a demonstration?' She does not give him time to respond, 'I will give you a demonstration and it will fit nicely in our plans anyway.'
She walks over to the door and reaches out to grasp the handle,
'Wait here,' she says.

The hostages look up as one as the woman yanks the door open and marches out in front of them.
'He is useless, bring me another.'
Her gaze wanders around the room before coming to rest on a dark skinned man in crisp white robes.
'Him, bring him here.'

The two guards who were ordered form the room rush forward and pick up the calm looking man by the armpits. They half carry him forward to where she stands as his feet struggle to keep up. She stops them before they enter the room.
'No, this we do in plain view. We need to send a message.'
The hostage is thrown to floor in front of her and he turns his face up to hers with venom flashing in is eyes. She smiles down at him,
'You are Saudi, yes?'
'My name is…'
'I don't care who you are. You are Saudi, yes?'
He nods, his piercing blue eyes betraying his anger at being treated this way by a woman.
'You bow to the Americans and you buy their weapons to kill innocents.'
His voice is calm as he replies to her accusations,
'We acquire weapons and equipment for defence, like all other nations.'
She points to the screen behind him where the dogfight has just finished between the two unfortunate Eurofighter aircraft and the MASTER,
'And this, you buy this for defence when you are already the most powerful nation in the region.'
'Our enemies adapt. As must we, it is the way of the world.'
'What of the innocents you have murdered in the name of your archaic laws?'
His anger causes his voice to rise,
'Our laws are our business. In my country you must live by the law or pay the consequences.'
She laughs. It is a cruel sound from such a pretty face.

'Beheading women for adultery because they have been raped? What kind of people does that to its own citizens?'

'It is not my place to make laws, but follow them. Is it not the same in this country? Or your country, wherever that is.'

She stays silent for a moment before replying.

'It is true. Laws are meant to be followed. So I tell you what I shall do, I shall create a law, right here and right now. I am in power here so that gives me the right to do so.' She grabs his chin and brings his gaze up to hers as she speaks venomously into his face, 'I declare that all Saudi nationals are pigs and must announce that this is true on pain of death. Do you abide by my laws, pig?'

The last word is said with such force that spit flies into his face. He wipes it softly away with his sleeve,

'I cannot do that. You have no right to declare such laws and I do not recognise your authority.'

His arrogant and defiant look infuriates her, she was hoping to see fear in his eyes.

'Pig, do you recognise this authority?' she says this as she pulls a large, black bladed knife from her belt. The silvery edge glints in the overhead lights where it has been honed to a razor-sharpness. He focuses his eyes between the blade and her face but remains silent.

'Stand up and announce to the world what a pig you are.'

'I cannot,' he says calmly.

Her eyes flicker to the two men in a silent command and they spring into action. One man forcefully places his knee in to the back of the kneeling Saudi figure and pulls backwards on his arms. The man cannot help but cry out and raise his head in pain and anger. The woman gives her knife to the other guard,
'Take his head.'
He blinks twice, rapidly, and swallows instinctively, his only concession to thinking about the command before taking the blade from her outstretched hand.
She leans forward to whisper in her victims ear, 'Allahu Akbar,' before taking two steps backwards. She watches in satisfaction as his forehead is grasped in one powerful hand and yanked back even further to expose his throat.
The point of the knife is pushed into the soft flesh just at the jaw-line under the ear and pulled forward with a sharp jerk. Blood spurts with each frenzied beat of the heart as the carotid artery is severed. The victim lets out a blood curdling scream while struggling to break free from his captors. The knife is plunged in again and the scream turns liquid before abruptly cutting off into a sickening, wheezing, gasping sound. The wheezing breaths turn to a bubbling gurgle as blood pours into the severed airway. The body stops its violent thrashing, instead it makes soft, fluttering movements. The sound of retching from those nearest the atrocity permeates around the room.
The woman stands triumphantly at the front of the onlookers and declares in a strong voice,
'You will do as I say or face the consequences. This is my only law.'

She turns away and strides back into the room unable to hide her look of excitement.
She grabs the man and pushes him down to the floor, unbuckling his belt and unzipping his trousers as she does so,
'What a rush, we must be quick.'
She never realised that such absolute power was such an aphrodisiac, she thinks as she impales herself upon him and moves rhythmically, at times, frenziedly until she reaches her climax.

CHAPTER 37

John Miller's chest is a searing ball of pain. He has a vague memory of people bursting into his workplace and then nothing more. What a strange dream, he thinks. He attempts to push himself up and out of his bed only to fall back with a low groan. That is when he realises it is not a dream. The memory comes flooding back. He has been shot.

He looks down at his chest expecting to see a gaping hole but is confused to see only a dark red patch on his shirt. He fumbles with his buttons and exposes his chest. The heavy crucifix, given to him by his mother is mangled and has been pushed into his pale, white skin breaking the flesh and causing the bleeding.. A deformed piece of grey metal is protruding from the centre of the heavy gold cross, or what used to be a cross before it was struck by the bullet. He takes a deep breath with trepidation and the pain increases and he realises he has probably sustained a few cracked ribs from the shot. The pain is making his head whirl and he is aware he is about to pass out again. Taking small, shallow breaths he puts his hand into his pocket and pulls out a small earpiece.

He places the Bluetooth device into his ear and presses the small button on the side as he looks around the area where he lies. He has been left in between the consoles and he is alone for the moment.

He rolls with great difficulty on to one side trying not to groan. He knows to make a sound will bring the gun bearing woman back.

He cups one hand to his mouth and says three numbers, nine, nine, nine. The voice activated software in his phone releases a dial tone in his ear and then three short beeps.
'Emergency services how can I help?'
John Miller starts to relay softly what he can remember of the situation to the woman on the other end of the line.

Wilks is listening to the discussion playing out in front of her. If it wasn't for the seriousness of the situation she would find it amusing as the men bicker like children in the playground over the next course of action.
'We don't know how many there are, we need to ascertain details before we react and possibly cause more deaths.'
'If we don't act we can guarantee more deaths. Where do you think that drone is headed? It is coming to London and so far we have no defence against it unless we stop it at the source.'
'What, by sending men on a suicide mission against an unknown threat in a heavily defended nuclear bunker? Do you realise what you are asking?'
Wilks hears the sound of her mobile ringing and fishes it off the table in front of her to answer it. She turns her head away from the argument going on to listen to the words coming down the line.
'Gentlemen,' she raises her voice to break their conversation and they stop to look at her, 'Gentlemen, thank you. We have a development.' She talks into the mouthpiece, 'I am putting you on speakerphone, you are speaking to the Prime Minister and the combined heads of COBRA .'

Wilks presses a button and places the phone on the table in front of her. The room is silent and attentive as they wait for whatever is coming.
'Go ahead,' says Wilks.
A softly spoken voice, wheezing, and in obvious pain, crackles from the small speaker.
'My name is John Miller, I am head of the flight control centre at TSI which has been attacked by gunmen and I have been shot.'
The Prime Minister leans forward in his chair, 'How badly are you hurt, John? How have you managed to call us?'
'I think they believe I am dead,' he stifles a cough, 'I am hidden between the workstations, I can't see anyone and it hurts too much to move. Their bullet ricocheted…' he lets out an involuntary groan as he breathes in to continue, '…so lucky, I am so lucky. When is help coming?'
The people around the table all look towards the PM at this question.
'It will be there soon, John, don't worry. You said you are head of flight control?'
'Yes, I am in charge of the MASTER control room.'
A murmur ripples around the room and the PM holds up his hand for silence.
'John, can you disable the MASTER drone? Can you abort its mission from where you are?'
'Yes, that is possible…'
'John, we don't have much time, abort the mission, do it now. Many lives are at stake.'
'Sir, I'm sorry. It is possible but only if I have the kill codes and they are with the CEO, James Emerson.' Another soft cough, 'Mason would have had them too, if Emerson is here, then perhaps you can get them from…'

'WHAT ARE YOU DOING?' A harsh voice breaks into the conversation. The PM stands up his face a mask of concern.
Coughing comes from the small speaker in perfect clarity,
'Help me, help me please.' Miller's voice.
There is a dull thud and short scream of pain.
Wilks notices how the Prime Ministers knuckles have turned white where he grips the edge of the table.
'Help you, you should be dead.'
There is a rattle of something falling to the floor and then cursing from a man.
'Drag him over to the others. We will wait and see what Leanne wants to do with him when she comes back.'
The sound of groaning and that of a body being dragged recedes into the distance.
Wilks stands up and walks over to the PM,
'I think he has dropped his phone deliberately, he has left a line open. I will get a trace on it and also enhance the signal. We may be able to glean information from it. Whoever this Miller is, he's a brave son of a bitch.' She realises her language,
'Sorry, sir.'
'No need to be sorry, you are right. Get it done Commissioner, we need all the help we can get.'
As Wilks walks over to the side of the room to use a landline the PM asks the rest of the COBRA group,
'What the hell are these kill codes and how do we get them? We must stop this aircraft from reaching London.'

CHAPTER 38

Graham reads through his Post-Mortem report on Zoe one more time and then starts typing up his conclusions.

1. Cause of death; repeated stab wounds to back of trunk and neck by bladed weapon. Indeterminate death blow due to frenzied attack with fifty (50) plus defined entry points. Zero defensive wounds to hands and arms. Victim died from extreme blood loss.

2. Fibres in oral cavity suggest a gag of some kind used to stifle victim's cries; lab results of fibres to follow.

3. Dismemberment completed post mortem in situ at victim's body discovered location.

4. Weapon used in cause of death, in all probability, is that used to dismember victim. Crude incisions coupled with snapping of bone and joints indicate no knowledge of surgical procedures in removing limbs.

5. In no way, apart from dismemberment of the body does this correspond to 'Ripper' murders by James Barnwell. Indications suggest a copy-cat murder using details available through media and press of the original crimes. Contra-indications between the cases include –
   i. Time of disappearance compared to time of death.
   ii. Cause of death.
   iii. In situ dismemberment.
   iv. Method of dismemberment.
   v. Message written on victims body.

Graham sits back in his chair and looks at the words on his screen. He is getting used to seeing and recording violent death and that fact is starting to worry him. Nobody should become immune to the level of destruction of a human body that he has witnessed. He looks up towards the ceiling, 'Maybe it's time I took a break.' he says wistfully. The head peeking round his door makes him jump with its words,
'Sounds like a great idea, where shall we go?'
Kate walks into the room with a smile on her face, 'Things not going so well?' she asks.
Graham smiles back at his new lover,
'Hey, how are you? I'm just finishing up my report on the park victim. Tell me, is it true that multiple wound victims are normally killed by someone they know?'
Kate sits down in the seat opposite Graham, rests her elbows on the table and crosses her hands in front of her,
'In the majority of these types of victims, that seems to be case, yes. Multiple wounds normally indicate a level of anger and hate that is associated with crimes of passion. A random killing will often be a single or double blow where the killer waits as the victim dies, or does not realise that a fatal blow has been struck. Also, in a study from the US, it has been confirmed in a vast number of investigations and convictions that multiple injuries to a victim are often caused by women. Males tend to initiate a dramatic, explosive method of killing; gunshot, head trauma, knife to the chest etc, whereas women in anger will slash out repeatedly at their intended target. It has always been theorised to be the case, and their studies seem to be proving the point.'

'Hmm, interesting. You see, our victim has over fifty stab wounds to her.'

'Posterior, anterior or both?'

'Does that make a difference?'

'Definitely. If spread over both sides of the body then the victim was probably struggling. The killer would have made indecisive stabs to begin with, almost as if they weren't sure if what they were doing should continue. But as the victim struggles to get away the attack rises in crescendo as the excitement and blood lust also increases. In this case the final blow will be the deepest, many psychologists have said that murderers who kill this way compare their feelings to sex and climax during the killing.'

'All of our victim's wounds were across the back of the upper body.'

Kate nods, 'Hate. The over-riding feeling would possibly have been hatred. The first blow would have been strong enough to fell the victim and…'

'Would there be enough time to place a gag in the mouth in this scenario?'

She shakes her head, 'No, this would have been quick and brutal. Unless of course the killer led the victim to the murder site. Was she blindfolded as well?'

'I have no indication of that from the post-mortem. No fibres, no constriction or breaking of the capillaries of or around the eyes.'

'So she was gagged to stop her screaming but left to see where she was going. It sounds like a classic threat scenario.' She sees the look of confusion on Graham's face, 'I mean, the killer was giving the victim a chance to live. Options were given, possibly, and only when the response is not what the killer wanted is the fatal blow struck.'

'But why continue an attack and especially why dismember the body afterwards?'

Kate shakes her head slowly,

'It all comes back to hatred. Not being able to stop the attack is often described by wives in murders of their husbands or lovers. They feel they want to inflict as much pain as possible on the person they have loved, to make their victim feel the pain they themselves have felt by the betrayal or loss of love they have experienced. The dismemberment, well, that I can't explain. That shows a level of barbarity and cold bloodedness that only the truly psychotic show.'

Graham lets out a long sigh,

'So we are looking for a psychotic lover.'

Kate leans forward, a serious expression on her face,

'And in all probability, a woman.'

Graham averts his eyes as he thinks of Peter's sister and her relationship with Zoe.

'Oh shit.' he says as he closes his eyes and wonders how he is going to explain this finding to his friend.

CHAPTER 39

'It is time to start phase two. Are you ready?' she asks the man who is doing up his belt and smiling at her.

'Certainly, where is your sister?'

'She is in the bunker controlling the drone.'

'Excellent, let's go make some money.'

He walks towards the door and, without facing her, pauses to say,

'Joanne, your mother would have been proud of you both.'

With these words he opens the door and walks quietly towards the hostages with his head bowed. Tears spring to her eyes at his words, the words from her father.

Wiping her eyes she grabs the small two way radio and presses the call button. The warbling sound lasts for a second before cutting off and the voice of her sister comes through.

'Go ahead.'

'We are starting phase two. Is everything in place?'

'We will input the data now, wait one moment.'

The transmitter goes silent and she can imagine her sister, Leanne, issuing commands to the men in the small command module.

'Completed, on my way.'

Joanne simply clicks the transmit button twice to acknowledge the comment and waits her sister's arrival.

Outside her father is talking quietly to a group of the hostages.

'She promised me safe passage and assured my safety for a ransom of $100,000, American. I paid it myself by transfer through her computer. She says it will be recompense for the victims and their families of air strikes and drone attacks in Pakistan and Afghanistan.'
The group mutter amongst themselves softly,
'How can you be sure she will do as she says?'
The man turns and points to the dead man on the stage,
'I can be sure of her reaction if I had not done it.'
The group is silenced by the forthright remark.
As his daughter appears in front of the group he nods slightly and moves backwards until he is against the wall where he sits down and waits.
He watches as she points to a man he was talking to,
'Bring him in.' she commands.
'There is no need for your men, I will come willingly,' the man says as he stands up and brushes down his trousers. He walks forward with a confidence he does not feel inside, but he knows that to show fear is a sign of weakness.
'I will do as you say.'
Over the next hour in ones and twos, the woman waits and watches as the hostages are led into the room and then afterwards, placed against the wall next to her father. The ones that refuse the deal of safety for $100,000 are placed near the main entrance doors away from everyone. Her father notes with satisfaction that there are more joining him than are moved away to the non-paying group.

No-one appears to notice the woman as she appears from a small side door and sits down on the floor. She has changed her clothes from that of the waitress into a smart business suit and her hair is free of the wig she used to disguise her appearance. She is the last person left to be led into the back room. As she makes her way onto the stage her sister exits the room and calls out to the group of twelve men near the door.
'You will have one more chance to rethink your options, the price is now $200,000.'
She points to the first man in line, a small, grey haired and understandably nervous looking man, 'You, what is your response?'
All eyes in the room are on him as he clasps his hands together in supplication,
'I cannot raise that money, I am just a photographer. I came here from a local newspaper to…'
The woman waves her hand and one of her men steps forward, raises his pistol and pulls the trigger. The man crumples, his life extinguished as easily as if he were an insect crushed beneath a foot.
She points to the next man in line,
'You, what is your response?'
His eyes visibly widen as he realises his life is about to end. His mouth opens and closes but no words escape.
'I will pay. I will pay for all of them.'
Emerson astounds himself as he speaks out and steps forward from the line of people that have paid their ransoms, 'Please let there be no more killings here.'
Joanne smiles at him,
'Come forward Mr Emerson, we will talk again and discuss other ways of payment.'

She calls out to her men,
'In five minutes kill one of them if I am not out to stop you. Then execute one every five minutes after that.' She turns back to the would be saviour, 'Come, come Mr Emerson, we shall do this in private. The clock is ticking and their lives are in your hands.'
She waves away her sister who is still standing near her on the small stage and waits as she walks over to the group against the wall.
Emerson knows what is required of him as enters the room after the woman.
'I will give you the codes, just don't…'
'Shut the door.'
He stops speaking and closes the door behind him.
'Sit down, please.'
He sits down in one of the chairs ensuring he is facing away from the body of his assistant which is still lying on the table.
'I will give you the codes,' he repeats, 'please, there has been enough death.'
'Of course you will give me the codes, but how will I know they are the correct ones? Should I just take your word for it?'
'Please, don't do this.'
Joanne shakes her head and smiles.
'When will you realise that I can do whatever I want. I am in charge, I say what happens and I say who lives and dies.'
She pulls out a mobile phone and dials a number, whilst it rings she asks Emerson,
'Give me a code, any code.'
Emerson nods, 'Golf 4-4-6-9.'
'What does that do?'

'It will return any Mark 3 UAV back to base immediately without any chance of reset by the pilot.'

'Hmm good,' she says as her head tilts to one side as the phone is answered.

'Hello again, how are you today…now, now, I told you I don't like it when you swear. Listen to me very carefully…Golf 4-4-6-9, I'll repeat that for you, Golf 4-4-6-9. Got that? Good. You have ten minutes to wire two million dollars to my account before I use it. You know the details. You have used the same account in the past. Oh and by the way, if you take the full ten minutes then you will have killed two of the hostages.'

A loud bang is heard from outside the door that relays down the phone line,

'Better make that *another* two hostages. Best you hurry. Bye now.' She hangs up on the caller and presses a few buttons on the net-book in front of her.

She looks over to Emerson and smiles,

'I guess now we wait.'

In his office in the main building of MI6, Leahy stares at the dead phone in his hand before shouting out,

'Mary! Get the PM on the line NOW.'

His hands fly across his keyboard as he types in the letter and number sequence given to him down the line. He pales as he sees the result of transmitting the code. There are currently fourteen missions in flight using the Mark 3 unmanned aircraft, four of them are critical, which means they are providing support for troops in contact.

He opens a new window on his computer that links him directly to the department's 'black ops' budget. As he is typing information on the keyboard, his phone rings. He barely pauses as he hits the speakerphone function,
'This is Leahy at MI6, sir. We have information regarding the ongoing crisis. I have identified the terrorists involved. I can send the information to you immediately. Are you at COBRA HQ?'
'Yes we are. Good work.'
'Are we on speaker sir?'
He hears a click,
'Not anymore. What is it?'
'Sir, Operation Dragonclaw has been compromised.'
He hears an angry sigh over the speaker,
'That is all too apparent. How the fuck has it happened?'
Leahy knows it is dangerous ground as the PM almost never swears.
'Circumstances beyond my control have occurred, but I assure you I am doing all I can to…'
'All you can, all you fucking can? Jesus, man, have you seen what happened in Cambridge. How are you going to bring that under control?'
'Sir, I…'
'Just get it done and get it done quickly.'
The PM hangs up the phone.
Leahy can almost see in his minds eye the force with which the phone was slammed down by the rattled PM.

He checks his watch. Barely three minutes has passed since the phone call demanding money. His finger poises over the 'Enter' key as he looks at the long string of numbers in front of him. He pauses and pushes a speed-dial button on his phone and then hits 'Enter'. Across the city a mobile phone rings twice before being answered,
'Masterson here. What's the situation, boss?'
'I need you to take a team to Norfolk and do a spot of clearing up. Events have rather taken a turn for the worse.'

CHAPTER 40

I watch as Masterson speaks on his mobile phone for a few seconds. He ends the call and looks at each of us in turn before speaking.

'We have to be quick, things are coming to a head and I think my boss has lost control.'

'What do you mean?' I ask.

'I will be assembling a team to take control of the Norfolk facility. What happened in Cambridge was not meant as part of his overall plan.'

I shake my head in confusion,

'Are you saying this whole event was orchestrated?'

Masterson nods his head slowly,

'Hijacking the MASTER project was a way to raise exposure to the world of its power. Mason and Emerson were both privy to this information but Mason wanted nothing to do with it. I was going to his home to protect him. I agreed with him you see, the destructive power of this aircraft should not be the main focus for the world. The energy systems and technology that allows it almost unlimited time in the air should be shared and developed by every nation, that was Mason's focus. Remember how I said certain members of the board were all about profit, well my boss and *his* boss are both stakeholders in TSI. Emerson went along with the plan, the government's plan, as it would increase the value of the project. We were involved to provide, shall we say, 'outside help', to facilitate the takeover. It appears they have gone rogue and now I have to go and remove them from the picture.'

He hands me the USB stick.

'Use this to stop the MASTER before it reaches London. I seem to recall you have a computer whizz kid working for you?'

I nod and say,

'Luke.'

'He will know what to do with the information on here. But you don't have much time. None of us have much time.'

I look down at the small device in my hand and wonder how many more people will die before the information on it can be used.

'JD, let's go.'

Angela stands up,

'What about me?' she asks.

We all look to Masterson who shrugs his shoulders, 'Looks like you have got the afternoon off. You can stay here with me for a few hours if you like, help me pack a bag or two.'

I notice how she smiles at his words and know that there is more than meets the eye between these two.

'Sure, that sounds better than sitting at home waiting for the world to end.' she says.

I grab JD's shoulder,

'Come on, let's get this to Luke and stop whatever is coming our way.' I look Masterson in the eye before leaving, 'You said your boss's boss is in on this. Is that who I think it is?'

He smiles grimly and nods his head.

I take a deep breath and release it out through puffed cheeks as I look up at the ceiling while shaking my head. I can only think of one thing that needs to be said, 'Good luck,' I offer.

'You too, we are both going to need it.' is Masterson's reply as JD and I head out of his front door to rendezvous with Luke.

CHAPTER 41

I let JD drive as I need to make a few calls. The first is to Luke who I want to make sure is in his office. He answers on the first ring.
'Luke, it's Peter Carter. We have some info on how to stop the drone, are you in your office?'
'Yes, but I have…'
I cut him off, 'Stay there, we will be with you in ten to fifteen minutes. Don't go anywhere!' I stress, and hang up.
I search through the contacts and find Wilks' number and hit dial. As she answers I don't give her time to respond,
'Ma'am, I have information on how to stop the TSI drone, it's a long story how it came about but I think we can disable it before it reaches London. I am on my way in to the office now to get Luke and his team to work on it.'
'Peter, what…' she pauses and I can almost see her brow furrowing in concentration as she processes the information, 'tell me later, right now the priority is to stop that aircraft before it can inflict any more damage.'
There is muffled speaking in the background that I can't make out.
'Ma'am,' I am not quite sure how to go on,
'…Ma'am, I think we have a situation which includes high ranking officials within our intelligence services and the government.'
The line goes silent and I almost check it to see if I lost the signal when Wilks comes back on the line,
'How far up the line are we talking?' she asks.
'The top.'

Again silence, but I know why this time.
'Peter, I will meet you at headquarters. I can be there in twenty minutes. Do not discuss this over an unsecure line.'
I nod and say, 'I understand. I will be in the IT security offices with Luke.'
'Be careful, Peter.'
The line really does go dead this time as she disconnects.

Wilks looks across the room to where the PM has just finished swearing down the phone to someone and then slammed the receiver down hard enough to crack the casing. Could it really be true, she thinks.
'Prime Minister,' she says as she stands up, 'I have an officer who has just relayed he may have found a way to stop any attacks on the capital.'
Wilks looks for any sign of reaction from the man opposite her. There is none.
'Go on.' he prompts.
'I don't know much more than that, I gave him permission to continue as time is of the essence in this matter as we are all aware. With your permission I would like to leave this COBRA meeting and liaise with him. I will of course keep this committee informed of any developments.'
The PM stares at her, rubbing his chin distractedly. Even from her position across the table, Wilks can hear the scratch of stubble under his fingers.
'Sir?' she asks.
He nods, 'Yes…yes of course. You should go and do what you can. Any developments should be relayed to me directly, understand?'
'Perfectly sir.'

With that he appears to dismiss her entirely as he turns to an aide and talks quietly into his ear. Wilks nods, to no-one in particular, gathers her briefcase and walks to the door.

'I'll come with you, if that's alright?' a voice says just to her left as she pulls on the door handle. She turns to find a man next to her.

'That's not a problem, the more minds working on this the better.' As they enter the corridor, Wilks holds out her hand, 'Patricia Wilks, Metropolitan Police, we haven't formally been introduced.

The thin, bespectacled man offers his own hand out and shakes hers with a surprisingly firm grip, 'Steven Mann, scientific advisor to our illustrious PM, but normally a professor at Cambridge.'

Wilks stops walking, 'Cambridge, my God. I am so sorry.'

He smiles weakly, 'I was in the city to meet with the Commons Select Committee and talk about GM crops this morning when COBRA was called together. Otherwise I would be...' he draws a shaky breath as his sentence tapers off.

'We will stop this and we will find the people who did this. I promise you.' Wilks says with belief that she didn't know she had. She repeats herself as she continues to hold his hand in hers, 'I promise you.'

CHAPTER 42

One of the perks of being the acting Commissioner is that Wilks does not need to drive anywhere anymore. Her car and driver are waiting for her in the underground car park. Her driver is a youthful looking but experienced police detective named Nick Herd, who she has come to know quite well over the last few months. He jumps out from the driver's seat as she approaches.

'Ma'am,' he says as he opens the rear passenger door for her, 'where to?'

'The Yard please, Nick. Full blues and twos and get there as fast as you like.'

He smiles in response. Like any professional driver he loves the thrill of speed, and to do it with lights flashing and sirens blaring to move other motorists out of the way is a rush in itself.

'I'll get you there in less than twenty minutes.' he promises as he closes the door.

Steven opens the door on his side of the vehicle himself and gets in without a word. Nick gets into the drivers seat, starts the engine and pulls out of the parking bay.

Wilks look towards to her guest,

'Hold on for the ride but don't worry, Nick is the best driver I know.' she says with a reassuring smile.

Steven smiles weakly back and carefully pulls his seatbelt across his body before opening the small briefcase he has with him. He takes a few sheets of A4 paper and hands them across to Wilks.

'These are the profiles that were sent through by MI6, did you see them in the meeting?'

Wilks shakes her head and reaches out to take them from him. She starts reading as the car accelerates out on to the streets of the city. Her concentration fades out the wail of the siren as she looks through the document.

---- CONFIDENTIAL – EYES ONLY ----

From: Leahy, A. MI6
Subject: Joanne and Leanne DuChamps

Names of certain terrorist members, organisations and attacks have been redacted to preserve the security of this department.

The above named subjects are known to this department in relation to a number of terrorism and criminal activities, most notably in their native France.
It is believed they were founding members of the failed group, AZF, which came to light in Spring 2001, when they carried out the bombing of the AZF chemical factory in Toulouse. Further activity included placing explosives on train lines with the view to extort money from the French government. These activities were mostly unsuccessful and the group dissipated.

The twins, non-identical, were born in Toulouse in 1985 to their mother, Carol DuChamps, a French national who died during the labour and their father, Ilias Badour, a Moroccan immigrant.
Badour has links with the Moroccan Islamic Combatant Group, known by its French acronym, GICM, and is thought to have significant connections to Al Qaeda. GICM has been behind a number of lethal bombings in Europe and the Middle East.

It has been confirmed that Badour recruited the two sisters, his daughters, into the GICM after the failure of AZF. It is unconfirmed if they had a part to play in the May 2004 bombings in Madrid, although analysts believe this may have been their initiation into the group. It is suspected through DNA evidence that Badour died in the Egyptian Sharm El Sheik bombings of July 23 2005, but this has not been confirmed.

Joanne is considered the more fanatical and bloodthirsty of the two sisters. In a report obtained from DELETED in interrogations of July 2007, he claimed to have been part of the group that placed explosives on commuter trains in Mumbai, India in July 2006. This attack killed 209 people and injured another 714. This devastating attack was co-ordinated by the two sisters.
Joanne DuChamps, it is claimed, felt this was a failed mission and blamed DELETED, the bomb maker, for the failings. His mutilated body was found hanging from a rail bridge some days after the attack. A video later released shows his torture and murder at the hands of a masked person. This person has been verified as Joanne DuChamps.

Leanne DucChamps, whilst apparently not as extremist as her sister, is still a person of concern. The subject has been implicated in the training and indoctrination of fighters and suicide bombers of many attacks. She is very persuasive. One man, DELETED, captured during a raid on DELETED compound, has described her as,
'...able to compel a snake to eat it's own tail...' with the ability to '...turn a normal teenager with hopes and dreams, into a bomb wearing, gun carrying freedom fighter who has only the promise of martyrdom to look forward to.' He truly seemed in awe of her.

Since their origins with AZF, it is apparent the subjects are financially motivated. After each attack, governments have been contacted and a ransom has been demanded to stop any further attacks. Many times this has been paid. After the DELETED attacks, such a ransom was demanded of the UK government. It was refused. We feel this is the motivation behind the current attacks on UK soil.

All members of this group are considered highly dangerous with a disregard for human life, including their own, with the exception of the DuChamps sisters. Their financial motivation shows a willingness to survive and may be a key factor in any negotiations that may occur.

Wilks lowers the document into her lap and looks out of the car window at the streets of her familiar city flashing by and wonders how people can turn into such animals.
'Not good reading is it?' says the man beside her, who is holding on tightly to the small plastic handle above the door as if his life depends on it. She shakes her head, agreeing with his words. Looking back down at the sheets of paper in her hands, she turns over the page to find copies of passports staring back at her. The two women in the photographs seem normal to her. One has a hint of a smile on her face as if wistfully dreaming of future holidays on a sunny beach somewhere, whilst the other stares impassively at the camera in a typical passport pose. The ringing of her phone breaks her hypnotic gaze into the black and white pages.
'Wilks,' she says answering whilst handing the file back to Steven, 'we are only a few minutes out. I will call you on the secure line from my office.'

CHAPTER 43

Luke is rapidly scanning through the files and documents he has managed to break into from Mason's email server and hard drives. After a slow start his password algorithm software finally managed to crack the barriers hiding the information from view. The phone call from Carter came just as he was reading about the kill codes and how to generate them to abort the drone's missions.

Still staring at the screen and trying to digest the complicated instructions, Luke whispers under his breath,

'I hope to God he has something easier to interpret than this.'

He scrolls down the page slowly thinking to himself that Mason had no need to encrypt his files if the instructions were this horrendously difficult to understand. He leans closer to the brightly lit screen as if this might bring the words to life, but it just ends up hurting his eyes. A large hand clasp him on the shoulder and makes him jump back into the real world.

'How's it going, Luke?' JD almost shouts in his ear, 'Carter's on his way up now but I have this for you.' He places the USB memory stick on the desk next to Luke's keyboard.

Picking it up, he twirls it in his fingers before asking,

'Has it been virus checked?'

JD shrugs his shoulders,

'Not a clue.'

Pushing his chair back, Luke takes the stick to a computer that is emblazoned with red and yellow tape.

'I just have to check it out in our standalone. I don't want to risk plugging it in to our network and uploading something that will take down our servers. Remember the Conficker worm from a few years ago? It contaminated half the police and military networks in a few days because simple checks were not carried out. I know this must be important, Peter said as much over the phone, but we cannot risk accessing the data on here without the proper procedures being carried out.'

'Do you think this could be a ploy to shut us down?' I ask the question as I walk into the room.

'Would you risk it for the sake of a few minutes?' he asks me.

I shake my head,

'Hurry it up. There's no knowing how much time we have.' I turn to JD, 'The live feed from the drone should soon be on a five minute delay to the news networks. Wilks is on her way in and she is going to go throw her weight behind the guys upstairs who are on it now, but it seems most of the major networks are happy to do this.'

'Most?' JD enquires.

'The BBC, Sky and ITN are all on our side, the problem lies with overseas channels. Not all will co-operate as much as we would like. Isn't freedom of the press a wonderful thing? Most are willing to compromise with a five minute delay, I wanted to stop the whole thing.'

Luke looks up from his chair,

'Why not use a recording from the last half hour and re-route that through the servers. Nothing much has happened and I think we could get away with it.'

'Isn't that a bit risky?' I say and JD nods along with me.

'Well, the pictures broadcast over the last hour are just general high-level stuff. Since it left the Cambridge area it seems to have been circling as if it is waiting instructions. I could loop that and switch the feed, I have already accessed the servers from information supplied by Mason's files.'

'Why didn't you tell me this on the phone?' I explode angrily.

'With all due respect, sir, you didn't give me a chance. I had only just managed to break through their firewall when you called,' he points to a monitor full of information that means nothing to me, 'it's all on there.'

The computer he is working on beeps three times in quick succession.

'Is there a problem?' I say as I fear the worst.

As he faces the screen I see his head shake from side to side,

'No, not really. It's just whoever you got this from has used it in the past to download porn and then not erased it properly. Is it yours?'

JD's mouth starts to turn upwards into a smile but my look stops it.

'Luke, stop pissing about, we don't have the time. Can we use it or not?'

'Sorry boss. Just checking the information on it now.'

As his fingers fly across the keyboard I struggle to keep up with different windows and folders that open across the screen.

'Yes!' he suddenly exclaims.

Both JD and I are on his shoulder in an instant looking intently as he points to a small yellow box. The writing underneath says simply,

Kill Codes.

He moves the mouse pointer over it and clicks twice to open it. He scrolls slowly down the list of documents and I am amazed he seems to know exactly what he is looking for. The mouse hovers over a document and he presses the mouse button to select it. As he scans the file he pauses and minimises the window to search through the rest of the folder behind it.

'Ok, here it is.'

His concentration is fully on the screen in front of him and I am just an observer as he works away. I want to ask questions, I want to find out what he has found, but I cannot risk breaking his train of thought.

'Oh you beauty.' he says as he turns to the two of us. 'It's all here, this is amazing. This will simplify the whole process.'

I hold up my hand, 'Luke, slow down. What the hell are you on about?'

'Mason left instructions on how to generate kill codes for the MASTER aircraft, but they are written for his engineers and make no sense unless you know the software protocols employed on it. This,' he pauses and points to the screen, '…this bypasses all that and generates a one time code. All I need to do is set up a handshake between the drone and us, run this .exe file and employ a new firewall to stop any unwanted access.'

My shoulders sag in relief and I let out a breath I did not realise I was holding.

'But…'

My head jerks towards him,
'What do you mean, but?'
'Boss, it's going to take some time and we have just the one shot at it.'
'One shot?'
Luke nods his head and switches the screen back to the document he had minimised,
'It says here, where is it, ah…failure to complete a correct communication procedure will result in node shutdown.'
'Please, Luke, in English.' I plead with him.
'Basically, if I can't get the drone's on board computer to acknowledge my communication request it will block any further attempts at communication until an over-ride command is given via it's home base.'
'Can we do it?' JD asks.
I shake my head and place my hand on Luke's shoulder,
'Can you do it?' I ask him.
'If I can find a way through his modified SCTP security, that's Stream Control Transmission Protocol…'
'Stop, stop, stop, Luke. Do what you have to do. How long do you think it will take?'
'With the re-routing of the video stream, I will have to do that first to throw the guys a curveball if I do manage to take control. They will still think they have it in a holding pattern while we ditch the damn thing into the ocean or something, and then breaking the codes. I don't know, maybe an hour, maybe two, it could even be more.'
'JD, stay here with Luke and help him out in any way he needs. I will find Wilks and tell her what is going on. We will need a plan B if this doesn't

work out. Luke, keep me informed of any development immediately.'

'No worries,' he stands up, his face serious, 'I'm sorry for earlier, I…'

'Luke, we were both out of line. There is a lot on everyone's plate at the moment,' I hold out my hand, 'are we good?'

He takes my hand and we both smile grimly. I release my grip and turn away from this young man who is probably our best bet at stopping this terrifying aircraft.

CHAPTER 44

'Prime Minister, I have an update on casualty figures from Cambridge.'
The Prime Minister looks up from the work he is doing with his assistant on a statement due for broadcast to the British public.
'Talk to me, Ben.' he says simply.
'It seems the initial figures may have been slightly overestimated…'
'Wait a moment. Is this from a reliable source?'
'Yes sir, the information has been collated from the five major hospitals dealing with the casualties.'
The PM pulls a notepad closer to him and picks his pen off the table,
'What are the hospitals?' he asks.
'Addenbrooks and Cambridge University Hospitals were both outside the blast radius and have been overwhelmed by casualties. They issued a black alert for assistance and have started to ship patients to Peterborough City Hospital, Milton Keynes A & E and The Princess of Wales Hospital in Ely. The most severe burns patients are going to Ely where they are being treated by Armed Forces trained doctors and nurses who have dealt with their type of injuries on overseas operations in the past.'
The PM is furiously scribbling the information down on his notepad as the aide, Ben, continues.
'These hospitals are now also close to capacity and have issued their own black alerts. We have offers of assistance from all major A & E departments from Cornwall to Edinburgh, but it has been considered prudent not to accept any London help

due to the threat of attack on the city.' He looks up from his Ipad, 'That information came straight from the surgeon general himself. He is expecting casualties in the city and wants to be ready to accept them.'

The PM nods his head thoughtfully and waves a hand for Ben to continue.

'Peterborough police have taken control of the scene due to local forces headquarters being within the blast radius. The scenes of crime officer has provided these figures from the incident and a map of the damage.'

Ben runs a few fingers over the surface of his tablet and an image appears on one of the flat panel screens on the wall of the room. Everyone stops to look and the room's quiet hum of conversation falls silent as a satellite map of Cambridge is shown.

'Here you can see a historic image of the Cambridge area,' he taps a finger and a small red dot appears on the screen, 'this is Cambridge Science Park and this large building is TSI headquarters. As you can see it is on the edge of the city with the busy A14 and junction 33 next to it,' he swipes his fingers again and a red circle overlays the TSI building, 'this is a one kilometre blast circle. It was assumed that anything within this area would be just complete annihilation. As you can see that includes most of the small town of Milton to the North. However, it appears that the location of the building next to the junction and the large concrete walls of the flyover have spared much of the town. The blast was either reflected back or forced upwards. Most casualties to the North are from broken glass or shock. To the South is as expected. From the site of the explosion to the Kings Hedges Road is gone.'

'How many people are we talking about here, Ben?' The PM asks softly.

'That is unknown at this time I am afraid, sir. We are still trying to access the records of the companies that are registered on the Science Park.' The map zooms out and the circle expands with it. 'This is the two kilometre blast radius. It is lucky that to the North and East of the site is mainly open land used for grazing and arable purposes. This circle represents the area of mass casualties we are dealing with, but again luck appears to have been with us.'

'Not luck…I don't believe in luck,' the PM states, 'God was watching out for us today.'

Everyone in the room knows the faith beliefs of the PM and whilst not all agree with it, they are all tolerant enough to respect his views. Even so, there are one or two raised eyebrows throughout the room at his statement.

Ben waits for him to saying something more, but it is silent in the room.

'Ummm, yes, well the casualty figures here have been revised dramatically. We were expecting a death rate of around 75% but I am happy to say this is extremely overstated. As you can see, the blast encompasses Chesterton and the Kings Hedges housing areas down to the junctions of Arbury and Milton road. Approximately 20,000 people live and work within this area making the projected casualty figure 15,000 dead or injured.'

Ben pauses and brings up another picture of the area next to the original.

'This is a satellite picture of the site from just twenty minutes ago. As you can see the Science Park is virtually obliterated, but the fireball we expected to spread outwards and cause the mass

casualty situation has done something unexpected. We are not completely sure but the fireball was pushed upwards at this point,' he creates an arrow near the Southern edge of the Science Park on the screen, 'one opinion is that there may have been underground fuel tanks here that ruptured in the first explosion forcing itself up into the air under extreme pressure. This ignited creating a wall of fire much like a jet engine's thrust, which deflected the blast and fireball enough to push it up and over the majority of area, this coupled with the reflection of the blast from the road junction saved countless lives.'
'A miracle, a true miracle.' This time the PM's words gain a few nods and words of agreement from around the room.
'We still have a mass casualty situation. Thousands have been injured from the shock wave and secondary damage. People were caught up in the fireball in certain areas, but here it is fortunate that with it being winter, the amount of clothing and layers being worn by people has protected many. Exposed areas have taken the worst damage as can be expected and we are getting reports of hundreds being blinded by the flames and flying glass. It is too early to tell if this will be permanent for the unfortunate victims or if their sight can be repaired.'
The PM stands up with his head bowed and asks, 'How many are we now saying have died?'
'Prime Minister, it is still too early to…'
'Ben,' he looks up and holds his gaze on his young aide, 'how many?'
'We have revised our figures down from tens of thousands and believe we are now looking at between four to eight thousand people have

perished or will succumb to their injuries over the next few days.'

The silence in the room as they all take their time to digest the information is deafening.

CHAPTER 45

The corridors are deserted as I make way through the building to find Wilks. The last time I can recall such quietness was back in 2007 when every available person was out on the streets attempting to deal with the terrorist attacks on the London transport system. I recall feeling unnerved back then by the unusual silence of the building which is normally full of mumbled conversations and movement. This time I am not unnerved but reassured by the absence of my colleagues. I know they are out on the streets of the city doing their best to protect the almost 8.5 million inhabitants from harm and they will do all it takes to complete that task, or die trying.
As I round a corner I hear up ahead a male and female voice in conversation and smile as I recognise Graham's tones then smile even more broadly as he and his companion step into view.
I only vaguely know her as the new psychologist employed by the department. I haven't had a chance to formally introduce myself to her, but from what I can see, it appears that Graham knows her very well. His hand is on her shoulder as he leans in to say something and they both have a smile on their faces. The smiles both drop as they see me and I feel I have intruded upon them.
'Peter, we have been looking for you.'
I don't like the sudden, serious look on Graham's face as he speaks to me.
'Well you've found me, Graham…and it's Miss Jeffery I believe?'

I hold out my hand and she steps forward to grasp it in hers. It is a surprisingly strong and firm grip. 'Please call me Kate. I'm sorry we haven't had a chance to meet before this, it seems our schedules have had us dancing around each other.'
'The apology is mine. I should have welcomed you to the department earlier, but...' I trail off.
'I understand. Things have been a little, shall we say crazy around here and it has been difficult to catch breath at times. It has certainly been a lot busier than my last position with the North Yorkshire force.'
I release her hand,
'Well, for what it's worth, welcome to the Met. Good to have you on board.' I turn slightly to Graham, 'What did you need me for? I am on my way to speak to Wilks if you want to walk with me.'
'Peter, we...' his eyes dart everywhere as I see he is uncomfortable with what he is about to say.
'Graham, calm down. We are friends, yes? Anything you have to say is OK.'
He takes a breath, a deep breath before continuing. 'It's to do with Zoe's murder. We believe there may be a significant suspect in the case.'
Even with the events unfolding around us, the murder of any single person even if it was someone I didn't know, is always on my mind. The fact we are talking about my sister's girlfriend makes only a slight difference in the urgency of the case to me.
'That's quick. What have you found?'
'Peter, it's hard to say this, we believe..umm, that is...'
Kate joins in,
'Peter, we believe that whoever killed Zoe was close to her.'

I am confused at the information,
'You mean a friend or a family member?' I ask
Kate shakes her head,
'I believe even closer and that they are probably a lover or a jealous ex-partner.'
'You're saying that Zoe was seeing someone else behind Helen's back? That's who we are looking for?'
The two of them look at each other before turning back to me. This time it is Graham who speaks up,
'We believe that Helen is going to be have to be questioned.'
I start laughing,
'You can't be serious. After what they have been through together you expect me to believe that she is a murderer now? Come on, Graham. What are you basing this on?'
Kate holds up a buff folder,
'This is the autopsy report and the profile made up of the suspect. I hate to say it, but it all points to someone that is especially close to the victim, shares a common bond and almost certainly a woman.'
I feel my laugh catch in my throat. It is quickly replaced by anger as I switch my gaze between the two of them,
'Oh fuck off. I cannot deal with this right now. There is about to be an imminent attack somewhere in the city, I mean we are talking a scale worse that 7/7, and you are here giving me a theory that my sister is a killer.' I look away, close my eyes and pinch the area between them with my thumb and forefinger to try and stop a huge outburst.
'I can only give you the evidence we have collected and...'
I interrupt her,

'Look…at the moment I cannot and will not talk about this.' She starts to speak again and I hold up my hand to stop her, 'No, this is not happening here and it is not going to be discussed in a corridor like this. I am going up to see the Commissioner and if and when this crisis is over…then…then we will talk this matter over further.'

I push past them roughly, take a few steps and stop as I consider their words,

'I will come down to your office, Graham, when I have finished with Wilks. You had better have a compelling reason for me to go out and arrest my sister on suspicion of murder.'

I leave them standing in the silent corridor as I walk away with my head reeling with unwanted and dangerous thoughts. Luckily my phone starts ringing to break me out of my confused state of mind.

'Luke, tell me some good news.' I say as I answer the call.

I can almost hear his infectious grin as he replies, 'It was easier than I thought. I'm in.'

CHAPTER 46

Emerson looks on as Joanne sits in front of him occasionally glancing up from the computer screen of her laptop between them on the desk. His ears strain for sounds outside the room as he hopes not to hear another gunshot. As he thinks that time must nearly be up for some unfortunate soul in the next room, Joanne smiles broadly, stands up and goes to the door. Opening it just a crack, she calls out,
'Release them and prepare to move.'
The look of disappointment on the gunman's face makes her quiver inside. The feel of the power she holds over the hostages and her own people is something she will never tire of. She closes the door and returns to the desk.
'Let's thank our benefactor shall we.'
Picking up the phone she again dials Leahy's number,
'Hello again,' she purrs into the phone as it is answered, 'thank you so much for your kind donation. I want to reassure you that it means a lot to us and we will cherish it with...'
'Cut the bullshit. What do you want?'
She shakes her head,
'Such harsh words just as I thought we were getting along.'
Leahy controls his urge to scream down the phone and instead repeats his words with a calmness he does not feel,
'What do you want?'
'I thought you would like to speak to an old friend. Would you like that?'

'What are you talking about? What old friend?'
Joanne smiles, 'Please hold for James Emerson, head of TSI…'
She holds the phone for out for him to take,
'It's for you.'
Through the earpiece a tinny voice can be heard,
'Emerson. Emerson? Are you there?'
He takes the phone from her outstretched hand and carefully places it to his ear,
'This is James Emerson. Who am I speaking to please?'
'My God I thought you were dead. Jim, it's Leahy.'
Emerson's eyes flick up to Joanne as Leahy continues, 'things have gone a little south with our plan, Jim.'
'Go on,' Emerson prompts, 'you don't say?'
'Listen, we have a plan to get you all out safely and…'
'What about MASTER? What about the deal?'
There is a pause on the line before Leahy continues, picking his words carefully,
'As far as we know everything is still on the table, perhaps we even have more bargaining power after the demonstration today.'
Emerson smiles coldly,
'Then that is all that matters, but I will expect more compensation for your ineptitude in the execution of the plan.'
'I really don't think that…'
'I don't give a rat's arse what you think. The deal for you is now ten per cent, not a penny more. Any arguments and I go to the press saying how you threatened and intimidated myself and Mason into selling our weapons platform to certain, shall we say, questionable countries. Do you understand?'

The answer is dripping with venom and unsaid threats,
'Oh, one hundred per cent old chap. But please, tell me, what makes you so sure you will get out of there alive today?'
Emerson smiles as he makes eye contact with the woman opposite,
'Tell me miss, would ten million dollars wired to your account ensure my safety?'
Her smile grows as she nods in affirmation,
'For that you get my personal reassurances that you and your people will walk away from this in one piece.'
He tilts his head slowly to one side to her,
'Then that seems to me like a good deal. Leahy? Did you catch that? Now if you excuse me, I have a few things to talk to this woman about, some of it concerns you and I am sure you will not wish to be bored with the details, so, this is goodbye for now. Toodle-oo…old chap.'
He hands the phone back and waits.
'Well that was an interesting conversation wasn't it?' she says into the telephone, 'now I really must be off, but just one more thing. We will be leaving shortly, we will have hostages with us and whilst I would love to guarantee their safety, if you try to stop us they will be killed.' As she says this, she theatrically and silently mouths 'Sorry' to Emerson. 'So you see that everything now depends on you. I will be leaving some people behind with the technical staff to keep control of the situation here, and when the time is right I will order them to surrender their arms and give themselves up to you. Until that time they will be in control of our little flying friend up there. It's purely for insurance purposes, I know you understand.'

'Do you really think…'
'Mr Leahy. I don't think, I know. It has been a pleasure doing business with you, but it is now time for our relationship to end. Goodbye.'
Leahy hears the line go dead and cannot control his rage any longer, throwing the phone across the room so it smashes against the wall.
'FUCK!'

Joanne gently places the phone down and looks across the desk,
'So, let's talk about this great idea of yours. Something to do with ten million dollars I seem to recall.' She stands up again and raises a finger, 'But please, just give me one second.'
Leaving the room she starts issuing commands to her people. A few moments later she is back opposite Emerson.
'OK, we have about ten minutes to discuss what we are going to do before I have to leave. Let's begin. Talk to me, James.'
Emerson sits back in his chair and starts to outline his plan to the woman in front of him.

CHAPTER 47

I cannot believe what I am hearing.

'Luke, you said it would take hours to hack into the communications. Are you saying you have control of the drone?'

'It was a simple case of backward engineering the communication protocol between the ground based unit and the aircraft. As soon as the 128 bit security protocol was cracked, well, then it was simple enough to break the handshake sequence which even though it was a higher 256 key algorithm, it was fairly easy to decode.'

I blink my eyes once or twice as I try to digest the information. I have to force myself not to ask, 'What the hell are you talking about?'

Instead I say,

'Good work, Luke. I take this to mean that we now control the MASTER and you are feeding a recording of the video back to whoever is controlling it?'

'Not only that, but I am changing the telemetry that is transmitted back to their ground station so they think they still have full control of the aircraft. It is just so cool.'

I pause, mid-stride,

'Luke…it is not cool what you are doing. You are currently saving countless lives by being in control of that thing.' I take a few seconds to think things through in my mind.

'Luke, is there a self destruct to that thing?' I ask.

He takes a few seconds to respond,

'There is, but I would need the correct codes. Then again, it would be easy enough to crash it into the ground. Would that be suitable?'
'You can do that so it would not endanger any life?'
'Give me a large enough area and even with the hydrogen on board it should be OK.'
'How big an area do you need?'
'Give me a second. Can I call you back?'
I imagine him sitting there running scenarios through his computer,
'You have control of it, yes?'
'I do.'
I cannot help but smile,
'Take your time. I will be with the commissioner and informing her of your progress.'
'But…'
'Luke, take your time. If you can ensure there is no way they can regain control then we can all walk away from this with our heads held high. Ring me back when you know the space required to destroy this thing safely.'
'Will do, boss.'
He hangs up, and for the first time today I feel a sense of relief that all will pan out in a way that may allow me to sleep tonight.
All I need to do now is find Wilks and update her on the situation.

JD is standing over Luke's shoulder as he watches the images of the MASTER drone on the screen.
'You really have control of this thing?' he asks.
Luke half turns, 'Sure, watch this.'
He presses a few buttons on the keyboard and moves his mouse a few times.
JD watches in astonishment as the picture suddenly hurtles ground-ward.

At what seems like the last moment before a crash the camera pulls upwards towards the sky again. 'Don't worry, the onboard camera is at full zoom. We were over a thousand metres above crashing into the ground. I have full control,' says Luke with a smile, 'now all I need to do is find a large enough area to crash the bastard. Let's see what is on the map.'

JD watches as Luke pulls up a window on the screen in front of them.

'Where is the MASTER at the moment, Luke?' JD asks.

'I currently have it in a holding pattern at 45,000 feet above Wembley Stadium. I figure that in a worst case scenario I can crash it on the pitch and the stands should absorb most of the explosion.'

'Jesus, after the hassle of getting that monstrosity built please do not crash it into that. Also I have to remind you that English football is struggling enough as it is.'

Luke laughs at his comment,

'Then again, I could always smash into Chelsea's pitch, it might give Arsenal a better chance this season. I am only using Wembley as a reference until I find a suitable area for it to crash land.'

He moves his mouse across the table in his attempts to seek out any large enough areas on the satellite maps.

'There is nothing suitable within the London metropolitan area. I think we will have to try further afield.'

His face suddenly turns serious,

'Shit, I know the best place. I used to go near there as a kid on camping trips. There is an old rocket testing area at a place called Pendine Sands in West Wales and I know there are no inhabited areas in miles around it.'

The phone, next to the monitor before them, starts ringing. JD beams one of his huge grins, picks up the handset and before answering, says to Luke, 'Do it, Luke. Let's take this piece of shit to Wales and dump it.'

CHAPTER 48

Once again, I find myself standing at the open door of Wilks' office feeling like a naughty schoolboy who is there to see the headmaster. Through the doorway I see her standing with her back to me as she talks on the telephone and gazes out over the city we have sworn to protect. Her head drops and she nods a slow acceptance to whatever is being said to her and turns around. Catching sight of me she offers a grim smile and beckons me in to her domain. She covers the mouthpiece with one hand, 'Close the door behind you, Peter. Just give me a moment.'

I push the door gently shut with a foreboding and see a man I don't recognise sitting in one of the soft armchairs that is against the back wall. I nod in the way of saying hello and turn my mind once again to the day's events. My thoughts are still jumbled with Graham's accusations against my sister and the fact that we have control of the MASTER aircraft. As Wilks finishes up her conversation I attempt to compose myself but I am concerned with her conversation.

'…Yes minister, I have been informed we now have control of the aircraft…' a pause, 'No, I will not relinquish that control until I have complete confidence that there is no way of the terrorists regaining the link.' A longer pause as she listens to the man on the telephone, 'That is your prerogative and…sir, I am being co-operative. I am only trying to protect the citizens of this city to the best of my abilities. At the moment that means my men will retain control until I have it in writing or a personal visit from the Prime Minister. She shakes her head and I see her eyes flick up to the ceiling in frustration, 'Then you go to the PM now and ask him to do just that.'
She ends the call,
'What an absolute idiot!'
I say nothing and wait for her to address me. I have been here enough times in the past to know that it will only take her a moment to bring her attention back to the world around her.
'Peter, thanks for coming up,' she waves her hand to the seated gentleman, 'this is Professor Steven Mann of Cambridge University. He is a specialist advisor to the PM.'
I extend a hand and get feeble handshake in return, 'I'm sorry about what happened, I know that no words can help in a time like this.'
'Please, it's OK. I um, I…' he looks to Wilks, 'can I use your phone? I want to check on some family and friends.'
'Certainly, Steven. We will give you some privacy.'
Before she can make a move to leave the room I say,
'I didn't realise you were expecting me and I also didn't know that the fact we now have control of the drone was common knowledge.'

Wilks sits down and looks up at me,
'I rang down to check on progress and spoke to JD. He told me you were coming up and he also explained the situation. What is worrying is that as soon as I finished the conversation with him, I get a secure call from a minister trying to order me to hand the drone over to him and the military will take over.' She lets out a long sigh, 'I need a coffee, what about you? Walk with me, we'll go to the cafeteria.'
She grabs her phone from the desk, stands up and briskly makes her way across the room. I open the door and stand aside.
'Always the perfect gentleman, Peter,' she says with a small smile, 'thank you.'
I look towards Professor Mann,
'Again, my apologies. I hope you manage to contact your family.'
With that I follow Wilks out of her office and fall in step beside her.
'Ma'am. what is going on here?' I ask.
'Have you spoken to anyone else about our control of the drone?' she asks.
'Of course not, I came to inform you first and discuss the information given to me about who was involved in this thing.'
Wilks stops and turns to me, 'In that case, I believe our department has been compromised. There is no other possibility that the news about the drone could have been found out so fast. My phone or my office has been bugged, and that worries me, no…that frightens me. Why is the office of the commissioner of the Metropolitan Police under surveillance?'
I shake my head,
'And who is doing it?' I ask.

'Let's get that coffee. We should be able to talk freely there.'

We walk in silence to the cafeteria, both lost and absorbed in our own thoughts.

Unsurprisingly the place is deserted when we walk in. We order our drinks and I follow Wilks as she looks around and picks a table in the far corner where we sit down opposite each other. Wilks places her phone next to her steaming coffee mug on the table.

'Before we start, ma'am, do you think the surveillance has anything to do with the internal investigation against me?'

I can see her considering this for a moment before she shakes her head.

'If that was the case then why would my office be under…' she trails off and I see her eyes drift out of focus as she thinks. 'Shit, that bastard, John Midgely! I'll bet he's in on this with his MI6 contacts.'

'MI6? Why are they involved in this?' I have to ask as I think to how Masterson and his boss are involved.

'MI6 gave Midgely information on you concerning your relationship with that journalist, Clark is it?'

I nod my head with shame and stay silent.

'They would have the power to do this and they would have the relationships within the government to steamroll through a surveillance operation of this magnitude. No-one is going to lightly authorise such a move against my office without some serious leverage.'

'We have had run-ins with them before. They blanketed the 'New Ripper' case with lies and smoke screens to suit their ends so why not the same with this investigation?'

Wilks takes a deep breath and considers her words before replying,

'But their involvement goes back to that case and I think they were using it as a way to keep on you.'

'What if they were keeping an eye on us. After all we are the only ones who knew of their involvement.'

I watch as Wilks nods her head in acknowledgement of my remark,

'Not forgetting JD, Luke and if I remember rightly, Dr. Young. I wonder…?'

Wilks picks up her phone and scrolls through her contacts,

'Let me just try something.'

Placing the phone to her ear she listens as it rings the number.

'Luke, it's Wilks. I need you to run a trace on a phone number…yes a private number,' she smiles grimly as Luke says something, 'Luke, I don't have a warrant and I don't have permission. What I need to know is can you tell if a call is being routed via different lines during the conversation?'

She looks over to me, 'Do you have your mobile on you?' she asks.

I nod and take it out of my jacket pocket and place it on the table.

'And how long would we have to stay on the line for you to confirm this?' another nod as she listens to Luke's advice, 'OK, I want you to tell JD to call Peter, use their numbers to determine if call re-routing is being used by either network. Do you think you can tell where it is being monitored from?'

I can tell from her expression that she is getting a negative response.

'OK, thanks Luke. I thought it was a long shot. Can you put JD on the line please? Thanks again.'
There is a pause as the phone is handed over in the offices downstairs from us,
'JD, when you ring Peter I need you to go along with everything he says…don't worry about the subject, just agree and say how the investigation is getting closer to the source. Call him from your mobile to his mobile in, let's say ten minutes,' she glances at her wrist, 'that should be enough time. Speak to you soon, and thanks.'
She hangs up the phone and focuses back on me,
'Tell me everything you know, Peter. Who are the principal players and why are they doing this?'
For the next eight minutes I go through the information given to me by Stuart Masterson and how it all seems to fit together. Our drinks go cold on the table as I talk. When I am done she leans forward and says,
'Right, this is what I want you to do.'
The ringing of a mobile phone breaks her instructions and I instinctively reach out to grab mine before I realise it is not my ring tone. Wilks looks down at the small screen of her own phone and frowns.
'With-held number.' she says absently as she picks up the phone. She looks at me and places it back down on the table before pressing the 'Speakerphone' button to answer.
'Wilks here.'
'Commissioner Wilks, you have made your point,' a man's voice emanates in perfect clarity from the small speaker, 'there is no need to trace any calls and there is no need for you, or I, to play any more games.'
I watch as Wilks leans forward slightly,

'You seem to have me at a disadvantage, who am I speaking to?'

'I rather thought you may have recognised my voice, we have met once before but I can forgive you as it was a rather brief encounter. I work for MI6, the name is Leahy, Andrew Leahy.'

CHAPTER 49

Joanne gently closes the door of the small room at the back of the hall behind her with a smile on her face. She stops for a moment and looks around, surveying the room, taking it all in. The screen beside her is still showing the MASTER in flight and its view of the fields, streets and houses of wherever it is at the moment. She glances down at her watch and her smile changes to a frown.
Looking back up to the screen she sees a landscape that is different to what she was expecting.
'You, what's been happening with this?' she asks as she points to the pictures on the screen.
The man she is talking to shrugs his shoulders, making the automatic weapon he is holding move around in a circular motion,
'It's just been flying around since we saw off the jets.'
She glances at her watch again,
'That must have caused the delay.'
She casts a short glance back at the video and tries to dismiss her misgivings.
'Is everything ready?'
She gets a nod in reply.
'Good. Let's go.'
As she moves towards the main doors she glances down at the dead who have been placed in a bloodied row to the side of the room. She points to the corpse of the RAF officer,
'Bring that one.'

One hundred meters away from the entrance to the small building, four men are intently studying a set of detailed drawings. Each of them are dressed almost identically in black Nomex flight suits over which they have a small array of webbing pouches and equipment attached. It is only the location of the pouches around their bodies that distinguish them when they put on their helmets and respirators, which at the moment lay on the ground next to their feet. Each has a Heckler and Koch MP5S 9mm sub-machine gun strapped to their body as well as an automatic 9mm pistol in a holster attached to their thigh. The pistol varies according to personal choice and is their weapon of last resort if the MP5 jams.

'What if we use an explosive charge here to force entry into the heating and ventilation ducts?' One man asks, pointing a twig towards an area of the drawing in front of them.

A short, squat, blonde haired man shakes his head, 'Too risky. These ducts go all through the bunker and any noise, and I mean even the slightest noise will reverberate through them like a drum. We need a silent entry.'

'C'mon Chunk, even with a diversion?' the first man counters.

The tallest of the quartet stands up to stretch his legs, rotate his torso to loosen the tightness he feels when immobile for any length of time and says, 'We can't do that. It's not like it's the embassy all over again. A diversion is going to make these guys feel threatened and they will probably start slotting the friendlies.'

'But Boss, the embassy diversion worked,' he doesn't want to lose his plan of action as he continues, 'we made a lot of noise, we went in, killed the bad guys and made it back in time for tea and medals.'

'Different scenario, Bomber. We had intel on the locations of hostages and of bad guys within the building. Here, shit, we don't even have any idea of the numbers involved or even where anyone is being held. I think we need to wait it out and only go noisy as a last resort.' He turns to the fourth member, who up to now has stayed quiet,

'Chuckles, your teams are in place?'

Even now he says nothing in response to the team leader, but nods and points to the tall building behind them and to the tree line.

'How many have eyes on?'

It is almost with reluctance that 'Chuckles' speaks, 'Two teams on the building, one on the edge of the scrub behind the bunker, don't want them nasty little buggers walking out the back door, and myself and Taff will be watching the main entrance and their vehicles from the main gate.'

'OK, Chunk, what do you have for me?'

The blonde haired guy stands up from his squatting position, followed by the rest of the group,

'Boss, their vehicles have all had GPS trackers fitted. I figure they will try and use them with hostages on board to drive away from here. We are still trying to work out likely routes, but with this being Norfolk and the edge of the civilised world, well I have to say their options are pretty limited. They can either go to the coast and take a boat or they have to drive out and the only real option is the A11.'

'What about airports they can use?'
'There's Norwich, about twenty minutes away and a few small grass strips around. If they choose that option I reckon they will pick one of the parachute schools around here and move out that way.
Harder to track and if they need to they can make it to Holland or France quite easily. From there, who knows.'
'Let's try not give them that opportunity eh?'
'Boss?' This time it is Bomber who speaks up, 'If we are thinking about their vehicles being used, what if my team take up residence in the luggage compartments. I can get two guys in each bus no problem.'
The tall figure looks over to the four black Mercedes minibuses that are lined up near the entrance. As he thinks through the options of just such a manoeuvre, Bomber speaks up again,
'It would be just like a stake out over the water, but with a better chance of being in the right place at the right time.'
He is referring to the times they have spent waiting around in muddy ditches and terrible weather in Northern Ireland waiting and hoping for the IRA or some other terrorist group to show themselves in the act of an 'aggressive action.' Unfortunately, most of the time is spent being uncomfortable with nothing to show for it.
The boss nods his head,
'Do it. But Bomber, I want comms from you at all times, understand? We don't know how long you will be there so we will rotate teams every 24 hours. When can you get in?'
Bomber smiles and says sheepishly,
'Well I have teams already in place…'
The stern look from the Boss silences him.

'Say again. You have teams in place without informing me?'
'When we putting the trackers in I thought it prudent to leave a guy in each bus to…'
'For fucks sake, Bomber! How long have they been in there?'
'Since we got here, Boss.'
'Shit, right, let's go with…'
'MOVEMENT FROM THE BUILDING!'
They all turn as one towards the cry from a uniformed policeman who is rapidly gesturing towards the building.
'WE GOT MOVEMENT!'

All eyes are riveted on the door of the building as it opens slightly. Countless weapons are raised to the aim and optical sights are checked for windage, elevation and any other measurements that will affect a perfect shot.
A hand is waved from the door,
'DON'T SHOOT. THEY HAVE A MESSAGE TO GIVE. DON'T SHOOT!'
A woman is pushed out to the edge of the door, her face a mask of terror. Everyone can see the barrel of a gun touching the back of her neck held in place with a short black strap.
'Show time boys, get to your positions and await my signal,' the Boss says as he starts walking slowly towards the hostage in the doorway. He takes measured steps and controls his breathing as he raises his hands and takes the hundred or so steps to get closer to the woman.
'I am here to help, don't struggle and don't panic. I know you are scared and I want you to know…'
A male voice from inside the doorway stops him,

'Shut up, little man. We are here to tell you our demands and what we are going to do, but first we have to show you how serious we are.'
Instinctively he rushes forward, shouting,
'No, don't, we know the seriousness of the situation.'
He is fully expecting to hear a gunshot and see the body of the woman crumple before him. Instead the door is pushed fully open and a man in a blue uniform is seen to be standing there. Gunshots ring out and everyone watches as the RAF officer's chest explodes in flowers of crimson before he collapses to the ground in an untidy heap.
The woman is pulled back into the doorway as the man's voice rings out again,
'Check his jacket pocket. There you will find our message. You can take his body back with you. You have my assurances that you will not be harmed but I make no such promises for the people I hold in here. You have ten minutes to prepare for us, so I suggest you hurry up.'
Rushing forward the Boss bends down to check the man's pulse but finds nothing beneath the cold dead skin. He looks up to the doorway in time to see a man staring down at him with a smile on his face,
'Ten minutes, chop-chop, little man.'
The door is pulled closed with a slam.
Grasping the dead man by the shoulders, he pulls him up to a seated position before hoisting him up into a fireman's lift and carrying him back to the police and ambulance vehicles.
He places the body gently onto a medical trolley.
'Sorry we were too late, sir,' he says softly to the figure lying before him, 'but we will slot the bastards who did this to you. I promise.'

With these words he carefully places his hand into the pockets of the bloodstained jacket and pulls out a sheet of handwritten paper.

The Chief Inspector of the Norfolk Police is already at his side as he unfolds the demands of the people inside the building. He scans it quickly before handing it over to the uniformed officer.

'They are on the move and now I think it is time I assume control of the next phase of this operation. What do you think, sir?'

The Chief Inspector is still reading what is on the sheet, but he has presence of mind to answer,

'We will offer you any support you need, I have a helicopter in the air at your disposal and as much manpower as required,' he looks up and addresses the man in black before him, 'we have to stop these bastards before anyone else gets hurt.'

'That's the plan, sir. I think we had best pull everyone back and see what they want to do next.'

Holding out his hand the Chief Inspector shakes hands with the special forces officer,

'Son, if these people do not see the inside of a court room, I have to say that is perfectly fine with me.'

He receives a smile and a nod in response as they part company, both shouting out orders to their respective teams.

CHAPTER 50

'Leahy of MI6, I do remember you now, but when we met I never caught your name. Or should I say, when you blocked a police investigation with your threats, you failed to give your name.'
'Now, now Commissioner, a lot of water has passed under the bridge since then. I do hope we can get along with the present matter rather than dredge up the past.'
Wilks covers the phone's mouthpiece with her hand and whispers to me,
'Call JD and get Luke to trace this call.'
I nod, stand up and walk over to the far side of the cafeteria. I can still hear her conversation.
'So, shall I call you Mr Leahy or Andrew?'
'Leahy is fine and…'
'OK then, Leahy it is. Why have you bugged my offices, put surveillance on my phones and who gave the authority to do such a thing against me?'
'I was going to ask, before I was interrupted, that as we are getting along so swimmingly and it is just that Commissioner seems, so, well just so formal. May I call you Patricia?'
'No you may not. Who gave you the authority and under what charges or criminal suspicion have I been accused of.'
'Hmm, alright. I guess I will just call you Pat. It's asier and less of a mouthful.'
'Leahy, who gave you the authority?' Wilks voice has risen slightly in volume and I can feel she is on the edge of losing control. I gesture with both my hands for her to calm down and I see her nod and sit back slightly.

I dial JD's number and he answers before the first ring has finished,

'Peter? I thought I was to ring you.'

I talk quickly and quietly into my phone,

'Change of plan, mate. Get Luke to run a trace on Wilks' number. She is currently talking to that bastard from MI6 we had a run in with the Ripper case.'

'Masterson's boss at MI6?'

'The one and only. We need to find out where he is. Can you get Luke on it?'

'Straight away Peter. What can I do?'

I pause as I wonder what any of us can do,

'Hang tight, JD and call me with me any details as soon as you have it.'

I don't give him a chance to respond as I hang up the phone and change the ring setting to vibrate. I listen in on Wilks and Leahy as I walk back to the table.

'Pat, it doesn't matter who gave me the authority. What matters is that I have it and I have enough damning evidence against you and your department to see everyone in it locked up for a very long time.'

'What the hell are you talking about?' she almost shouts into the phone.

'Embezzlement of public funds, bribery of officials to garner your position, I mean, it's not everyone who can make the jump from Chief Inspector to Commissioner in such a short space of time as you did. We also have details of bribery to look the other way in certain crimes. How else can you explain the deposit of £30,000 into your bank account a few months ago?'

I see Wilks looking confused, then angry,

'What money? I haven't had any money placed in my account, especially anything like that.'
'You see, this is where I hold all the aces, Pat. I can make that happen, or I can make it go away. All I need is for you to relinquish control of the MASTER aircraft and give me the means to dispose of it in my own way. None of the charges will ever come to pass. You and your department will carry on as normal, DCI Carter will not have to go to prison, and you know what happens to coppers in prison, don't you, Pat? Oh, by the way, I presume you have me on speakerphone, so, hi DCI Carter, hope you are having a good day.'
I say nothing but stand there looking as confused as Wilks. All I can do is wonder how the world got so crazy so quickly.
Leahy continues,
'Not the talkative type I see. No matter. Now, Pat, where were we? Oh yes, the MASTER. I need full control and I need it now.'
Wilks features harden and I see her fists clench on the table,
'Now you listen to me, Leahy, I will not be bullied or threatened by a…'
Leahy's furious voice explodes from the phone on the table,
'No, you listen here you fucking bitch, give me control, or your life and the life of everyone you care for is over. Do you understand?'
There is a pause as Wilks and I both look at each other in amazement as the ranting going on,
'Do you fucking understand?' he asks again even louder.
Wilks stands up and snatches the phone of the table and holds it in front of her mouth. She speaks softly,

'I know cheap threats when I see them and even though you can probably do all that you say, that does not concern me. What I am worried about is the fact that a major figure in our country's intelligence circuit is frightened enough by someone like me and my team that he has to make threats.'

'Listen to me you...'

'No, Mr Leahy, you listen to me,' she continues on in the same soft, confident tones as before, 'control of this aircraft will not be relinquished until I have an order from the Prime Minister explaining the reasoning behind it. As I don't believe that such an order is due anytime soon I will endeavour to protect the citizens of this city, and this country by disposing of the threat in a way that I deem to be suitable. Do your worst, Mr Leahy. We are ready for you.'

Wilks ends the call as Leahy shouts unintelligibly down the phone.

I notice she is trembling as she places the phone back on the table. I take a seat opposite her and grabbing her hand in mine, I look her straight in the eye and say all that I can think of,

'Excellent work, Commissioner, you have made me and this department proud.'

'Peter, I am not sure what the consequences of my actions will be, but thank you.'

I feel my pocket vibrate and I release her hand to pull out my phone,

'What have you got, JD?' I answer.

'We've got a number and Luke has even pulled up a location.'

I look at Wilks,

'They've cracked it,' I am just about to ask for the details when Wilks' phone rings again.

Her eyes widen and I nod,
'JD, do another trace, make sure it's correct. I want to nail this guy,' I pause as my mind races, 'JD, can Luke record the call on Wilks' number?'
I hear him mumble something on the other end of the line,
'He says it's possible but he might miss the beginning of the conversation as he sets it up.'
'Get him to do it. I will call you back.'
I hang up and look at Wilks,
'We are recording this one. Get him to threaten you and the department and we have him.' I say with a smile. I see her relax. She nods and reaches out to the phone.
'Wilks here.'
'Commissioner Wilks, please hold one moment for the Prime Minister.'

CHAPTER 51

'Everybody, move back behind the perimeter fence. The hostages and their captors will be leaving the building. No-one, I repeat no-one is to attempt to stop them.'

The police start following orders from their senior officer. Cars are started and moved out of the way of the main gate until a path is cleared. The Chief Inspector looks over towards the small huddle of men dressed in black and whispers under his breath,

'Good luck son,' before turning his attention back to his own men.

The Special Forces team listen intently to their Boss as he outlines the situation for them.

'In a few minutes they are going to be exiting the building. It is our worst case scenario. According to their instructions, three groups will head towards the minibuses and board them. There will be a number of terrorists within each group and each will be armed and also wearing a suicide vest. They say they are not afraid to die and we know from our own experiences that this is not a problem for these guys. There will be a group of players and hostages left inside the bunker who are acting as insurance.

Once the first three groups reach their destination, a call will be made and then they will make their way out and also attempt to reach freedom. Only when all groups know they are free will the hostages be released.

As a goodwill gesture they say that the technical staff and other employees of TSI will remain in the underground sections of the bunker. We have been told we can enter the building when the last bus leaves to get them out.'

'Fucking goodwill gesture? Jesus Christ, Boss! Who the fuck are these guys?' It is Bomber who releases the frustration they all feel.

'I know where you are all coming from and I feel your pain, but we have an ace in the hole…or rather an ace in the busses. Bomber has placed a team in each one as well as a tracker device. We will know where they are and have eyes on them at all times, whilst we follow at a safe distance. Bomber, get on the net and let your guys know they are on silent running,' he addresses the rest of the group, 'Their demands are simple. If they see anyone following them, they kill all the hostages and as many civilians as they can. Any questions?'

'Yes Boss, just one.'

Everyone looks to the normally silent Chuckles in astonishment.

'What is it Chuckles?'

He points a finger up to the sky,

'By following, do they mean the TV choppers as well?'

Like a group of mean looking and well armed meerkats the group all crane their necks up as one to look to the sky.

'Shit,' the Boss turns and starts running towards the police line which is now further away and shouts as he runs, 'Get those fucking helicopters out of the air, now!'

The Chief Inspector is one of the first to react and turns to see the tall, black clad figure running towards them.

'..et…cking hel..ers out…..now.'
Over the noise around him he cannot make out the words, but the gesturing and pointing makes him look skywards. Realisation hits him like a soft hammer.
'The press, damn it, the press have to go.'
He grabs the nearest officer,
'Get the press liaison officer. We have a crisis here that needs resolving immediately. Tell him those helicopters have to leave the area or people are going to die.'
'Yes sir,' the young woman replies and stumbles away quickly to the Crisis Response Centre to relay the Chief's commands.
As he turns back to the man running towards him, the Chief Inspector notices the door to the building is being pushed open.
'Oh no,' is all he can say, 'It's too late.'

Hostages and terrorists start leaving the building. Each is tied together and each one is wearing a balaclava. It is almost impossible to tell captors from their captives. Now and again you spot a barrel of a gun poking out of a jacket or held discreetly by the side of a person, but in the throng of people there is no chance of distinguishing friend from foe.
The first group of around twenty people cross the short distance of ten or fifteen metres to make their way towards one of the black Mercedes minibuses and climb aboard. The blacked out windows mask all movement from inside and when the door closes it is like the group have vanished into thin air.

A second group leave the building in the same manner and enter a second minibus. As the third group starts to exit the building it stops suddenly. A woman's voice rings out,
'We said no surveillance. Why are there helicopters still here?'
Again the Special Forces officer takes control. He had stopped running towards the police lines when the first group appeared. He now raises his hands and walks back towards the group of obviously terrified people.
'We are doing all we can to remove them. They are press helicopters and we have people talking to them now to explain the situation and asking them to move on. They will be gone in a few minutes.'
Joanne looks to the figure walking towards her and the small crowd of people that surround her,
'Not good enough. You were given explicit instructions. If you don't follow instructions then consequences must be met.'
'Wait,' he shouts out, knowing he must act quickly to avoid bloodshed, 'I guarantee they will be removed from the area. We are following your instructions because we don't want anyone else to get hurt.'
'You guarantee this?'
He is now within five metres of the group and stops. He lowers his arms to his sides and looks intently towards the source of the voice. He thinks he can make out a small figure that appears to be staring at him through the eyepieces of the black balaclava that covers her head. He takes a deep breath and looks directly at the figure,
'I can.'

He sees movement and notices a stubby barrel move up until he is staring down the black metal tube. It is not the first time he has had a weapon pointed at him and just as before he notices how time stands still. His only focus is on the black, gaping hole that at any moment could spit death his way. He wonders if he will see the muzzle flash or even see the bullet before it hits him. He drags his eyes away from the gun barrel and looks up to the figure holding it. He sees her eyes watching him with the intensity of a hungry lion watching a wounded gazelle. He braces his body for the shot. He feels rather than hears the changing sound of the rotor blades above him and it takes all his willpower to look up and see the two helicopters peeling away. It is then he notices he has been holding his breath and he lets out a long drawn out sigh between his pursed lips. He brings his eyes back down to the woman with the gun,
'I told you they would go,' he says with a smile as his body relaxes from the adrenaline that has been coursing through his veins. He can almost believe he sees her eyes smile.
'You did. Thank you, but our instructions were explicit. You had ten minutes.'
He doesn't even have time to change his expression as the bullet smacks into his forehead. His brain has a millisecond to process that he does not hear the shot, but he has managed to see the bullet in flight as it screws its way through the air towards him.
'Well fuck me...' are his last thoughts before the blackness descends.

The sound of the shot and the sight of the body falling to the floor creates a vacuum of sound in the area. The echo of the shot reverberates and fades away, just like the life of the man on the floor.
The woman's voice rings out to jolt everyone back to life,
'When we issue an order it must be obeyed without any hesitation. The consequences for non compliance will not be pleasant for anyone.'
The group moves forward again and boards the third small bus. Before the door closes on the vehicle, a figure appears in the doorway. A hand goes up to the balaclava and removes it. Joanne looks out to the assembled men and women of the emergency services and armed forces.
'If I feel anything is out of the ordinary,' she looks from the body of the man in black just a few meters away, back up to the stunned crowd, 'Everyone dies.'
She steps back and with a small hiss of hydraulics, the door closes to shut her away from view.
The rumble of the diesel engines breaks the silence as all three vehicles start up. They move off in their small convoy, past the police, past the cordon and out of the gate and perimeter fence that marks the boundary of the site.
Hundreds of eyes watch their progress.
Nobody follows.

CHAPTER 52

As we wait for the Prime Minister my phone again vibrates urgently with a small rumble. It's JD,
'Peter, we have a trace. It's coming from the same location so we can confirm it's our same guy. We are just setting up the recording so keep him talking.'
I wave my hand to grab Wilks' attention,
'They have a trace on this call,' I whisper to her, 'They say it's from the same location as Leahy.'
Her eyes narrow, she nods grimly at me and places a finger to her lips and then points at her phone. Once again I move away to have a whispered conversation,
'Are you sure it's the same?' I ask.
'No doubt about it. It's routed through a switchboard, uh, wait a second, here are the GPS co-ordinates. Latitude 51.4878, Longitude -0.124639.'
'Sorry, JD, that means absolutely nothing to me. Can you pull it up from there?'
'Sure thing, I wasn't thinking for a moment there, just relaying the information we have here. One second...'
The line goes silent for a moment.
'Well I should have guessed this. The address it refers to is 85 Albert Embankment.'
'MI6 main building,' I confirm.
'That's the place.'
'Thanks again, JD.'
'No problem...what the...'

I hear a commotion over the line of shouts and orders being issued but can't quite hear distinct words.

'Uh, Peter, we are, we uhmm, we seem to be having a bit of a situation here.'

'What's going on, who's there with you?'

'We have a few members of the, what I presume to be military, here with us at the moment and they are demanding we move away to give them control of the MASTER drone. Any chance of…'

His voice is cut off and I hear someone ask,

'Who are you speaking to?'

I cannot help but smile, even with the current situation as I hear JD's answer,

'Fuck off action-man and give me my phone back. This is police business and I am pretty sure the last time I checked we were not under martial law. So why not just crawl back to your tank or your fox-hole or wherever you and your cronies came from and let us do our job.'

A man's voice erupts out of the phone at me,

'Who is this?'

'I am Detective Chief Inspector Carter of the Homicide and Serious Crimes Unit and you are hindering an investigation which is a criminal offence. Now why don't you tell me who you are, so I can start on the paper-work.'

'Certainly, Inspector, you are speaking to Captain Andrew Phillips of the Royal Military Police and we have been given authority by the Crown to take control of the situation developing here. If you need confirmation why not pop down so we can have a chat. Or better yet, ring my employer. Just call 118 118 and ask for Her Majesty, they will put you right through.'

I am about to reply when I realise he has hung up on me. I storm back over to Wilks not caring who hears me on her phone,

'We have a problem. The military police are attempting to stage a coup and take control of this case and the MASTER. I have to go and sort this out.'

Before she can reply a very familiar voice is heard from her phone,

'I wouldn't do that Inspector, you see those men are there on my authority. As soon as we intercepted your ability to control the rogue aircraft an emergency operation was brought into play. I am sure you understand that the military are much more capable of dealing with this situation than police officers. No offence of course.'

I open my mouth to give an angry retort, but Wilks answers before me,

'None taken of course, Prime Minister. We are just concerned of the legality of the situation and the speed with which this appears to have come to fruition.'

'Ah, Commissioner Wilks, I am sorry you were bypassed by the whole thing. Once these plans come into motion they take on a momentum all of their own. We had our own team attempting to regain control, but your team, and you must thank them wholeheartedly for me, managed to beat ours to the finish line. Well done by the way.'

'And this had nothing to do with the surveillance operation on myself and my department?'

'Surveillance, Commissioner? I am afraid I don't know what you are talking about.'

'Sir, do you know a man by the name of Leahy, he works out of MI6?'

'I meet a lot of people as PM, Commissioner. I cannot be expected to remember everyone and their names,' his voice is guarded.

'I understand that, sir, it's just that Leahy and myself were having a conversation just moments before you called. I and officers in my department were personally threatened unless we handed control over to him. I find it a huge coincidence that you rang demanding the same thing within seconds of me refusing to be blackmailed by him.'

'I see,' then he pauses a beat, 'Patricia, you say blackmail. That is a serious accusation against a fellow officer. Are you sure his words were not misconstrued in some way?'

'No, he was pretty emphatic and clear about the whole situation that would befall us should I refuse. Which I did, by the way. Refuse that is, unless I had authority from you. Again, a pretty big coincidence. You see, sir, in our line of work we do come across the odd coincidence, but never one after another. That is when the word used to describe it becomes, what we call, evidence.'

'Commissioner, be careful what you are saying.'

'I would but then we have another small coincidence. We traced the call that Leahy made to me earlier to a location, which unsurprisingly is the MI6 offices. Not an issue as he works for that organisation. But then I also ordered a trace on this call as I believed he would call back with more threats, sorry, more offers of redeployment of myself and others in this department. Instead I have the Prime Minister calling and as luck would have it, he is calling from the same location as our previous caller.

What I find strange about this fact is that I left you in the cabinet office buildings in Whitehall during a COBRA meeting just over an hour ago.'
'Commissioner Wilks, this conversation is coming to an end. I called you out of courtesy to inform you of the military take over of your control of the MASTER aircraft. That courtesy has been thrown back in my face with accusations that I do not care for. I will…'
Wilks cuts in to his indignant speech,
'Prime Minister, I am informing you that I and my staff will not rest until we get to the bottom of this fiasco. Thousands of people have died and I will point the finger of blame at you, this government and any other department that may be involved. I will not allow the wool to be pulled over the eyes of the people of this country and I do not care who you are, you are not above the laws of this land.'
There is silence. I can hear the sound of the cafeteria clock slowly ticking away. I count twelve heavy 'ticks' before there is a reply.
'You must be very, very careful with your actions here, Commissioner. This is a debate that is far beyond your office and involves matters of national and international security that you have no knowledge of. People have died and that is a tragedy, but we are aiming to avoid many more deaths, not just in the United Kingdom, but around the whole globe. I cannot and I will not discuss this with you here and now, but before you take any measures I ask that we meet face to face. I will endeavour to answer your questions at that meeting. For now, I urge you to get your department to stand aside and for the greater good of this country, allow the military access to whatever they require.'

'Do you really think…'

'Commissioner,' his voice turns softer, 'Patricia, please don't force me into making it an order. Co-operate with me and I will co-operate with you. For now you will have to trust me that we both want the same thing, an end to the violence and death today.'

It is now Wilks turn to pause. I can see the conflict on her face as she struggles to hear the words of the Prime Minister against the evidence before her. Finally she makes a decision and I can see it is against what she believes,

'I give your men full control, but I want my staff to be in on the loop. They cracked this thing and they deserve to be there at the end.'

'That is only to be expected. Thank you, Patricia.'

She reaches out and presses the small red button to end the call.

'What a fucked up, crazy day, eh Peter?'

I can only nod my head in agreement with her sentiments.

'Best you get down to JD and help diffuse the situation there. I will be down shortly but I just have a few more calls to make.'

CHAPTER 53

Stuart Masterson is seated in the back of the Merlin helicopter along with his team of six men as it speeds over the countryside above Norfolk. With his headphones on, provided by the aircrew on board, he hears the pilot say,
'Five minutes to destination and touchdown.'
He gives a thumbs-up to the co-pilot who is looking through the narrow doorway of the cockpit and gets one in return before the helmeted head disappears back to its duties. Stuart holds up his right hand with all fingers splayed outward to tell his group how long to landing. He gets sets of thumbs up and nods to confirm their understanding. He looks out of the window at the green and yellow fields as they cruise by. Three large, black vehicles catch his eye as they travel down a small country lane before they are lost from view behind trees. The aircraft makes a hard turn to the left and all he sees is sky before it settles back into its normal attitude of flight.
'Sorry about that,' the voice appears in his headset, 'We were given orders from air traffic to avoid this area, we have to re-route slightly but it won't delay us by more than a minute or two.'
Masterson shrugs his shoulders and smiles. He can never understand why, with miles and miles of open sky, that it is easy to stray into areas you are not allowed. His mind moves on to the entry procedure of the bunker he has devised and he looks down at the blueprints on his tablet computer once again. He doesn't give the black minibuses a second thought.

Seven minutes later he is striding out of the large, grey helicopter even as its engines and rotors are still running. He bows his frame slightly and walks towards the group of men dressed all in black that are standing in what looks to be deep conversation. As he gets closer he sees they are all standing over a man who is laying on the ground. Thinking it is a demonstration of some kind, he is about to make a joke about it, when he catches the words being said, 'May the road rise up to meet you.
May the wind be always at your back.
May the sun shine warm upon your face;
The rains fall soft upon your fields and until we meet again,
May God hold you in the palm of His hand.
We will avenge you, brother.'
He stops in his tracks as he recognises the poem and the smile dies on his face. He waits and stands a respectful distance away for the few seconds the Special Forces team needs. They turn away and one or two of them look towards him.
He can see the look of confusion on some of their faces. It is as if they know his face but can't quite place it. As they look at each other he walks forward until he is close enough to smell the sweat and adrenaline on each one of them.
'Fuck me, isn't anyone going to say hello?' He asks with a smile then realises after his surgery there will be subtle differences to his face that they may not recognise.

'Christ, it's me...Stephens. Bomber you big wanker, we were on selection together then spent a few years on D squadron. I remember that time in Oman when we got lost near the only bar for a hundred miles. You fell in love with that Russian bird, the one with whiskers on her chin. What was her name?...Dimitri, wasn't it?'

'Bloody hell, is that you Stephens?. What are you doing here?'

Bomber's face breaks out into a huge smile and he grabs Masterson and places him in a bear hug that would crush a normal man.

'I am here to chew gum and kick some arse...'

a chorus from the group breaks out,

'And I'm all out of gum!'

Bomber releases his old friend and his face turns sombre,

'What the fuck happened to your face. It's like you decided to whack it repeatedly against a tree and the tree won. You were ugly before, but now...shit! Seriously mate, what are you doing here?'

'The firm I'm working for now sent me here with these guys,' Masterson gestures over his shoulder to his team, 'The face, well sometimes we all have to take a hit for the team. I asked to look a lot less handsome and a whole lot more ugly. I showed them a photo of you and this is what they gave me.'

'Plastic surgery?' Bomber asks.

Masterson nods,

'We have come to offer assistance and sort this mess out.'

Even with the death of a friend so recent there are smiles and handshakes as they come forward. These men are often surrounded by death, to lose colleagues and a friend is not unknown to them. Bomber shakes his head,

'You're too late. The fuckers have blown the coop. We have a few left inside but the main group have left in a shed load of wagons about ten minutes ago.'
'Who the fuck authorised that?'
A cultured voice speaks out,
'I did, now who the fuck are you?'
Masterson turns to see a police Chief Inspector standing behind him. He stretches out a hand,
'No names from me but pleased to meet you, sir. I have been sent here to, oh hold on one second,' he fishes in his trouser pocket and pulls out a piece of paper,' This is for you. My boss gave it to me.'
The Chief Inspector takes the folded up paper, opens it and as soon as he sees the signature and seal upon it, hands it back.
'Carry on. If you need any assistance we will be over at the incident command tent near the main gate. You can't miss it.'
With that the senior officer walks away wondering what the world is coming to when the police are being pushed to one side like this. Masterson feels sorry for the man as he watches him walk slowly away, his head bowed under the weight of command.
He turns back to Bomber,
'What happened here?'
'They were leaving, that's the shit of it. Two groups had got into their black vans and the third lot had just exited the building when they noticed the press helicopters. The boss had arranged for them to leave but she slotted him right in front of us. There was fuck all we could do.'
'And you just let them walk away?'
Bombers grin widens,

'Not quite. Walk with me,' he gestures to Masterson's team, 'leave them here to catch up with the guys, I recognise most of 'em so it would be good for them to catch up.'

Masterson lets out a whistle and holds up two fingers for his team to see and walks off with his old friend from his SAS days. As they walk he realises what he noticed on the way in,

'They left in three black vans didn't they? Mercs or something like that?'

Without breaking stride, Bomber turns his head with a puzzled frown upon it,

'How did you know that?'

'We flew over them on the way here. Our pilot even had to do a pretty radical manoeuvre to get us out of their way. Damn it.'

'No problem, we know where they are and we have eyes and bodies on the targets.'

'Well that is one piece of good news at least.'

They are walking towards a large white van that would not look out of place on a building site. To an untrained eye it is just a battered old, long-wheel base workman's vehicle. Masterson looks along the roof line and sees the tiny array of antennas built into the metal. He also notices the way it sits a little too heavy on its axles, even with the strengthened suspension.

'I remember helping design these buggers,' he says absently, 'I can't believe they finally got them made up.'

'One of the best things to come out of the chop shop since the pinkies. Come on, let's show you how the magic is made.'

Bomber opens the rear door and before them sit three people hunched over a suite of electronics and computers that would send shivers down the collective spines of many security firms.

'Get in and shut the bloody door, it's freezing out there.'

Bomber smiles,

'That's Tommy, always whinging.'

They both get into the back of the van making the small space feel even more cramped.

Masterson looks around to get his bearings and finds immediately what he is looking for.

'The trackers, you beauty. What's the plan?'

'We have four teams here. Three are following the vans at a very safe distance and are being directed from this location. The last team is mine that you saw outside. We're waiting for the fourth group to exit before we all make our move. The best thing is that I have a man inside each vehicle, if things go pear shaped they can use their initiative to save as many hostages as possible and stop the bad guys escaping.'

'Who do you think is control of the terrorist group?'

'My best bet is the bitch that shot up the Boss. She seemed to be the only one who was in any leadership position and she showed her face like she didn't have a care in the world. Tommy, bring up her up.'

An image appears on one of the screens. Masterson sighs,

'I know her, or should I say I know of her. She's a nasty, vicious one. Which vehicle is she in?'

'Number three.'

'I'm going after her. Can you direct me onto her location? I can use the Merlin to follow but to have your eyes on would be a great help.'

Bomber picks up a small radio from a rack at the side of the van,
'Take this, it's set up with our frequencies. Get her and don't bring her back.'
Taking the radio, Masterson shakes his friends hand, exits the vehicle and jogs over to his team.
'Listen up, weapons are hot, we will engage with caution.'
The helicopter is already starting up as they run towards the open doorway of the crew cabin.
'Collateral damage is to be kept to a minimum but if you feel you have a shot, take it.'
As they strap themselves in they feel the reassuring vibration of the engines and then they are pressed down into their seats as the heavy helicopter takes off vertically. Looking out of his window once more, Masterson sees men hurrying about and moves his head to get a better view.
'What the…'
On the ground, Bomber is walking back to his team when people start streaming out of the building in front of them. The rattle of gunfire and screams starts to fill the air. He un-slings his weapon, crouches and attempts to seek out targets.
The scene is chaos, men and women are running in all directions as they exit the building. Bomber sees one woman stumble forward as if slapped forcefully in the back before a large red stain appears at her waist. She falls to the ground and lays still.

He moves his weapon in an arc behind her and sees a man holding a short stubby automatic pistol spraying it indiscriminately into the crowd.
Bomber releases his safety catch and squeezes the trigger. The push into his shoulder of the recoil is like an old friends welcome slap, and as his sights come back down into the aim he sees the man lying face down on the floor with blood forming a large pool around his head.
He shouts out,
'CONTACT, CONTACT, CONTACT,' and starts looking for more targets. There are plenty to choose from.

On the minibus, Joanne is speaking rapidly into her telephone,
'Keep up the diversion, kill all the hostages if you have to and when the time is right…you know what to do. Good luck.'
She looks around at the passengers. Her eyes rest on her fathers face and he smiles back at her. Sitting next to him is her sister who also smiles back. One by one she looks at each of the people on board, smiling and nodding before announcing,
'We have done it. They will not be able to stop us now.'
A cheer rings out as each one of her organisation who is sitting before her relishes in the accomplishments they have achieved. The only person who is silent is James Emerson.

CHAPTER 54

I pause as I survey the scene in the Met's IT offices. JD is being pushed against the wall, which given his size and strength is no mean feat. The two men holding him there are obviously used to dealing with strong guys. Over their camouflage uniform they are wearing red armbands with MP in thick black letters emblazoned on them and their biceps are bulging with the strain of keeping my friend in one place. JD, to his credit, is not giving up easily and it must be like trying to hold an angry bear in place. I almost have a little sympathy for the two military policemen…almost.

'JD, stop resisting. Gents, please let him go, you have my assurances he will restrain himself from doing you any harm.'

A tall man with a severe crew-cut steps into my face. I hate having my personal space invaded in such a way. It reminds me of playground bullies trying to assert authority through intimidation. I glance down at his chest, noting the name,

'Captain Phillips,' I say as I hold out my right hand whilst pushing him gently but firmly a pace backwards with my left, 'DCI Carter, we spoke on the phone a few moments ago.'

I see him bristling with anger but his training gets the better of him and he extends his own hand out to shake mine. Like a typical bully he attempts to crush my hand with his grip but I am used to JD's vice like handshake and I smile as he squeezes.

'I am here to offer the Met's co-operation,' I pull back my hand sharply causing Phillips to stumble slightly towards me. I lean in quickly and whisper in his ear, 'Let's stop pissing about shall we?'
I release him and wait for his response.
He looks at me for a moment, his eyes hard and angry. I am not sure if he is going to take a swing at me and I tense my body. Instead he smiles at me,
'Finally someone who knows what they're doing. Roberts, Mansfield, let go of him, his boss is here.'
The two MPs step away cautiously from JD and I see that one of them has a large red mark on the left side of his face. I look from him to JD and he just shrugs his shoulders as a way of explanation. I shake my head and turn back to Phillips.
'Captain, the Commissioner has sent me down to give you what you need. She has spoken to the Prime Minister and we will do as you ask, but, our guys go with you.'
As I say this I point to JD and Luke.
Phillips raises his chin slightly,
'No, that's not acceptable. Your man here assaulted one of my men and I don't want him anywhere near this operation. I will take the computer guy only.'
'Then I am afraid you will be going nowhere with our information. It is not a request.'
Luke turns around in his seat,
'Inspector Carter, it's alright. We need to sort this mess out and they only need me as I was the one who broke the security protocols.'
I see JD shake his head.
'Why do you need to take Luke away when we have control here?' I ask.

'Your facilities here are limited and we have specialists who are trained in what we need to do at another location.'

'Where?'

'Classified information.'

'Your specialists, what do they need?' Luke asks.

'Son, if I knew that I wouldn't need the specialists.'

Luke continues, 'In that case how do you know our equipment here is limited compared to yours?'

The question goes unanswered, so he continues, 'Look, I have control of this thing from here, there is now way of guaranteeing that if you make me move to another location and these guys,' he gestures to JD and myself, 'They don't have the skill sets to do what I do.'

I would love to argue the point but I know he's correct.

'Luke is right. You stay here, bring in as many guys as you want to assist but we are staying right here. JD can stay outside the room but he will be here. What do you say?'

Phillips nods, 'If I give you co-ordinates can you program them in to the drone?' He asks Luke.

'No problem that's easily done.'

'Mansfield, get on to HQ and tell them to send the team out. We have a go.'

The guy who JD punched, leaves the room to make the call as he pulls a mobile phone from his pocket.

Taking a notepad out, Phillips flicks through the pages,

'I need you to program these in, 51°33'11"N 000°25'06"W.'

Luke starts typing in the numbers, but pauses before hitting enter,

'Zero degrees, that's back towards London.' He says.

'We are bringing it to RAF Northolt. That is where we will destroy it.' Phillips replies as he leans over Luke's shoulder and hits the 'Enter' key himself. 'Now do you think you can stop anyone else form taking command of that aircraft?'
'Certainly.'
'Can you show me how?'
Phillips pulls up a chair and sits down next to Luke to watch as the young IT wizard shows off his skills.
'JD, step outside with me a moment,' I say.
As we leave the room the MP, Mansfield, is walking back in. He glares at JD as he pushes past.
'I am not going to ask,' I say, 'But that has to end here. I need you to keep an eye on these guys. I don't trust any of them but as long they are going to destroy this thing, I'm happy to go along with them. Wilks will be down shortly, let her deal with it. I have to go and find Graham and I may need your help in a little while. Can you come down as soon as she gets here.'
I see JD wants to question me but I can't let him, not until I have the full facts from Graham,
'I'll explain it all in full when you come down, OK?'
'I'll be there when you need me.' He replies.
I walk away, wondering if I am ready for what Graham is about to tell me.

CHAPTER 55

Identify a target, fire, move.
Bomber has been trained to do this so many times it feels like second nature. He sees his team doing the exact same thing as they pick off men and women who are carrying and using weapons. Some of the terrorists get lucky, not all of his team members will be walking away from this fire-fight, but the odds are evening up for the men in black. Another man drops to the ground as Bomber feels the push of his weapon into his shoulder and he is up and moving forward again. Always moving forward. He is only now a few short paces from the doorway. The movement of it draws his eye and the weapon comes up to track it instinctively. It only opens a few inches and Bomber misses the small objects that are tossed out. One of his men doesn't.
The cry of, 'GRENADE' barely registers but the soft bump of something against his foot causes him to look down.
'Ahh shit…'

Pushing off with his left foot in an attempt to sprint away is not enough. The force of the explosion catapults him in the air. There is no pain as he feels he is on a cushion of warm wind that has pushed him out of the way. He lands heavily and feels his shoulder crunch into the hard concrete and he loses his grip on the rifle. It clatters away out of reach. Blinking dust and smoke from his eyes, Bomber reaches down to grab his pistol from its thigh holster. He scrabble for a second, unable to find it before his hand comes across something sharp sticking up and proud. He looks slowly down his own body to see his hand grasping the stark white and splintered bone of his dismembered leg. As he loses focus, the pain washes across him before he mercifully passes out, the blood pumping relentlessly from the mangled messy stump. It takes just thirty seconds for the blood flow to slow to a trickle and stop as the heart gives up its fight to keep him alive.
The door opens once again and a man appears holding a green coloured tube. He points it at the nearest vehicle and presses a button on the top of the tube. Smoke pours from the tube and two seconds later the small rocket hits the battered white van with a huge roar.

In the helicopter, Masterson is receiving directions over the radio towards the terrorist's vehicles when it suddenly goes silent. He tries to regain communications but, nothing. The last words said were,
'…heading towards the city centre.'
Pushing his head through into the cockpit he shouts,

'Get us to the city as quick as you can. We need to find those three vehicles before they vanish altogether.'

The helicopter thrusts forward as the pilot twists the throttle to bring the aircraft up to its maximum air speed. Everyone is at a window scouring the roads and countryside as it speeds past for the three vehicles.

'Spotted,' the cry goes out from the co-pilot and he raises an arm to point, 'Two clock just past the roundabout.'

Masterson follows the direction and sees the three black minibuses.

'Don't lose them. Whatever you do, don't lose them.' He shouts.

The Merlin's pilot keeps behind at a distance and height that should make it difficult for anyone in the vehicles to see the aircraft. As they approach the city centre, Norwich Castle sitting atop its small hill becomes prominent. One of the minibuses veers off and disappears into an underground car park.

'Do I stay with those two?' The pilot asks Masterson.

It takes a split second for Masterson to think through his options,

'Take us down. We will get out at the castle as it's right above where they went in. We may find them. When we debus, you get back up and don't lose those other two vehicles. I'll leave two men with you.'

A nod and a thumbs up is given and for a second the bottom falls out of the world as the helicopter punches down out of the sky.

People scatter as it rushes to the ground. Some stand firmly rooted and take pictures and videos with their mobile phones. Not even the sight of men with guns jumping down and running towards them can make them move. They stand rooted to the spot, their phones their protection against the real world.

Masterson and his team ignore them as they all move forward as one towards the gated entrance and rush out onto the busy city street. He looks left and sees a sign proclaiming, 'Castle Mall Entrance', with an arrow pointing the way.

He leads his men forward, into the crowded shopping mall. They have entered on the second floor, directly to their front is an elevator going down and to their left and right, the mall sweeps around before meeting up at the far end. He quickly glances at the information map at the entrance and sees the car park is on the far side. He directs two men each to the left and right and takes the remaining man with him.

As they rush through the shoppers there are only a few that let out a horrified gasp. Many just look at them with a disgust as they push by, as if to ask, 'What's the rush, why can't you queue like the rest of us?'

The smell of coffee and soap mingle together with freshly baked doughnuts as they move towards the car parking area. Masterson spots a young security guard standing next to a lingerie shop. The young man is staring into the window when he catches the reflection of Masterson behind him. He turns, guiltily and his eyes widen as he takes in the weapons being held in front of him.

'Uh…uh…uh…' he stutters.

'We are with the anti-terrorist squad. Get on your radio and lock the place down. Then get your control room to contact the police for reinforcements an also tell them to bring up any footage they have of a black minibus entering your car park about five minutes ago.'

The security guards nods rapidly and fumbles with his radio microphone attached to his jacket.

'Son, follow me and stay close. I will need the information you get.'

Two minutes later they are all standing near the lobby that forms the entrance to the car parking floors. The security guard holds his hand to his ear and the small headphone that sits discreetly there.

'A black minibus came in and parked on level two. Multiple occupants exited the vehicle, most are coming this way.'

Masterson looks around. Behind him are the large glass windows of a Boots store and to the left is a smaller window, brightly painted and offering a children's play area. Not the best place to stage a possible fire-fight. He points to the members of his team and issues commands,

'Stairwell left, cover the elevator, I'm going down to level two. Stop everyone who comes through,'

He looks at the security guard, 'You said most are coming this way, what about the rest?'

'Uhm, four people got into a car, two women, two men.'

'What make and is the car still there?'

The question is repeated on the radio and the answer is immediate,

'Silver Honda and it's still there.'

'Take me to level two. Is there a security or service elevator?'

'A lift, yes. We use it for deliveries.'

'Let's go.'

The lift is huge, scuffed and unlike the rest of the mall, dirty from neglect. It is clear that the cleaning staff only give it a cursory wipe around once a year, if that often. Just like every other establishment, the areas not visited by customers or dignitaries is a shit-hole, thinks Masterson.

The guard tilts his head to one side and says, 'The car is on the move. It's just leaving the slot now.'

'When we stop which direction will they be in?'

'Uhm, left. Yes left of us and coming directly towards us.'

The lift bumps to a halt and the doors slide open with a soft ping. Masterson explodes through the gap his weapon up in his shoulder his eyes looking down the squat, black barrel. A small car starts reversing out of one of the spaces nearly hitting him. The woman inside screams as she sees the gun and her head ducks down out of sight behind the seat. At the end of the row a silver bonnet appears as it turns the tight bend to come towards him. Through the windshield he sees two women in the front seats. He takes a firm stance with the weapon pointed at the vehicle and shouts out, 'Stop the car and get out, slowly.'

The Honda rolls to a gentle halt. The two women look at each other, saying something.

'Don't do it, don't do it,' Masterson says under his breath.

His thumb flicks the safety off and he walks forward a few steps. The women both look towards him again, the passenger drops suddenly in her seat and the car jerks towards him, the engine racing. His finger finds its place on the trigger and is smoothly squeezed.

His first shot stars the windscreen dead center. He adjusts his aim and fires three shots in quick succession at the driver. The passenger reappears and hoists herself out of the window holding a pistol in both hands. She fires off a shot and Masterson hears the hum of it pass him by with the sound of a bee caught in a bottle. His hips swivel slightly and he fires three more shots at the passenger. He feels no satisfaction as he watches her get pushed backwards as if by an unseen hand and plucked from the vehicle. The rear wheel bounces over her arm as it continues on its collision course with his body. He manages two more shots at the driver before he throws himself out of the way at the very last moment. The bumper catches his outstretched foot and spins him round so as he lands on the floor he watches the car speed away. Without warning it veers sharply to the left and smashes into the parked cars. The impact lifts the rear wheels off the ground and half turns the car around so it is side on to him.

He checks behind him at the woman on the floor, he can see that she is no longer a threat to him. He gingerly gets to his feet, his right leg is painful but he manages to put weight on it. He hobbles slowly, painfully towards the Honda.

As he gets closer he sees the driver has been hit several times in the chest, but somehow she is still breathing. Her breaths come out in rapid gasps and Masterson knows that unless medical help comes fast, she has no chance. He pulls open the rear passenger door and a man falls out and lands on the concrete with a sickening thud. A bullet has caught him in the chin and most of the bottom quarter of his face has gone.

Another man cowers on the back seat. His hands splayed out in front of his face to ward of whatever is coming. Masterson points the barrel at him,
'Are you hurt?'
The man lowers his hands slowly at the question,
'No. They were going to use me as a hostage. They were…'
He looks around at the gore covered car, turns to his right and throws up against the still closed door,
'Is she dead?' He asks.
'As good as.' Masterson replies.
Masterson recognises the man from TV interviews recently,
'Let's get you out of the vehicle Mr Emerson and cleaned up.'
As the shaken Emerson clambers out of the vehicle he takes a look into the drivers seat and pales again,
'Oh God,' he grabs Masterson's arm, 'I didn't mean her, I was talking about the woman in charge. The one who calls herself Joanne.'
As Masterson lowers his weapon he hears the sounds of sirens in the distance as he scans the parking lot. Tilting his head to the front seats he looks through the open window at the driver,
'Looks like you might get lucky after all,' he says.
He watches as the woman takes a deep, liquid sounding breath, shudders and lays still.
'Or maybe not.'

CHAPTER 56

With everything going on today I have not been able to think about Zoe's murder. Mercifully I have also not been able to think about Julia and what I need to say to her. I pause in the corridor. This may be the last chance I get to speak to her for a while. Especially if what Graham is implicating is true. I rub my forehead, feeling the first signs of a headache coming on. I make the decision and pull out my phone. I dial her parent's number as I assume that is where she will have returned to. I am greeted by the sound of Nektarios, her father, as he answers.
'Ella, hello.'
'Nektarios, hello. It's Peter. Is Julia there?'
There is a slight pause,
'Give me a moment please. I will just go and check the bookings.'
I hear a door open and close and the sound of Nektarios breathing as he walks somewhere. Another door opens and I hear it close none too gently.
'Peter, you have hurt my daughter terribly. You know this?'
'It was never my intention to...'
'Always we never mean to do these things, but it has happened. I am glad you called, I needed to talk to you privately, that is why I left the room. Julia's mother does not want me to speak to you, but I feel I must. It is a father's responsibility after all.'
I sigh. This is not how I planned this to go, an irate father berating me down the phone.

'Peter, we have all done things in our life we regret. It is only with age we look back and realise that sometimes these things helped shape our future for the better. Is it true what they are saying about you and this journalist?'

'Parts of it are true. I wish to God they weren't but...'

'Water under the bridge. Let it flow fast enough and it washes away the hurt. You know in my country it is not unusual for a young man to do as you have done, it does not make it right, but the couple must talk about it to make sure it does not happen again. You are lucky my friend, I like you and more importantly, Julia loves you. She will be strong for you, but only for a while. If you do not fight for her, she will not fight for you, do you understand?'

'I do, but there is so much going on here, and what do I say, it's just...'

'You have to be with her. Take it one day at a time and you have to let her know from your heart and your soul what she means to you. If you do not do this she will go. She is just like her mother in many ways. I did a similar thing once, it was hard for Anna and myself to overcome but a strong woman will fight for her love and believe me, Anna fought. I still have the scars to prove it.'

He lets out a low chuckle,

'So you will go to Julia, yes?'

'As soon as I can I will come over to see her.'

'Hmm, well that is where we have a little problem. You see, Julia has gone to her Uncle's house for a while.'

'Her Uncle? Where?'

'She has gone to stay with Anna's brother, Babis, in Crete. She thought it would be good to get away for a while. If you want Julia back, you must go to Crete and show her your love.'

I stand there quietly thinking of how my life is going to pieces. Nektarios whispers into the phone, 'Anna is coming I have to go. Fly to Crete and get Julia back. Good luck son.'

He hangs up on me and I am left holding a silent phone to my ear. There is nothing else I can do or say so I make my way down to Graham's office, my footsteps heavy on the tiled floor.

I don't even bother to knock on his door, just grasp the handle, turn it and walk in. Graham looks up from his desk and sees my expression,

'I am so sorry Peter for expressing my theories the way I did. I want you to know it was unprofessional of me and I should not have let it happen.'

I see that he thinks I am looking morose because of Helen and her possible part in Zoe's murder. I shake my head at him and force a weak smile on my face,

'Graham, you did what you thought was right and you came to me as a friend. I don't have many and I can't afford to push any away, especially at times like these. Now I am going to sit down here,' I pull one of his chairs out and plonk myself down in it, 'You are going to make a pot of your strongest coffee, and we are going to sit here and go through the evidence. If it is Helen, I want to be sure. I can have no margin of error with this as you can understand.'

Graham's response is to open one of his desk drawers, remove a square, foil wrapped block of ground coffee and walk over to his machine. As he prepares the coffee, neither of us say a word. It is only when the steaming cups are placed on the table before us that he pulls out a folder and starts talking.

Thirty minutes later he has me convinced. The evidence against my sister is compelling. I drain the last dregs of my now cold coffee.
'I think I need a refill before I go and arrest my sister on a murder charge. Any chance of one?'
Graham looks grim as he picks up my cup and pours more steaming coffee into it.
'If I had known it was tea break, I would have brought the biscuits. Wilks is overseeing those army idiots and...'
It is JD's voice that erupts from the doorway. His smile freezes on his lips as he sees the expressions on our faces,
'Jesus, who died?' he asks.
As we let our coffee go cold once again, Graham and I run through our earlier conversation with him. It is not long before the three of us sit in the office, silent, staring at the bottom of our empty cups with sombre thoughts running through each of our minds.

CHAPTER 57

Running now as fast as his damaged ankle can manage, Masterson reaches the lobby where his men had lain in wait. On the floor surrounded by his own people, the local police and a couple of bemused security guards, are twenty to thirty people, all face down with their hands tied behind their backs using plastic tie-wraps.
'What happened? How many injured?'
The man standing nearest him replies without even moving his eyes from the people on the floor, 'None. They came up here, either through the stairwell or in the lift, saw our weapons and surrendered.'
Masterson scans the face on the floor quickly,
'The girl in charge is not here,' he roughly grabs one of the men up off the floor. A policeman moves forward as if to restrain him but Masterson just glares at him, 'Back off, this is my operation.' He slams the man against the wall of the lobby with a force to make him grunt,
'Where is she? Where is Joanne?'
He receives a smile in response and the man glances at the large multi-faced clock in the mall,
'It's too late,' he faces Masterson again, 'Too late for everyone.'
He sees something in the mans eyes and makes an instant decision,
'Everyone out. We need to get everyone out of here right now.'

He starts running for the exit, forgetting the terrorist who is standing against the wall and laughing now. His team leave their prisoners on the floor and sprint for the exit which is mercifully near. The police hesitate, they have prisoners to look after. They start raising the people nearest them to their feet.

Masterson bursts through the door into the cold sunshine and feels a tremor beneath his feet that almost knocks him to the floor. A loud roar follows and the glass on the entrance doors blows outward covering his back with small glazed pieces of safety glass. He looks back into the entrance. People are staggering out, bloody, with clothes and skin torn and ripped. He watches as a woman suddenly grasps her throat and falls to the floor twitching. A young boy standing next to her does the same and then it is like a rolling nightmare as the people escaping the explosion start dropping to the ground.

'Gas! Get away from the building. They have used fucking gas.'

One of his men near the doors starts choking and Masterson almost moves forward to help him. He catches the man's eyes and is waved away as the dying man coughs painfully and spasms rack his body. Masterson starts pushing people away from the entrance, yelling and threatening them to get people to move. He is hoping the poisonous air will dissipate in the open space. A pigeon falls to the ground near his feet, then another. The small feathery bodies jerk a few times then stop. He looks up to see a small flock of the birds, disturbed by the explosion, flying round in circles above the castle. One by one they falter in flight and drop to the ground.

Masterson breathes a big sigh of relief and stops in his tracks,

'It's being blown away,' he grabs one of his men by the shoulders, 'Get on the blower, we need a decontamination team down here,' The man turns away to speak into his radio and Masterson grabs him and spins him around again, 'Tell them to bring plenty of body bags.'

CHAPTER 58

Wilks is fascinated by the set of screens before her showing the landscape cruise by,
'What altitude is this thing at?' She asks.
'Currently 42,000 feet but we will be descending fairly rapidly in a minute or so.' Luke responds.
'The resolution is amazing.'
Wilks can clearly pick out people walking along the streets. She watches as a young mother bends over to her pram and pulls out a young baby. She can almost make out the features on the womans face.
'Start the descent now and begin the landing sequence.' Phillips voice breaks her concentration.
'What are your plans once it is on the ground?' She asks him.
'I have orders to destroy it. It will be placed in an old hardened aircraft shelter, the doors will close and we will self destruct the machine remotely. That way there is no chance of any collateral damage and our government do not want a weapon of this kind to fall into the wrong hands.'
Wilks nods her approval and watches Luke as he directs the MASTER down to the airfield at RAF Northolt.
It takes a few minutes of descent before the aircraft gently touches down on the runway. Luke manoeuvres it to a large open area near the runway threshold,
'Where now, Captain?'
'I'll take it from here. It will be easier than trying to give you directions like some sort of backseat driver.'

Luke turns to Wilks a questioning look on his face. She nods her approval and he pushes his seat aside to let Phillips in. He stands up, closes his eyes and stretches his shoulders to relax the knotted muscles that have been hunched over the keyboard for the last few hours. A hand slams into his back and his arm is grabbed and forced up and behind his back. His eyes fly open and he sees the MP, Roberts, holding a pistol at Wilks.

'Civilians need to be removed from this area. I am sorry if it seems a little drastic, but operational security is important. You are not allowed to know the final location of the aircrafts remains.'

Wilks stands there impassively, staring at the young man with the gun,

'You could have just asked us to leave, Captain. Why the sudden aggressive tactics?' She says calmly.

'Ma'am, I don't have time. Please leave the room immediately, or you will be assisted to leave.'

Luke is trying not to grunt with the pain in his shoulder and arm, and failing. He gives out a little groan with each breath.

'Let him go, we will leave together, quietly and peacefully.'

Mansfield pushes Luke away and towards the Commissioner, motioning with his head the direction he wants them to go.

Luke rubs his shoulder with a wince as they both walk out of the room,

'Jesus,' he says, 'is everyone in the army such a knob?'

Wilks smiles grimly,

'It's something you learn by experience, Luke,' she says as the door slams shut behind them, 'I need to make a phone call. Are you coming?'

Luke stares at the closed door to his offices for a moment,
'It looks like I've got nothing better to do, so why not?'

CHAPTER 59

'Sir, we have news from Norfolk.'
The Prime Minster stops writing, places his pen down and looks up to the aide that is standing in the doorway. He waits for a moment before prompting,
'Go on.'
'It's not good news I am afraid, sir. It seems that the TSI bunker was the scene of some heavy fighting. The terrorists that were left, for some reason, decided to start firing. Some hostages were forced from the building as they tried to escape, the terrorists were shooting at them. Our forces on the ground have contained the situation but there are many dead and injured. The bunker was stormed and we have been told it is a massacre inside. Those terrorists that were not killed by gunfire used their last rounds of ammunition to kill themselves. There is not a single terrorist left alive in the bunker. We have multiple wounded casualties from the TSI staff, many of which are critical.'
'What about the escaping vehicles? What is happening with them?'
'Two vehicles were stopped on the outskirts of Norwich. It appears our special forces had personnel inside them that managed to overpower the terrorist on board each one.'
The Prime Minister interrupts,
'You say terrorist, like it's singular.'

'That is correct sir. One terrorist on each bus forcing a hostage to drive. This is the good news, sir. We have saved forty two people from these buses with no harm. The people here include our own Chief of Defence Staff and many foreign dignitaries. They are saying they had to pay a ransom to be released.'

'The third bus?'

The aide pauses, nervous how to continue, 'Another disaster. The vehicle split up from the other two and entered a shopping mall in the center of the city. We are unclear exactly of the details, but it appears that the majority of the terrorist group were on this bus.'

'Please don't tell me we let them get away.' The Prime Minister says, thumping the desk in frustration.

'No sir. As I say, the exact details are unclear at the moment, we have a version that talks of a shooting incident and we have stories of men and women giving themselves up voluntarily. All we know for sure is that at some point a huge explosion rocked the interior of the mall. As if that was not bad enough it has been reported that some form of chemical weapon was also used. Some of those injured in the blast succumbed to a form of gas or poison very shortly afterwards. The Chemical and Biological Response Team are on their way to the scene but we are looking at hundreds of casualties from within the building and the immediate area.'

The room falls silent as the PM absorbs the information.

'Will this day never end?' He asks no one in particular, 'Does this mean that all of the terrorists have perished either in the bunker or in the city?'

'Our first reports indicate that this is the case, sir.'

'Thank God for small mercies. What about the MASTER aircraft?'

The aide pulls a out a separate piece of paper and hands it over,

'This has just reached us from Northolt via our secure line.'

The PM takes it and places it on the desk in front of him to read. After a few seconds he smiles slightly,

'Prepare a press statement. Try and make as positive a spin as you can on this tragedy. Force the issue that all terrorists have been captured or killed and the drone has been destroyed by a team of our technicians. Say it was crashed into the sea to avoid any further damage or threat to our population. Get Claire on it, she can write a good story. Tell her she has thirty minutes to get it drafted before I address the nation.'

CHAPTER 60

48 HOURS LATER

Masterson is sitting in his car as he watches the television reports on the seven inch screen in the dashboard. The newsmen and women are speaking to survivors and the injured from the largest terrorist attack on British and European soil. The nation is in mourning and the hundreds of thousands of flowers placed around the devastated sites in Cambridge and Norwich show the loss, hurt and anger that everyone is feeling. He shakes his head as he listens to the attacks that have occurred on Mosques, Synagogues and other buildings where white, Anglo-Saxon males look out of place. Many are saying there has been a rise in membership of far-right parties that promote hate and ignorance.
He shakes his head as he sees that the terrorists have achieved their aim of creating fear on the streets of nearly every city, town and village across the UK.
He picks up his phone and dials a number. It is answered on the third ring,
'What do you want?'
'I quit,' says Masterson, 'I've had enough and I'm getting out.'
He hears a small, cultured laugh from the man on the phone,
'You can't quit, old boy. You belong to me and only I can say when it's time for your employment to be relinquished.'
'I quit.'

Masterson hangs up the phone and picks up the other object on the table. The metal glistens softly in the streetlight as he turns the pistol in his hand. He picks up a stubby metal tube and carefully screws it on the end of the barrel before looking out at the windows of the building opposite. Placing the pistol inside his North Face down jacket he exits the car and again looks up at the building. This time he is focussed on one window in particular.

'I quit.' He repeats as he walks towards the door. The security guard on the desk looks up, recognises him and stands up,

'Sorry to hear about Bomber and the rest of the crew. They were good men, good brothers, good fighters.'

Masterson walks across to the desk and they hug,

'He's in isn't he?' he asks as they pull away from each other.

The guard confirms his question with a nod.

'Isn't it about time you had your tea break and locked the door?'

The man checks his watch,

'Not for another...' he glances up and stares into Masterson's cold eyes, 'Yeah, you're right. It is that time,' he turns away and pauses, 'I never liked this job anyway.'

Masterson walks towards the elevators, presses the button and waits for the doors to open. Behind him he hears the locks click into place on the heavy doors,

'Oh, he has a guest. She came in a while back, could be a hooker but then you never know.'

Masterson raises his arm in acknowledgement as the ping of the elevator announces its arrival. He steps in and presses the button for the penthouse suite.

Removing the pistol from his jacket, he pulls back on the top slide and chambers a round into the barrel of the handgun. He releases the safety with his thumb and holds it down by his side. The soft ping from the elevator once again sounds and the doors open. He steps out into a spacious lobby and makes his way confidently across it and into a large welcoming dining area. A bar sits in one corner, two half-empty glasses of what looks like whisky sit upon it. He goes over and sniffs one, the distinctive aroma of Laphroaig makes his tastebuds water. He takes a small sip and feels the peaty liquid glide down his throat. He places it back down and continues on.

He hears the sound of voices to his right and stops to listen. Definitely a man and a woman but he cannot make out what is being said. He opens the door and steps into the room.

Leahy looks up in surprise from behind his large mahogany desk,

'What the hell do you think you are doing walking in here like this,' he says angrily and rising up out of his chair.

Masterson raises his pistol and fires once. The sound is like someone dropping a delicate china cup onto a soft carpeted floor. The ejection mechanism as it racks back makes more noise than the bullet entering Leahy's forehead. He slumps back into his chair, the surprised look still on his face as blood seeps from the wound above his right eye and slowly channels down his face.

'I quit,' says Masterson, dropping the pistol to his side again. He is about to turn around and walk away when he realises the woman has not moved.

She does not even seem perturbed by the death in front of her. He studies her carefully and something tugs at his memory.

'Do we have a problem here?' She asks without moving.

'Turn around, slowly.' He commands.

The woman stands up, and following his commands, turns slowly until she is facing him. Her eyes show no recognition but Masterson knows the face.

'You!'

Her hands move slightly where they are holding her purse in front of her. He raises the pistol,

'Stop right there. What are you doing here?'

Joanne studies the man before her carefully,

'I was asked by a man who paid me a lot of money to find Mr Leahy and kill him. You seem to have saved me a lot of bother.'

'Who paid you? I know many people who would love to see him dead, but why you? And why now?'

She steps sideways away from the chair,

'You seem to have me at a disadvantage. You seem to know me, but I have never laid eyes on you before.'

He fires a shot that punches a small neat hole in her left shin. She falls to the ground screaming. As she falls a small silver pistol drops out of her left hand where it was hidden behind her purse.

'Who paid you? Tell me and live, don't tell me and we see how long you can suffer or I run out of ideas.'

'Just kill me,' she hisses through the pain, 'Why should I help you?'

He aims the pistol theatrically and pulls the trigger again. A hole appears in her other shin, causing blood to spurt out in a red fountain. He moves forward quickly and clamps a hand over her mouth to stifle her screams.
'Now we both know I am not joking around here, who paid you?'
Tears are streaming for her face as she threatens to pass out from the pain. He slaps her once on each cheek, hard enough to raise bright red marks on her skin. Her breathing is forced,
'Emerson. He is head of TSI. Now call me some help, please.'
Masterson steps back and checks his clothing for any blood. There is a small spot on his right trouser cuff and shoe. He steps back into the dining room and reappears a moment later with a clean napkin. He dabs away the blood and throws the towel to the bleeding woman.
'Use this to stem the flow,' he says, 'and tell me everything.'
Ten minutes later he knows all he needs to know. He stands up from his chair,
'Thank you, Joanne. I am afraid it's time for us to say goodbye.'
He presses the barrel of the pistol against her forehead.
'You said you would let me live.' She screams.
'I lied.'
He pulls the trigger.
Before he leaves he picks up the four ejected cases and places them in his pocket, takes one last look around the room, and walks out. He walks out of the apartment, out of the building and into his car.
'How did it go? You were there a long time? Did he need persuading?'

Angela Wilson looks at him from the passenger seat as he settles himself into his own seat.
'He took a little persuading but I think he got the message.'
He starts the big Lexus and pulls away from the curb,
'How do you fancy a little holiday? Somewhere warm at this time of year would be nice wouldn't it?'
Angela smiles and leans over to kiss his cheek,
'Sounds great to me, let's go.'

CHAPTER 61

The case against my sister is building momentum. JD has been put in charge of the investigation as the Commissioner rightly thinks that I will have a conflict of interest in the situation. I still cannot believe she could do such a thing, but even I am convinced of her guilt. I wonder what may have caused her to do such a thing and can come up with nothing. I look at my watch for the tenth time is as many minutes. I know that before long there will be a knock on her door and JD will be standing there with a warrant for her arrest. I am struggling with the fact that I have been forbidden to speak to her at all during the investigation. It will be at least a week before I get the chance to ask her any questions now. My phone rings. It's JD.
'We are just about to get Helen now. I thought you may want to know.'
His voice sounds apologetic.
'Thanks JD. I just wish…'
I don't know what I am wishing. The events of the last few days and the developments with Helen have really fucked me up.
'I know Peter, I know. I will be looking after her whilst she is charged. I will try and make it as easy as possible for her.'
I mumble my thanks again and hang up explaining I have to go. I don't even give him a chance to respond. Once again I am running away. Running away from my family when times get hard. I look up at the large display board in front of me.

The departure lounge at Gatwick Airport is mercifully quiet at this time of the morning. My flight to Athens is the first of the day and I arrived here early as I could not sleep. How could I when I know how the day is going to unfold for my sister. I sit back in my chair and let out another deep sigh. It is going to be a long day for everyone. My flight takes just under four hours, in that time Helen will have been processed into the system and sitting in a cell somewhere. She will probably be cursing me the whole time. I have a three hour wait in the Greek's Capital airport before the short flight over to Chania in Crete. By the time I arrive there she will have had her first meeting with a lawyer and have heard all the evidence against her. I wonder if she will confess when she hears that. Part of me wants her to as I do not want the prolonged agony of the investigation to continue for either of us. But part of me wants her to fight it, to protest that she is innocent. I want that doubt to remain.

My phone rings again. I answer it without looking, thinking it is JD to tell me he has my sister in custody.

'Peter? Is that you Peter?'

My blood runs cold,

'Ann?'

'Oh Peter, where are you? I have been...'

'You were attacked, do you remember anything?'

'Nothing, the doctors say I have been unconscious for days? Is that true?'

'Yes. Yes it is.'

'They say you saved me. Peter, thank you, I love you.'

I stay silent.

'Peter? I said I love you, thank you.'

I still cannot bring myself to say anything.

'At least they have said the baby is OK.'
Ice running through my veins now and my head starts spinning,
'What? What baby are you talking about?'
Already I know and fear the answer,
'My baby...our baby.'
I slowly pull the phone away from my face hearing Ann's voice recede into the distance,
'Peter...Peter...Peter...'
I hang up and for good measure turn the phone off.
'Flight number EZY6643 to Athens now boarding at Gate 122.'
The call is repeated as I somehow manage to push myself off the uncomfortable chair and walk unsteadily away. I don't have a clue where I am going or what am I doing, but Nektarios' advice rings in my head,
'Take it one day at a time, son. One day at a time.'

Printed in Great
Britain
by Amazon